MW01285161

# A Duck & Cover Adventure Book 4

Benjamin Wallace

Copyright © 2018 by Benjamin Wallace.
All rights reserved.

*Invictus* by William Ernest Henley

Copyright © 2018 by Benjamin Wallace.
All rights reserved.

ISBN-13: 978-1722038939
ISBN-10: 1722038934

This is a work of fiction. Names, characters, places, and incidents are the product of the author's imagination. Any resemblance to actual persons, living or dead, events, or locales is entirely coincidental.

Cover design by Monkey Paw Creative.

From the pages of the best-selling Duck & Cover Adventures comes thirteen stories of those who survived the apocalypse. Some would go on to be heroes, others villains, some were dogs and will stay dogs, but they all must contend with the horrors of the new world and find a way to survive in the wasteland that was America.

**Get this laugh-out-loud collection of stories from the Duck & Cover Adventures post-apocalyptic series now when you sign up for my Readers' Group.**

To get your copy of TALES OF THE APOCALYPSE and be the first to know about new releases and other exclusive content, you just need to tell me where to send it.

Visit
**http://benjaminwallacebooks.com/join-my-readers-group/**
to get your free book now.

*To all the haters.*

# Prelude

---

*Before you embark on a journey of revenge, dig two graves.*

    *A wise man once said that. A wise man that, apparently, didn't have many enemies. Which is quite admirable considering he spent his whole life telling people what to do. If your whole life is going around and being a bossy little shit and you only end up with enough enemies to just fill two holes, you've beaten the odds. Offering unsolicited advice is not an endearing quality.*

    *Of course, in his infinite bossiness, what the man meant was to dig one grave for your victim and one for yourself, as revenge is a less-than-noble pursuit and would surely damn the soul of those that seek it. That would be a best-case scenario. Worst case it could lead them to their literal death.*

    *It worked well enough as a metaphor, but in all practicality, it was bad advice. Especially since the world ended.*

    *For one thing, no one really dug graves anymore. Maybe for a loved one, but not really for someone they didn't care for—much less hated enough to murder. The simple fact was that grave digging was hard work. It was far easier to leave your enemy's corpse for the countless scavengers. Buzzards had to eat, too.*

    *It may seem cruel but, since the collapse of polite society, morality* had become somewhat squishy. Most people still tried to be good and certainly thought of themselves that way, but the definition of good had become rather difficult to pin down. Almost anything could be justified in a world without indoor plumbing.

"Steal a loaf of bread to feed my starving family" soon became "raid a farming commune, pillage, rape and plunder to maintain my status in the gang so my family can eat and I don't get shanked in the middle of the night for that warm blanket I pulled off a rotting corpse outside of Biloxi last winter."

The justification of violence became easy enough for anyone, but it was even easier in a mob that backed up your messed-up moral view. Because of this, it was rare that the target of revenge was ever just a single person. Entire groups were targeted for their associations—real or perceived.

On one hand this made turning the other cheek a rather popular option. It was easier to forgive Donovan's Death Adders and forget that they had swooped into your town in the dead of night, murdered half the population, burned the grain stores and pissed in the water supply than it was to take up arms and chase a hundred maniacs on motorcycles into the wasteland.

Of course, impossible odds didn't stop everyone. After the bombs fell, civilization collapsed and the Earth turned murderous some pretty terrible things happened. Man showed what he was truly capable of and a little urine in the drinking water was really on the low side of offenses.

But some things, quite obviously, justified revenge. Those that had lost everything had lost their common sense as well, and the impossible odds of going up against a gang weren't enough to deter them.

Those that followed this path of self-destruction were often afforded a quiet respect. A stranger seeking righteous vengeance was usually treated with more kindness than your run-of-the-mill stranger. They were given food and shelter and a certain amount of reverence. They were dead men walking, after all. But people everywhere wanted to see justice done even if they weren't about to see to it themselves. It was a romantic idea at best. Justice had died in the bombs with just about everything else.

There were rumors of the rare, successful rampage. A lone madman wandering into a raider camp with nothing to lose and somehow emerging with justice done and memories of loved ones avenged. Of course, there were also stories of a city back east, or west, or north, untouched by the apocalypse. And another one of a city filled with talking moose. People liked to believe strange things and justice being served fell into that category.

The smarter revenge-seeker would plan the long game and take an Edward Dantes approach. That would have a better chance of success. But, while watching your enemies succumb to their own weaknesses, hang themselves by their own misdeeds and drown in their own hubris in a complex web of traps and ruses of your own devising would be satisfying, it wasn't quite practical in a world where even the plants could eat you on any given Tuesday. Time was always an issue in the wasteland.

With Dumas's plans out the window and a full frontal assault tantamount to suicide, those truly entitled to revenge had little choice but to sigh and whisper, "Before you embark on a journey of revenge, dig two graves."

But sometimes, revenge is worth that stain on your soul.

And sometimes, two graves aren't enough.

Sometimes you need an entire cemetery.

If you decide to bury the bastards at all.


- A journal entry from the post-apocalyptic nomadic warrior dated "final entry"

# 1

---

The semi-truck belched a plume of black smoke as it crossed the Rainbow Bridge over the Niagara River.

The once-popular crossing between nations was now a maze of barriers and burnt-out cars. Some of the hulks had been placed intentionally; other twisted wrecks had been left to burn as examples to others. The Peterbilt found another gear and shuddered as it picked up speed. The improvised plow that served as its front bumper wasn't bothered by the obstacles. It barreled into them, creating a shower of sparks and sending several of the barricades plunging into the river below as the men charged with guarding the bridge scrambled out of the way.

There was no time to revel in their panic. There wasn't even time to enjoy the view of the falls as he raced across the bridge with his foot pressed to the floor.

More men gathered atop the barrier that towered in front of him. People called them the Great Canadian Gates, but Canada had nothing to do with it. The end of the world had happened so fast that the world's governments didn't have time to close the borders, much less construct a massive structure like this. Just like so many other things on that day, Canada was and then simply wasn't.

The fifty-foot wall was never meant to protect Canada or its people. It was built to solidify the power of the tyrant Invictus by closing some people in and shutting others out. This was Alasis in all its horror.

They opened fire from the top of the gates. Most of the bullets bounced harmlessly off the metal plate he had welded across the cab. The thickness of the plate and the distance made the projectiles little more than a distraction. Even the guard on the 50-caliber machine gun, despite his best efforts, wasn't getting through.

As he neared the gates and reduced the range, the larger rounds buried deeper into the shield. A string of dents appeared over his head as the bullets pounded the metal. His instincts told him to cringe and lay off the gas, so he pushed the pedal harder against the truck's floor and sat up tall in the seat.

The engine burped another blast of soot as he geared down and sped up. The dog in the seat next to him barked its encouragement at the action. The hair on its back bristled. He knew why they were here and was as willing to throw himself against the gates as the driver was.

They had taken everything from so many. Few that had survived the end of the world had been untouched by the monsters behind these walls. They had seized power with such speed and violence that no one could stand against them. They orchestrated the terror of every man, woman and child that struggled to scrape out an existence in the post-apocalyptic world. No one could stop them.

But someone had to try. It was suicide. Deep down he knew it, but the rage inside him had kept that knowledge buried as he planned and prepared for today. They had taken everything from him. Despite his best attempts to flee their grip, they had taken everyone he cared about.

The dog barked as if it could see the man on the gate hoisting the rocket launcher onto his shoulder. The driver saw it too and pulled hard on the steering wheel as the canister on the guard's shoulder flashed.

The rig swung hard right toward the edge of the bridge and crashed through the concrete barrier that had once protected pedestrians from motor vehicle traffic.

The rocket struck to his left and tore a hole through the bridge's deck. He felt the concussion slam into the metal plate he had welded to the door.

It pushed the truck farther right and he scraped the safety rail, throwing a cascade of sparks toward the river below.

The dog howled and scrambled as it slid across the seat. He felt himself falling as well and fought to crank the wheel back to the left while trying to ignore the thought of going over the edge of the Rainbow Bridge. He'd never know exactly how close he came to ending his assault in the cold waters of the Niagara River, but he knew it wasn't far.

Veering right, he straightened the rig once more and sped toward the gates. Even the dog let out what sounded like a sigh of relief. He looked at his faithful companion and grinned. "It's our turn, boy."

The dog barked in agreement as the driver pulled a black box from the dash. Four dozen wires spilled from the back of the box and ran up into the truck's console. There they split into two harnessed bundles bound together with electrical tape. Half went to the left of the truck, the rest to the right, but they all served the same purpose. He thumbed back the red switch cover and mashed the button beneath.

Every launch shook the truck from left to right and back again as the rocket pods mounted on the rig spit out their payload. The narrow slit he had cut in the armor filled with fire as forty-eight rockets streamed toward the gates. For a long moment he couldn't see anything else. Briefly, their fiery tails faded and for a split second he could see again.

It was only a fraction of a second before the explosions blinded him once more, but in that fraction, time slowed. He saw the men on the gates. He saw them realize someone had decided to fight back. He saw them understand that the fortress of fear they hid behind wouldn't stand forever. He saw them realize that the hell they had wrought on others had finally come for them. And, in a much more practical sense, he saw them realize that the wall they were standing on was about to be obliterated.

But there was only time for that realization to drive them to fear. Not action. And it was sweet.

The rockets delivered their explosive warheads in a blast that shook the bridge beneath him. He lost sight of the men and the gates themselves as fire erupted and raced up into the sky, baking the metal that lined the once impenetrable obstacle.

Fire turned to smoke and the wind over the river carried it away. The gates still stood. The men had been thrown from the perches. The structure had been shaken and the gates still stood. But there was a hole.

"Get down, boy!"

The dog responded by dropping to the floor under the dash and burrowing into a cocoon of foam and blankets.

He aimed for the hole and never touched the brakes.

The rig bounced as it collided with the debris. The trailer scraped against the remains of the gate. Metal twisted and screeched and screamed as the momentum drove them through the crack in Alasis's armor. Despite the seatbelt's best effort to hold him in place, he was thrown around the cab. He felt the bruise form across his chest almost instantly as the strap snapped taut across his body.

The sound and the bouncing got worse and it felt as if the cab would tip over at several points, but it always righted itself as it forced its way through the hole in the great gates.

One final crash sent him surging forward. He was bloodied and bruised but he was inside the walls of the tyrant's stronghold. His eyes went to the other side of the cab, searching for movement in the piles of blankets, and found it instantly.

The dog stuck his nose out of the pile and cast a damning gaze at the driver.

"That's step one," he sighed as he unbuckled his seatbelt and crawled into the back of the cab. "C'mon."

Step two was no less subtle. The engine fired through low flow pipes that quickly filled the trailer with exhaust and chaos. The ramp crashed down, crushing one of the braver guards that had approached the truck. The Shelby leapt out of the trailer and into the streets of Alasis.

Getting through the customs pavilion was surprisingly easy. The plaza was lightly guarded and it wasn't until he drove through that he realized he had always wanted to charge across a border, crashing through wooden barricades while guards dove for cover, shouting at him in a foreign language. Or, in this case, it would be a foreign accent. He idly wondered if they would have screamed at him in English only, or followed it with the French translation as well.

Even though the idea of nations had been long since obliterated, it was interesting to see how Canada had once welcomed foreigners into their country. He imagined it was important to have some sort of landmark that displayed the nation's culture as soon as one left the customs plaza, but he was surprised to see just how much Canada's version of Planet Hollywood looked like their American cousin's. He wasn't sure what he was expecting. An Alan Thicke-centric theme perhaps? At the very least a Lorne Greene statue or a Leslie Nielsen fountain couldn't have hurt.

He shot past the restaurant, a mall, and then hung a left. Rumors about the city's tyrant were plentiful and often conflicting. While some said he was formerly an important political figure, others claimed he had risen from next to nothing to rule. Some said he was a younger man while others claimed he was north of sixty. Some rumors claimed he practiced cannibalism by eating the hearts of victims, while others said he was vegan and warned about starting any conversation with him for fear of getting a lecture about the diet's health benefits and altruism.

For every rumor, there was another to contradict it. But all of them had the despot living at the Fallsview Casino, and he wasn't far from the hotel tower.

Shots rang out behind him as the guards rallied their defense. Several cars were on his tail now, so he hung a right just past a wax museum. The back end of the GT500 slid out and the dog barked as it tried to steady itself in the passenger seat.

Motels and convenience stores were a blur as he watched the rearview mirror. Two of the pursuit vehicles made the turn while others continued down Victoria Avenue as they spread out to cover the city. Another wax museum and a block of motels passed by and he veered right to follow the street through a residential neighborhood.

A pickup blocked the end of the street, so he cut across the yard, sending mud and sod at the guards as they raised their weapons to shoot. He felt the Mustang's ground effects scrape against the curb on the way up and back down. A 4x4 may have been a better option.

The tires regained their grip on the road and he cornered left a couple of times trying to lose his pursuers inside the neighborhood of old homes. But he kept sight of his goal. The hotels along the river were the tallest buildings in the town and he used them as reference points as he swerved through the streets.

There was no end to the number of men and women trying to kill him. The longer he was on the road, the thicker the streets became with armed sentries. He doubled back through the neighborhood, and the quiet homes he had passed earlier were now covered with armed men firing at him from their porches.

He wouldn't last long on these mean streets of Niagara Falls.

Drifting around another corner put him in line with the Fallsview Casino. He straightened the Mustang and unleashed all 550hp in a final charge that would take him to his target's doorstep. He made it half a block when the plow shot out of a side street and scooped the Ford off the ground.

He screamed as the car flipped sideways and back in the air

before crashing onto the hood and sliding off the side of the road. They were spinning. Was it the car? Or was it just him? Everything went dim.

Hovering somewhere just shy of consciousness, but never fully able to wake up, his mind filled the time with bitter thoughts. It reminded him that it was his own fault for being here, ultimately. It was his fault for always trying to do the right thing. The right thing had put him on the wrong side of Alasis's men. The right thing had pissed off the wrong people. The right thing had cost him everything. His love. His freedom. And ultimately, the right thing would cost him his life.

The bouts of awareness were brief. But he knew they had pulled him from the car. They had tossed him into a truck and moved him somewhere. He was briefly in an elevator and now he was in a chair somewhere quite windy.

"Is it him?"

"We think so."

"Wake him."

The command was followed by a slap across his face that cranked his neck to the right farther than he thought it was designed to go. He tried to pull away as a back-hand followed and sent him toppling over backward. In trying to catch himself, he discovered that his hands were bound behind his back. His full weight crashed onto his wrists. He felt one snap. He couldn't feel the other one at all. There was nothing he could do but scream in pain. Every kick he made to relieve the pressure only made the pain in his wrist worse.

"Get him up."

He opened his eyes as the hand that had struck him down lifted him back into a seated position.

"Are you the Librarian?" The man that asked the question was wearing a stupid helmet with a bullet hole in the temple. Behind him was a shattered window that looked over the city below.

He didn't answer. He looked around the room. There were several large men in colorful cloaks standing by. He wanted to see his dog. But he didn't. What had they done to his friend? Had he gotten away after the crash? Did he survive the crash?

"Who are you?"

It was Invictus who spoke. It had to be him. This was the man who had taken everything from him. The man he had come to kill. He pulled at the ropes and the pain in his wrists nearly made him lose consciousness again. He grit his teeth against the pain and seethed, "I'm the man who's going to kill you."

"Of course you are," laughed Invictus. "Are you the Librarian?"

He didn't answer. He only stared, locking eyes with the man who had orchestrated the misery of so many.

Invictus turned to one of the guards. "Bring it in."

One of the cloaked men nodded and opened the door to the room. "Bring it."

Two more guards walked into the room carrying a wire dog crate between them. His best friend whimpered inside.

"Put it on the ledge," Invictus said.

They did as ordered and the dog instinctively moved to the side of the crate farthest from the window. Slowly. He was hurt.

"What are you doing?"

"Are you the Librarian?" Invictus asked, and kicked the cage closer to the edge.

"Stop that! Leave him alone!"

Invictus kicked the cage once more. The dog yelped and tried to back away, but he had already reached the limits of the cage.

"Are you the Librarian?!"

"I don't know what you're talking about!" He screamed. He couldn't lose his dog, too.

Another kick. Another yelp.

"Are you the Librarian?!"

He struggled against the ropes. He couldn't feel the pain in his wrists anymore. He had to get free. "No! I don't know who that is!"

Invictus backed away from the dog crate and nodded at the guards. "I believe you."

Before he could breathe a sigh of relief, they hoisted him and the chair from the ground and tossed him across the room. He collided with the crate and both he and his only true friend in the apocalypse rolled out the shattered window and fell to the ground fifty stories below.

# 2

The joys of staying at a Days Inn had changed since the end of the world. Locating the ice maker and hoping your floor had both a snack AND soda vending machine had been replaced by the act of rolling the bed to make sure there weren't giant scorpions hiding in the dirty sheets. Jerry had just finished giving the pillowcase a solid stomping when Chewy barked and ran to the window. The canine's keen ears must have somehow picked up the first sounds of the disturbance on the bridge.

Jerry, with his far more inferior ears, didn't look up until the first explosion.

He joined the mastiff at the window and together they stared out toward the river. A column of black smoke rose up from the bridge connecting the former nations. He raced across the room and pulled a monocular from his bag before returning to the window.

The gate was a twisted wreck and through the eyepiece he could see guards scrambling to confront the threat.

"That's ballsy," he said to the dog.

The dog woofed in agreement.

"Do you think it will work?"

The dog said nothing.

"I hope it works," he said in a none-too-convincing tone and tossed the scope on the bed.

The dog shot him an accusatory look.

"What? I mean it." He mostly meant it. Invictus and his allies deserved nothing short of eradication and as long as it happened, it would be a good thing, objectively. But, deep down, he wanted to be the one to pull the trigger. He wanted to be the one who got to look the tyrant in the eye and accuse him of his crimes before taking revenge.

If he was being honest, the feeling wasn't deep down at all. It was all he had thought about for weeks. Rage had consumed him, driven him since he buried his wife. He knew it was dangerous to let it control him. He knew it was foolish. It would lead to mistakes and it could get him killed. But he decided he didn't care. For the first time in his life he embraced it and let it pick his path. And it had led him here, to a run-down Days Inn in Niagara Falls.

He dismissed the commotion on the other side of the river. A lone frontal assault was suicide. He knew it. That's why he hadn't tried it himself. He was at least able to convince his rage of that. The idea that someone else might deny him his revenge passed through his mind once more. He sighed and wished whoever it was Godspeed. They deserved that much.

"C'mon, Chewy," he called. "We've still got work to do."

It had grown cloudy while they were inside, and it became clear that the "glowing city on the river," as Alasis liked to bill itself, was more marketing than it was truth.

Ever since Tesla harnessed the power of the falls, the city had provided electricity to a good portion of the Northeast, so it wasn't a surprise it had been well defended against missiles during the end of the world. The city had survived the war relatively unscathed. But it hadn't weathered the apocalypse well at all. The streets were filthy and the buildings were run down. People's baser instincts had taken a greater toll on the city than Armageddon ever could.

The power was on. This much was true. It was the largest city left with reliable electric delivery thanks to the power stations that surrounded the falls. But with the clouds casting their gloom over the area, it was clear that not all parts of the city got equal treatment. Lights shone inside some buildings, but with a few notable exceptions, the lights outside weren't lit. Streetlights were dark, and neglected exterior signage flickered at best. What had been the Canadian side of the river appeared much brighter. This was no surprise. The government of Alasis occupied that side and left its peasants in the dark.

In the dark, but not unwatched. There were enough posters around to make Big Brother green with envy, and every one of them reminded the citizens how good they had it. "Invictus is for us," declared one poster featuring a majestic interpretation of the tyrant behind the city-state. He stood rigid, looking off to the right in a silver helm that echoed that of an ancient Roman commander. Another poster was a constructivist image of the hydro-electric dam with a glowing city in the distance that claimed Alasis as "The power of the North." Others encouraged support of the Legion or demanded that citizens "Labor hard!"

The Roman theme was carried out all over town. Jerry identified two of the Alasis Legionaries by their polished metal helmets and the crimson capes that hung from their shoulders. They had traded their lances and shields for automatic rifles, but even these bore their tyrant's crest. The soldiers' appearance stood in stark contrast to the dilapidated buildings along the street.

One of the soldiers caught him staring and called him out with an all too predictable *Halt!*

"Halt?" Jerry mumbled to himself. "Really?" He halted and turned toward the soldiers.

The pair marched toward him with the confidence of a bully-- that certain swagger that could only be bought with stolen lunch money. They stopped in front of him and studied him with a sneer. "I don't recognize you."

It wasn't a statement. It was an accusation. It was clear from the way the Legionary spoke and the way he held himself that the guard was accustomed to being feared and respected. Jerry could only imagine how brutal the Alasis guards must have been to the citizens to warrant this expectation. Their tactics were no doubt ruthless, and their application of law and order must have been distributed swiftly and without mercy. It was the only way to explain why a man in a cape thought he deserved respect.

"I'm new in town," Jerry explained. When that prompted no response, he added, "Just got in this morning."

They looked at him without expression. Judging him, but giving no sign of their verdict. It was an awkward silence for those who were being judged.

"I like your cape," Jerry said with a nod to the cape.

This got things moving.

"Turn around and put your hands on the wall."

"Did I do something wrong?" he asked as he turned slowly toward the nearest wall.

The guard grabbed him by the shoulder and shoved him into the bricks. "I haven't decided yet."

Jerry was able to put his hands out before his face smacked into the wall of someplace called Smoking Joe's Indian Trading Post. This stopped him from hitting his face, but it was enough to trigger a reflexive thought that said, "Take his gun, use him as a human shield, shoot the other guard and then strangle this dick with his own cape. It will be funny." His inner monologue had been rather violent ever since he'd been consumed with rage. But he wasn't here to cause problems. Yet.

The frisking was a little rougher than necessary. The guard grabbed rather than patted and left bruises along his legs and waist. They found nothing. There was nothing to find. Alasis wasn't big on having the underclass armed and had made possession of everything short of a spork a capital offense. And you had better have a good reason for carrying that spork.

Satisfied that he was unarmed but not content to stop the

oppression the guard punched him in the lower back and Jerry dropped to the ground. Short of breath, he wheezed a command to the dog. She was fiercely loyal, and he could see her getting riled up. Even though the command sounded like a cough, the dog understood and remained still.

The guard grabbed him by the throat and pulled him to his feet. He leaned in close and snarled, "I'm going to tell you something about me. I don't like change. I like things just the way they are. And you? You're change. You're something different in my life that I now have to adjust to. And, if you ask me, that sounds a little unfair. I don't like extra work. Therefore, I don't like you. Or your stupid dog. Do you get me?"

With the hand around his throat, Jerry couldn't answer if he wanted to. He could snap the guard's wrist and break his neck or gouge out his eye with a thumb, but that was his inner monologue talking again. All he could really do at this point was nod and let the soldier think he'd won.

"Welcome to Alasis," the Legionary said, and buried a fist in Jerry's stomach that doubled him over and made him consider throwing up.

The last bit of air exploded from his lungs and he collapsed to the ground once again. He struggled to get his breath while the guard walked away. It was all he could do to wheeze, "Thank you."

The guard acknowledged the sound with a glance over his shoulder but never broke his stride as he and his partner walked on down the street to find another victim.

Chewy padded over and licked his face.

"I'm fine, girl. Just a bit of acting," he said, though he sat against the wall for a full minute or two before even bothering to stand. The compliance and kindness had been an act, but the blow to his stomach had been a little too method for him. The guard had a mean right sucker punch and even though he knew it was coming, it really did knock the wind out of him.

After that the pair encountered several more patrols on their walk through town and did their best to avoid them. From the number of troops on the streets, it was clear that Invictus didn't trust his peasants to keep the peace, or their allegiance to him, all by themselves.

Most of the troops walked their beats, but he spotted several others in patrol vehicles driving up and down the streets. There was no consistency in their make or model, but each had been treated to a matching paint scheme with the Alasis crest painted on by someone possessing a high degree of skill. At a distance the crests looked like decals. It wasn't until one drove by him that he saw that the vigilant eagle insignias were hand-painted. A vulture would have been more fitting, but the eagle looked mean enough.

The guards certainly looked better than the people on the streets. They milled about with no apparent destination in mind— if they milled at all. Many sat huddled on the stoops of the old homes or in the entryways to the former businesses. Jerry and Chewy passed through several crowded shanty towns that filled the parking lots and alleyways. No one seemed eager to talk. Not even to beg. They looked hungry and defeated. A few toiled away, hammering and cutting at pieces of scrap metal. But, even with this din, the general demeanor of the people and the roar of the falls in the distance made the town eerily quiet.

His destination was less so.

The first person to ever go over the falls in a barrel was a woman named Annie Taylor. After testing the contraption on a cat, she survived the plummet and walked away with little more than a slight gash on her head and a really pissed off cat. The first man went over ten years later and broke both his ankles, but otherwise figuratively walked away unharmed. The third person to go over the falls was Charles Stephens, and they only found his arm. Just one. Still strapped inside his custom-built barrel. There was a good chance the bar, Charlie's Arm, was named in his honor.

As Jerry approached he could hear the pounding of the odd drum and the occasional feedback of an electric guitar through the walls. Flyers posted in the windows informed him a band would be performing later that night, so he assumed he was hearing the sound check. It had been years since he'd heard electric instruments.

"Harmeggedon," he read aloud. He looked at Chewy. "Harmeggedon. They could have called themselves anything. Shit, they could have called themselves the Beatles and gotten away with it. But they went with Harmeggedon. Kind of makes you think we were asking for it all along, doesn't it?"

The dog said nothing.

He opened the door and a wave of sound and smell hit him hard in the face. The singer was giving the microphone a run-through, and Jerry was glad to know he wouldn't have to be there for the show.

"Strike the match!" the singer screamed. "Set the blaze! Watch it grow! Make them—"

"Okay," the sound man interrupted. "I think we've got it. You can stop singing now, please."

Harmeggedon's singer threw the horns, gave a *whooo* and wandered off stage.

The meager crowd in the bar applauded his departure. It wasn't as large a crowd as Jerry expected, and he attributed the low number of loiterers to the building-sized bouncer that greeted him inside the doorway. The man said hello and had him against the wall for another rough frisking before Jerry could even return the greeting.

"He's okay, Doorway," the woman behind the bar called across the room.

The call had caused only one or two of the patrons to look up from their drinks. The light crowd looked well fed and sturdy, unlike most of the people he had passed on the street. If they had money to buy drinks it must have meant they were some of the few in town with work.

Aside from the few patrons and the bouncer, there was a man

and a woman tending the bar and a kid mopping up something nasty in the corner.

Jerry sat down at the bar, wondering how, after living through the actual apocalypse, people could find so much fascination with it. Maybe embracing it or making light of it was their way of dealing with the pain and misery it had wrought upon the Earth. In Harmeggedon's case, however, it seemed like a cheap marketing gimmick.

"You want a Posthopocalypse?" the woman tending the bar asked.

"I'm sorry, a what?"

She pointed to a sign above her head. Posthopocalypse was a 90-minute India Pale Ale. Its name was written in a mushroom cloud stemming from a beer bottle. Beneath the bottle was another line promising that the beer would "Blow his mind."

"You want one?" she asked again.

"Do you have a lager?"

"Sorry. But I did just tap a blonde you might like," she said with a wink.

"Give me two," he said, ignoring the terrible joke, and the bartender headed off to the taps.

Unlike just about everything else, the apocalypse did not destroy the craft beer trend. In fact, it made it worse. After the end of the world, everyone was forced to make their own beer so they figured why not capitalize on it. Every town had at least one person with some home brewing experience and a penchant for puns, so the trend continued through the chaos and killing and thrived on this side of Armageddon.

The bartender set the beers in front of him and he took a sip.

"What do you think of the old Ablondic Tom, there?"

"The what?"

She pointed at the beer in his hand.

Jerry took another drink and gave her a thumbs-up in hopes it would be enough. He had to admit it wasn't a bad beer. Actually, it was one of the better beers he'd had in a while. Still, part of him longed for a simple, shitty Budweiser. But he dismissed those cravings as nostalgia.

"So are you going to keep pretending you don't know me?" Jerry asked the bartender.

She grabbed a rag and started wiping down the bar in front of him. "That's usually what you want."

Jerry picked up the second beer and set it on the ground. Chewy gave it such a cautious sniff that he thought she might be part mastiff, part hipster. The Ablondic Tom passed her sniff test and she started lapping it up. He left her to her beer and turned back to the woman.

"A lot of things have changed, Liv."

"Oh," she mocked. "Then you should buy me a beer and tell me all about it."

Jerry nodded with a smile as she grabbed a beer of her own and slid over the bar.

"What do you want?" she asked, taking a seat. There was no *it's good to see you* or *how have you been*.

"We need to talk."

She wrapped a hand around the glass and took a drink. With a swig down, she set the glass on the bar and smiled. "So. The legendary Librarian. In my little old town."

"When you told me you were heading this way I kind of figured you'd be running the place by now." He was only half kidding. She could talk almost anyone out of anything. Possibly even an empire.

"Who says I'm not? I may not have a fancy red cape, but who's to say I'm not the one pulling the strings around here? And just to keep everyone fooled, instead of living across the river in the relative lap of luxury, I'm hiding out in this shit hole to throw everyone off."

"If that were the case, I wouldn't be here."

"What are you doing here?" she asked. "I wouldn't say it's the best likeness, but your face is plastered all over town between the words WANTED and DEAD. There's no OR anymore. They took that off a week ago."

"I'm here to kill Invictus."

Liv had a thousand laughs in her vocabulary, and each one was designed to do one of a thousand things. Break a heart or make it dance. Sway a vote or stay a hand. But this was the first time he'd heard this particular one and figured it might be the first time he heard her laugh betray actual amusement. "Is that right?"

Jerry stared at her with dead eyes and took a drink of his own.

"Just you and that dog of yours?"

He shook his head and set the glass down. "No. We're going to have some help."

"You're the most wanted man in the city. Who's going to help you?"

"You are."

This laugh began genuine and turned sarcastic somewhere in the middle.

"I'm not kidding," Jerry said.

"I know you're not." She slapped a hand on his knee and shook it. "That's what's so funny."

"You owe me, Liv."

She raised the glass for another drink. "I don't owe you that much."

"You owe me, Liv."

"I owe a lot of people. And if you get me killed, they're not going to be too happy with me, or you. So quit being so selfish and get out of my bar."

"You owe me your life."

"That's right, and it isn't worth what you're asking." She stood up to leave. "Thanks for the beer."

"Sit down." His voice was cold. Colder than even he expected. It stopped the woman in her tracks and she turned back to him with a raised eyebrow and a tilted head.

"Oh my," she said with a hand to her chest. "There's that big bad Librarian all the girls talk about."

He just gestured to the barstool.

She sat and smiled. "It always makes me laugh, the way they all talk about you. Especially here. On one side of the river you're a monster. The greatest threat to everything Invictus has built. They blame you for everything that doesn't go right. Over here, on this side of the river, you're a damn Davy Crocket. You should hear the way they talk about you, some kind of icon of liberty. If either side ever met you they would be greatly disappointed."

"Liv—"

She slammed the glass down on the bar. "Do you have any idea how much better my life would be if I turned you in?"

"You know better than to cross me."

She smiled and nodded in agreement. "I do. But this town is full of people that don't. Liberty is one thing. But a ticket to the other side of the river is something else."

"We'll see about that. I just need you to arrange a meeting for me."

She stared at him for a long moment. "You know, I could never tell if you were an optimist or an idiot."

"In the end, does it really make a difference?"

She shrugged. "I guess not."

"Does that mean you'll help me?"

"Oh, that's a hell no. I've got a good thing going here. But don't you worry. Your secret is safe with me, O' Hero of New Hope. Besides, no one would believe me if I told them it was you." She stood and turned to leave once more.

Chewy sneezed and knocked the glass of beer over. Jerry wasn't worried about the mess. First of all, it wouldn't show in a place like this, and the dog was sure to lick it up. He looked for the kid with the mop to tell him not to bother, but the child had disappeared. He turned back to Liv. "You forget that I know more than a few secrets of yours."

"See, that's just it. You can threaten me all you want but I know you. And that's not you at all. You're not going to like hearing this since you're out for revenge and all, but you're one of the good guys, Jerry. Hell, you may be the last good guy left on Earth. And good guys don't blackmail. They can't go around threatening the innocent. If they did, they wouldn't be so good anymore. So no, I won't help you. But I will tell you this: If you really want to kill Invictus, you'd better hurry."

"What do you mean?"

"Let's just say you're not the only person looking for revenge."

# 3

Mr. Christopher sat cradling the stump of his left arm in his remaining hand. He could still feel fingers that were no longer there. They itched. And having an itch he couldn't scratch was almost as annoying as the raspy breath that was coming from the man sitting next to him wearing the bear mask.

"Do you have to wear that mask?" he asked as he shifted in his seat trying to find some way to hold his arm that didn't hurt.

"What? You got a problem with bears, Stumpy?" The voice was muffled by the mask but the sarcasm came through loud and clear. And the sarcasm stung a bit more coming from a bear. "You mad they ate your hand?"

Christopher fought the urge to strangle the driver with his one good hand and answered instead. "It wasn't the bear, it was the bastard with the ax," he explained for the third time. "So, I have no problem with the look of your mask, it's the sound your rank breath makes coming out of it."

"Do you want a ride or don't you?" the bear asked.

"Just drive, Teddy Ruxpin."

"My car, my rules. The mask stays on. You don't like it you can walk your crippled ass back home."

Christopher sighed and tried to pull his hat down to shield his face against the wind. He couldn't decide if the lack of a windshield bothered him more than his chauffeur wearing an animal mask. In the end, he decided that both were horrible.

And he hated to admit it, but the bear had a point. He was lucky to get a ride back to Alasis at all. The Librarian had taken out most of the men and women Invictus had sent against him. The rest had been chased off by a biker gang that had found its way to Tolerance. He had given up finding a ride and started walking when Winnie the shithead came across him on the road north.

He was also lucky to be alive. After being shackled to the Librarian and put in a bear fight, he should be grateful that he only lost his hand. That he wasn't killed in the crossfire was miracle enough. Yes, he realized he should be grateful, but he was pissed. His left arm throbbed, his head ached and all he could think about was getting back to Alasis and finding a way to get his revenge.

It wasn't just that the man had cut off his hand. The Librarian had proven to be the only mark Christopher could not deliver and if he didn't rectify that, it could put his standing in the city in jeopardy. No one wanted to be seen as a failure in the eyes of Invictus. Mr. Christopher knew he could run, but he would be found. His best chance now was to limp home with a plan to make the situation right and if that meant being driven home by an asthmatic bear, so be it.

He did his best to block out the raspy breath and the hacking cough and pulled his hat down over his face to try to get some sleep. He had finally found a corner where the wind wasn't horrible when the car lurched and the bear screamed.

Instinctively he reached for a gun that wasn't there with a hand he no longer had. A second crash knocked the hat from his head and he sat up in time to see the pickup truck ram them again.

The man in the bear mask growled and swerved left, aiming for the truck. But the truck slammed on its brakes long enough that the bear missed and their car turned sideways on the road. Having been modified with an emphasis on scariness over performance, the car quickly lost control and began to roll.

Christopher did what he could to stabilize himself as he was tossed around. His right hand found part of the roll cage and grabbed the support, while his left arm flailed about as the car rolled down the highway before it came to rest on its right side. Christopher could feel the cement on his back and the driver on top of his chest. The man in the mask was still alive and struggling to stand up. Mr. Christopher shoved at him with his good hand and tried to free himself from the restraints. The Winnie's wheezing was worse than ever, but the man managed to get to his feet and crawl out the driver side door.

A gunshot sounded and the wheezing stopped. The man fell back in the car and landed on top of Christopher with blood pouring from under the bear's face. Christopher did his best to remain calm and was able to wiggle out through the missing windshield onto the road. Getting to his feet proved much more difficult. His legs fell from underneath him as he tried to rise and he still wasn't used to not having his left hand to support him. Every time he tried, he drove the stump into the ground and pain shot up his arm. He stumbled backward toward the edge of the road, searching desperately for his attacker.

The pickup truck just sat there in the dark with hazard lights flashing, painting the road a sickening amber.

He couldn't see the driver. He couldn't see where the shot had come from. All he could see was smoke coming off the wrecked car. Everything was silent. Even the pickup truck had turned off its engine. He stumbled as he backed closer to the shoulder and fell to the ground. The pain was overwhelming. His legs hurt, his arm hurt and now his head hurt. He wasn't sure he could trust his senses. He strained to hear anything and thought he heard footsteps, but he couldn't be certain. He tried to pinpoint the sound. It had to be coming from the truck but he couldn't see a thing. He couldn't say if it was his own mind or a voice from out of the darkness, but it came as a hoarse whisper. One word. "Run."

Mr. Christopher rolled over backward, off the shoulder and down to the ditch that ran alongside the highway. Somewhere along the way he found his feet and began to run. He dashed through a drainage pipe to the other side of the road hoping that he could shake the mysterious assailant. The pipe was filled with branches and other trash that the storm waters had brought over the years, and they tangled his feet and drove him to the ground several more times before he cleared the pipe. Once on the other side, he turned north and ran through the ditch. He desperately wanted to look over his shoulder but was afraid of what he would see.

He ran up the ditch, across the service road and found himself in the parking lot of a restaurant that had been known for its Southern style and older clientele. He scrambled up the porch and ran to one of the windows, picked up a rocking chair, tossed it through the pane of glass and followed it inside.

Tripping over a display of painted rocks, he stumbled through the bric-a-brac that had filled the shelves of the restaurant's old country store. He looked for anything he could use as a weapon, but the only thing of substance was a metal sign that said "Live. Laugh. Love." Swung hard enough, it could leave a gash. He shook it to test its strength and it gave off a nice wobbly sound that assured him he was screwed.

The wooden porch out front thunked as footsteps fell across its planks. Christopher set the sign down on the counter and raced out of the country store and into the dining room. It was a mess of overturned tables and chairs, as if there had been an Old West gunfight or an irresistible early bird special. Getting around the solid furniture wasn't easy or quiet, and he couldn't hear anything over his own escape. When he finally stopped, he could feel eyes on him.

Whispering. This time he knew it wasn't in his own head. It was low and ragged but not forced. His attacker wasn't trying to sound scary. He just was. "Christoph."

His name wasn't Christoph but it was close enough to scare the shit out of him. His heart stopped. His palm sweat. "Who's there?"

He could hear the footsteps moving through the store scattering the kitschy crap that had fallen from the shelves to litter the floor. The whisper repeated itself.

"Christoph."

"Show yourself!" He stumbled backward and tripped over a chair. By the time he looked back up, the figure was standing in the entrance to the dining room. The shadow wasn't tall, but it was broad enough to be a threat.

"What do you want, you coward?" he screamed in a shaking voice he would never have recognized as his own. He was always the one in control. He pulled the strings. He set the traps and he did the scaring. He wasn't used to being alone or being unprepared. He had made his reputation by being cold and calculating. Now it was all he could do to pull himself up straight and not tremble at the knees. "Who are you?"

"I'm surprised you don't remember me."

Christopher's back was against the waiter's stand and he felt around behind it for a weapon. All he could find was a piece of silverware and he couldn't tell from the handle what it was. He gripped it tightly in his hand and silently hoped it wasn't a spoon. It wasn't much, but it was something and it gave him some sense of control. "I forget a lot of people."

"Yeah," the shadowy figure said. "That seems like your style. But I thought you might remember me. Because of you someone very important to me is dead."

Christopher had killed a lot of people. And when you broadened it to include people who died because of him, it certainly didn't help narrow down the shadow's identity. "That doesn't give me much to go on."

"How's the hand?"

No. It couldn't be him. Christopher's list of enemies wasn't short, but few people had as much reason to hate him as the Librarian. From what he heard, the girl his bounty had been traveling with was killed by the Skinners. The man had already left him to die once at the hands of a bear or the outraged citizens of Tolerance. Why would he bother tracking him down now? How could he know he escaped? He gripped the eating utensil tighter in his hand as the shadow stepped forward into the light.

It wasn't him. It wasn't the Librarian. It was one of those damn hillbillies he'd hired. The short one with the scars on his face. "Oh thank God it's only you, Willie."

The man responded with a scream and grabbed one of the chairs from the floor. He yelled as he hurled the chair across the dining room, "I ain't Willie!"

"I'm sorry. Look—"

"My name is Coy!"

"Look, Coy–"

Coy growled as he came closer, "I mean, I was Coy. But now you can call me...The Coyote."

Mr. Christopher couldn't help but chuckle as he asked, "Why?"

"Because, eating Willie changes a man."

The words rolled around Christopher's head for a moment before he stammered, "You can't mean what you just said."

"Oh, I'm afraid so, Christoph. You see, your friends made me eat my friend. They cut him up and cooked him like bacon and fed him to me strip by strip."

"But, why did you eat him?"

"Because they told me Willie was bacon!" Coy grabbed another chair and smashed it against the wall. "And I like bacon! And I was hungry! And you can't blame a man for wanting bacon when he's hungry!"

Christopher held up his stump in an effort to calm the man. "Look, Coy—"

"The Coyote dammit!"

"Coyote—"

"The Coyote!"

"The Coyote, I'm sorry you ate your friend. But that wasn't me.

That was the Skinners! You can't blame me for that. They're the ones you want."

"Oh, I've got a whole list, Christoph. It's long and the spelling may not be 100% all the way right, but your name is on it. If it weren't for you, I'd have never gotten into this whole mess. Willie would still be alive and I'd be back home doing sweet jumps on the Coy-O-Te."

"I... I thought you were The Coyote."

"I am The Coyote! My bike is the Coy-O-Te. Are you stupid or something?"

"I'm sorry, but you can understand my confusion. Both those things sound the same."

"But, they're spelled different. Completely different!"

"You always were an idiot, Coy."

"Maybe. I don't win a lot of arguments. But that's not my fault. I was better at arguing back when we had me mes to help."

"Me mes?"

"Yeah. Little pictures with words on 'em. I was never the best with words, but Ole Spongebob...he always knew what to say."

"Memes? You mean memes?"

"Are those the pictures?"

"Yes. Memes."

"Then that's what I mean."

"So, Spongebob made you smarter?"

Coy rushed forward and got in Christopher's face. The breath and spittle were horrendous. "Watch what you say about—"

Christopher stabbed Coy in the chest with the silverware.

It was a spoon.

Dammit.

The Coyote grabbed Christopher's hand, twisted the spoon free and sent it clattering to the floor. Christopher tried to punch him with his other hand, but it only caused him pain. Coy caught him with a backhand, kicked out his legs and knocked him to the floor.

Mr. Christopher coughed in pain and cradled his wounded arm in his free hand as The Coyote squatted down in front of him.

"A week ago, that would have worked. Coy would have fallen for that or been scared. But not The Coyote. You see, Chris? I didn't just change my name. When you feed a man his friend, it has a certain affect."

"You mean effect," Mr. Christopher winced. "Nothing's changed, Coy. You're still a moron."

Coy smiled through missing teeth and grabbed Christopher's wrist. He slammed the man's hand against the wooden stand and drove a knife through the palm.

Mr. Christopher screamed and tried to pull it free but The Coyote wouldn't let him.

He pinned the bounty hunter against the wall. "You're going to help me, Chris. I want to make sure my list of names isn't missing any...names. So we're going to talk. And then I'm going to kill you."

# 4

They started following him as soon as he left Charlie's Arm. Two men and one big, hairy dog. The men weren't dressed any different from the other people in town, but they appeared a little less downtrodden and walked with more confidence than the general populace.

The dog was a Newfoundland covered in dark brown fur and a fair amount of drool. It was a massive creature, but the breed's dopey expression gave it a friendly enough look as it loped along beside the man.

The dog's owner had a friendly, if not suspicious look, about him. It was like if he ever had to kill you, he wouldn't hesitate, but he'd probably say sorry while he did it. Relatively clean and recently shaven, he was easy enough to pick out of the crowd. The other man was grizzled, had an unkempt beard and wore a pissy expression like he was the kind of man that used to get upset and yell at strangers on the internet. Now that there was nowhere left to vent, the irritation came out in his face. He had hard blue eyes that had seen things and squinted in every direction.

Jerry and Chewy walked toward the river and one of the men

soon peeled off the tail. Thinking they had gone unnoticed, the other man and his dog stayed behind them.

The Librarian played along and went about his business. They passed more and more guards as they approached the Rainbow Bridge. The entrance was now barricaded and defended by two dozen men in black capes who, judging by their expressions, were even less friendly than the pair he had encountered earlier. He gave them a wide berth and acted disinterested in the bridge itself, but a cursory glance revealed a flurry of activity on the span as the men worked to repair the damage from the morning's attack.

The Librarian turned and continued upstream to an observation deck that jutted out over the river. At Prospect Point a tower rose from the base of the river to well above street level, while the observation deck itself connected to the street and ran out past the tower and over the river to give visitors a limited view of Horseshoe Falls. The tower itself had once served as access to boat tours below. Visitors once rode the elevator down to the river, where they would board the famous Maid of the Mist fleet of ships for an up-close and very wet view of the great wonder.

A glance over his shoulder revealed that the man and his dog were still doing their best to act like they weren't following him. Jerry made his way down the observation deck as if he hadn't seen the pair and looked toward the Falls. Even if the Maid of the Mist fleet hadn't washed away years ago, it wouldn't have been much of a tour. The base of the Falls had become a collection point for the drifting hulks and abandoned ships of the Great Lakes. They said that every vessel left afloat would eventually find its way here. And many already had. Several large ships were already piled up in the plunge pool beneath the Falls, unaware or uncaring that they were ruining the view.

Despite the cold weather, there were several other spectators on the platform with him. No one seemed particularly interested in the view. He guessed that even something as spectacular as the Falls would become a boring sight if you had to look at it every day. More than likely, they were watching for visitors. Tourism had certainly slowed after the end of the world but Alasis, and anywhere with electric light, drew its fair share of travelers. The ideal ones would be more focused on the Falls than their valuables. He stared at the Falls and looked the part of the easy mark, but no one approached him. Chewy saw to that. The dog's mere presence made everyone else's pockets easier to pick.

He loitered for twenty minutes before making his way back to town. The man and his dog had disappeared. In their place was their companion from earlier. The grizzled tail looked out over the river and paid no attention to Jerry as he passed. He and Chewy turned upstream and crossed the smaller American Falls by way of a footbridge to Goat Island before making their way to Terrapin Point.

This lookout area sat just above the Horseshoe Falls and provided an excellent view of the rusting boats in the river below. It also gave him a better view of what he had really been looking at back at the platform. A casino tower was directly across the river. The lights were on inside and from his vantage point it barely looked like time had touched the building at all. But it had certainly been corrupted. Invictus had made the tower his capital and his residence. Even from here, Jerry could see the fortifications ringing the base of the building. They looked considerable.

To get his revenge, he would have to get inside and find Invictus without getting killed by the hundreds of soldiers that no doubt filled the building. That was going to take some doing.

The military presence on Goat Island was thick itself and a short stroll revealed why. Pulled by the mighty force of the Falls, a fishing trawler had found its way downriver. Before it could join the others at the bottom, a salvage crew had tethered it and set to work stripping it of any valuable materials. Citizens formed the work crew, but more crimson-caped guards oversaw the operation. They didn't have the friendliest management style. It consisted mainly of swearing and threatening to shoot everyone. But, even if it wasn't the most HR compliant approach, it was effective, and the citizens moved about quickly unloading the cargo from the ship and then heading back for more.

Jerry took the 1st Street Bridge back into town and met his tail there. The man and the Newfoundland let him pass without incident and waited before following him once more. Despite the fact that the man and his dog had been shadowing him all day, he wasn't getting a dangerous feeling from the pair like he did from the other man. Still, he was getting tired of being followed and he decided it was finally time for everyone to meet.

Leading Chewy through one of the many shantytowns, he began a series of stair-step maneuvers through the narrow avenues formed by the hovels. It wouldn't shake the man following him. He knew that. But it would make deciding where to introduce himself his decision.

He finally decided it would be a former postal box shop. He was far enough ahead of his tail now that he had to wait to be spotted. Once the man caught sight of him, he darted into the shop through a broken window and screamed for Chewy to follow.

Like everywhere else after the apocalypse, the place had been ransacked. But it had never been repurposed, and the floor was littered with torn packages and the contents that scavengers had found useless. Slipping and sliding on the shipping materials, he rushed through the shop and out the back door where he stopped, waited and then clotheslined his tail as the man chased after him.

The Newfie scrambled out the door and growled at the Librarian. Chewy crashed into the dog and the two began to circle one another, growling and snarling. There were a few false charges from each dog but it was mostly a show of force at this point.

The man leapt from the ground quicker than Jerry expected. He didn't attack. He just held his throat and coughed.

"I don't like being followed." Jerry took a step forward but the man put up his hand like he didn't want to fight.

Another hand landed on Jerry's shoulder and the Librarian spun to find the second tail. The man with the pissy look on his face was in the process of throwing a left hook. Jerry deflected it with his forearm and pulled his left arm into his waist to absorb a body blow from the man's right. He blocked another combination of punches before he had a chance to counter.

The dogs continued their dance to determine dominance and the teeth were really starting to come out now. Chewy had the weight advantage by a few pounds but her size wasn't enough to deter the Newfie.

Jerry took an unconventional stance. His right arm was dominant, but he led with it nonetheless. He had always reasoned that he'd land more jabs than power punches and figured it was best to have those do the most damage. He snuck two through the man's defenses and put Mr. Pissy back on his heels.

The other man was back on his feet now and grabbed Jerry from behind in a bear hug and pinned his arms to his side.

"Easy now," was all the man could say before Jerry reacted.

He stepped to the right and back, placing his leg behind his attacker's while reaching for the man's opposite ankle. He lifted the leg, reared back and drop slammed the man onto the concrete.

His other attacker moved in with an insult and a quick right that caught Jerry on the side of the neck. The left followed predictably, and Jerry was able to step inside of the hook. He exploded forward, carrying himself and the man back across the alleyway and into the side of a dumpster. Jerry pinned him there and drove fist after fist into the man's ribs while his enemy responded with hammer blows to Jerry's back.

The dogs' growling turned to snarls and Jerry could hear the sound of snapping jaws over the grunts he and his opponent were putting out.

"Lord Stanley, heel," came the command, and half the growling ceased. Chewy wasn't quite ready to disengage. The voice then addressed the man on the dumpster. "Let him go."

"The hell with that. He's still hitting me."

"Just stop. Both of you, please. Guy, we just want to talk."

The fists on his back started getting lighter and lighter and finally stopped.

Jerry stood up and stared at his attacker. The man's face was ragged and rough, but it had been that way long before Jerry had started hitting it. His eyes were cold and the windows to a black soul. But he could see that the fight was over. He put one more fist in the man's stomach and dropped him to the ground.

He turned to face the other man and called Chewy off. The growling stopped and the mastiff moved to her master's side.

"We know who you are," the man said.

The man against the dumpster coughed with a nod and began the long process of standing up.

"You know who I am?" Jerry asked.

"We know why you're here. It's why we're all here. We all have a score to settle across the river."

"So you don't know who I am."

"We know your type. A post-apocalyptic nomadic warrior. You're a loner with a code. You stand up for what's right. You help people. And in doing that, you ran afoul of Invictus and his killers. He didn't like you standing up for people and struck back. So now you're here to get even. Does that sound about right?"

Jerry didn't say anything.

The man just shrugged. "We can smell our own." He stuck out his hand and stepped closer. "The name's Joshua."

Jerry looked at the outstretched hand but did not shake it.

Joshua chuckled and pointed to the man by the dumpster. "That's Lu—"

"No names," the man interrupted and spat on the ground.

Joshua continued. "I'm sure my story isn't that different from yours, though mine started on the other side of the border."

"I've heard of you," Jerry said. "They call you the Mad Max with Manners."

"People say things." Joshua blushed a bit and gave him a sheepish grin. "But I'm no hero. I just want to do what's right. And doing what's right got me on the wrong side of Alasis. He started up in Canada, you know? Invictus. I guess he figured it would be easier to conquer us Canucks. No less spirit, but not nearly as many guns as you all have in the States. But Armageddon was enough to finally piss us all off and we did what we could to fight back."

The Newfoundland barked at his side.

"Oh, of course you've already met Lord Stanley."

"Lord Stanley?" Jerry asked.

"I just call him that for short," Joshua said. "He's actually Son of Lord Stanley."

"Don't do this, Bob and Doug," the man by the dumpster groaned.

"That's right," Joshua continued. "He's Lord Stanley's pup."

"No one likes it when you do that," he groaned.

Jerry rolled his eyes. "You're really playing to type, aren't you?"

"Are you going to help us or not?" This came from the man against the dumpster. His demeanor wasn't nearly as cheery as Joshua's.

"I don't know," Jerry replied. "It kind of goes against the whole lone warrior mystique. Don't you think?"

"But you're not alone," Lucas said. "You're not the only one that wants to see Invictus pay for all he's done."

Jerry shook his head. "Sorry fellas. Teaming up has never really worked out for me."

"So you're going to take on a whole army by yourself?" The grizzled warrior asked. "You're not too bright."

"I think you guys know the drill. Contact the Resistance. Win their trust. Give a rousing speech and overthrow the dictator. It's fairly standard stuff."

"You think we didn't try that?" He threw an elbow into the dumpster for effect. The receptacle boomed but it also hurt his elbow. He did his best to hide the pain as he continued. "We all tried that. This town has the most stubborn resistance I've ever seen."

Jerry shrugged. "Yeah, but you've never seen one of my 'rise up' speeches. I'm told they're quite good."

"It doesn't matter. They've got an army of people. One of the most organized I've ever seen. But they won't listen. They won't listen to anyone except the Librarian. They've got it in their heads that he's their leader or something. The whole city walks around with books in their arms in protest. They shush people, in protest. They really have a thing for this guy. It's annoying."

"Well, I guess I'm in luck then." The news was shocking to him. He had never set out to be a leader. Or an inspiration, or a legend. He had always run from his reputation. It had been nothing but trouble. But, now it looked like it might finally pay off. It was finally time to own up to who he was, and he might as well start with these two.

"I am the Librarian."

He wasn't sure what he expected but the laughter wasn't part of it. The Canadian tried to stifle his, but the man at the dumpster needed a minute before he could even speak again.

"You can't be the Librarian. I'm the Librarian." He doubled over laughing again. He pointed at Joshua. "And he's the Librarian."

Jerry narrowed his eyes. "I see."

Joshua composed himself first. "Don't bother, buddy. We've all tried telling them we're the Librarian. It doesn't work."

"But, I am—"

Another burst of laughter from the grizzled man cut him off.

"Never mind," Jerry said and started walking away.

"Wait," Joshua said and chased after him. "We're sorry. We didn't mean to laugh. We're serious here. I don't know who you are but it's obvious you can handle yourself. Invictus needs to be stopped and the more men we have the better."

More people could mean a better chance at toppling Invictus's army. But it also increased the chance of betrayal. The horrors of Eternal Hope, Colorado flashed through his mind. That had been the result of misplaced trust and it was a mistake he couldn't afford to make again. And, selfishly, Invictus was his to kill. He looked at Joshua and whistled for his dog. She stood up, and Chewy and The Librarian walked away.

# 5

He worked his way down the hall, doing his best not to touch the walls. They were cold enough in the summer and this time of year he worried his hands might stick to them like a tongue on a lamp post. Touching them was unavoidable, however, as the floor slanted beneath him. Planking had been put down to level it out but that was shaky at best. Some of the wooden planks floated in puddles of water. One shifted under his weight and a *sploosh* sent a rush of near-freezing water up his pant leg. It clung to his shin and sent a shiver through his body as he tried to steady himself. He reached out instinctively and touched the wall. His hand didn't stick. It was silly to think it would. But the metal was almost painfully cold and he pulled his hand back quickly.

The boy looked down and found himself ankle deep in the water and swore. He looked at his sock and remembered something his parents had told him. Before the world as everyone had known it ended, people use to complain about everything. Especially stupid things. They would complain about having to wait in line. It didn't matter what was at the end of the line. They would complain even if it was something amazing. They would complain about things not moving fast enough and they would complain about things happening too fast. Food was one of their favorite things to complain about. But no one complained about food now. One of the things his parents said they liked about the end of the world was that, despite losing almost everything, people complained a lot less. They said it put things in perspective and that he should always think before complaining. So he thought long and hard before he finally decided that cold wet socks still sucked and he should be free to bitch about them.

He shook what water he could off his foot and staggered on down the hallway. There were voices ahead and they were arguing. The adults told him it was called debating, but he knew arguing when he heard it. He was ten. He wasn't stupid. Some resistance. They spent more time fighting each other than the enemy.

The child pushed back the shoddy wooden door and stepped inside as quietly as a crappy, crooked homemade door would allow. He didn't want them to hear him. He didn't want to interrupt. It wasn't courtesy as much as that he liked it when the adults argued. They used the best words. Especially when they didn't know he was there.

They were really going at it this time. Gatsby was yelling at Pride and she was just waiting for her chance to fight back. She always had the best comebacks because Gatsby was an idiot. The boy smiled as he realized no one saw him come in.

"It's time to act," the woman said. "Lelawala is ready. We can—"

"No," Gatsby interrupted. "There's still planning to do."

"The planning is done, man." Fahrenheit said. The boy liked Fahrenheit. He was a big man with a deep voice and everything about his look said he should be scary, but he was one of the kindest and calmest men on the council.

"The attack plan, yeah." Gatsby conceded. "But what about everything that comes after?" Gatsby walked over to a table covered with papers and started shuffling through them. "If we topple Invictus and don't have a plan to put in place once he's gone, this will all be for nothing. Now, I have a list of slogans we could use to let the world know that we're a free city once again."

"Slogans?" Fahrenheit chuckled. "Are you serious with this?"

"Yes," he said, and began to read some of the ideas. "Niagara's Back! The Falls Have Risen! What Went Down Has Now Come Up!"

"Those are terrible, man." Fahrenheit said.

"They are pretty bad," Pride agreed.

"I thought the last one was pretty clever," Gatsby said. "It's an idiom. But, like a flipped idiom."

"You're an idiot," Pride said.

"It's idiom," Gatsby explained slowly.

"It's stupid is what it is," Fahrenheit replied.

"Well maybe instead of pissing all over my ideas, you'd like to contribute some of your own." Gatsby didn't take criticism well. He didn't really do anything well. The kid wondered how he had even become the head of the council.

"I don't know," Fahrenheit mulled. "How about, 'Niagara Falls. Free again.'"

"Actually, that's pretty good," Gatsby admitted. "It's not that poetic but straight to the point may be what we need. I'm going to submit it for consideration."

"This is a waste of time," Pride said and started rifling through the paper herself. "Flags. Uniforms. Are these lyrics to an anthem?"

"Yeah, Rise Up Niagara Falls. It's an id—"

"Shut up," she said, and slammed the papers on the table. "None of this matters if we don't rise up and take the bastard down."

"Hey, Oliver." It was Fahrenheit that saw him first. The man walked over and tussled the boy's hair.

Oliver hated that. It was condescending. Just like his codename. Which he didn't get to pick. He had wanted to be Harry Potter. But they said there was already a Harry Potter in the Resistance and it would only lead to confusion. "There's another kid in the Resistance?" he had asked.

"No, Harry's like 40 or something," they had explained.

"You'd think he would pick something different then."

They shrugged and told him it was the only book Harry had ever read. So that guy got to be Harry and he had to be Oliver. Like the damn orphan. And they tussled his hair. And he hated how they treated him like a kid. Sure, he was a kid, but he was a part of the Resistance, too. He should at least get to pick his own name. But, as much as he hated the tussling and his name, he liked Fahrenheit well enough. "Hey, F."

"What are you doing here?"

"I need to talk to Pride. Do you think it will be much longer before she puts Gatsby in his place and he just gets mad and gives up?"

Fahrenheit checked his wrist for a watch that didn't exist. "It shouldn't be much longer now."

And it wasn't.

"We need to do something!" Pride pounded the table with her fist.

Gatsby countered by mocking her fist smash. "We are doing something!"

"Keeping your piss in glass jars isn't what I'd call doing something," Pride snapped.

"That's because you're forgetting that I know how these things work. I marched with the Resistance for eight years. We stood up to tyranny then and that's what I'm doing now."

"Why do you keep your pee in jars?" Oliver asked.

Gatsby noticed Oliver and looked annoyed at the interruption, but he answered anyway. "So you can throw it on fascists."

"Why? Does it hurt them?"

"No, it doesn't hurt them," Gatsby mocked. "It's because it's gross."

"Does that make them stop being mean?"

"What? Of course not, Oliver!" Gatsby shouted. "If I threw pee on you would you still like me?"

"I don't like you now," Oliver said.

Gatsby swore under his breath and then addressed the room.

"Look, the piss, the slogans, these are all proven tactics, okay? If only we still had hashtags, that would be something."

"What are hashtags?" asked the boy. "Will they stop people from being mean?"

Gatsby threw up his hands in frustration and turned away from the discussion. Pride did her best to hide a smile and waved the boy over. "What are you doing here, Oliver?"

Even coming from her, he hated the sound of his nickname and it made him wince. She caught the wince.

"Is something wrong, Oliver?"

"No." He wasn't normally shy. Shy went hungry in Alasis. But around her, he often found it difficult to find his voice. He was only ten but he wasn't blind. She was beautiful. "It's just that...I don't really like my codename."

"What's his problem now?" Gatsby asked as he got over his tantrum.

"He doesn't like his codename," Pride said.

"So?" Gatsby asked. "Who cares?"

"Easy for you to say," Oliver snapped. "You picked your own."

"So what? I picked yours, too. What are you complaining about?"

"Don't you think naming an actual orphan after a Dickensian stereotype is a tad cruel?" Oliver asked.

"Quit trying to sound so smart," Gatsby said. "We all get our names from books. So, I'm sorry I couldn't name you Autobot or something. When you grow up and read a book, maybe then we'll talk about you choosing a name. Until then you're the adorable little orphan, just like in that movie with the cat. What do you think about that, Oliver?"

"I think you're an ass," the boy said.

"Oh, what the hell do you know? You're just a kid."

Oliver took a deep breath and said, "Whenever you feel like criticizing someone, just remember that all the people in this world haven't had the advantages that you've had."

"What does that have to do with anything?" Gatsby asked.

"He's quoting the book, genius," Pride said.

"What book?" Gatsby asked.

"*The Great Gatsby*, Gatsby," Fahrenheit said.

"Oh," Gatsby waved it off. "I never read it."

"Then why did you pick the name?" Pride asked.

"He was the hot guy. All the chicks wanted him. Because he was a magician or something."

Fahrenheit laughed. "Seriously?"

"Yeah," Gatsby shrugged. "What?"

"He wasn't a magician," Fahrenheit said.

"Oh no? Then why did they call him The GREAT Gatsby, smart guy?"

Fahrenheit doubled over laughing. "You are some kind of stupid, man."

Gatsby rushed across the room to argue closer and Oliver was left alone with Pride. She knelt down and put her hand on the boy's shoulder. That made his knees weak. "You didn't come all the way down here because of your name. What is it?"

Oliver looked around and decided to whisper the answer for effect. "He's here."

Intrigued, she leaned in closer, and that was a point for Oliver.

"Who's here?" she asked quietly.

"The Librarian."

"The Librarian?" she asked loud enough for everyone to hear. "Where did you see him?"

This brought Gatsby back into the conversation. "What's he talking about?"

"Over at Charlie's Arm. He was talking to Liv like they knew each other."

"I don't think it was him, Oliver," Pride said with a degree of sadness in her voice. Most of it was intended to comfort him.

"You don't think it was who?" Gatsby asked.

"The Librarian," Oliver insisted. "I saw him at Charlie's."

"The Librarian? You've got some imagination, kid." Gatsby laughed then grew even more condescending. "I know, why don't you put that imagination to good use and imagine us up some lunch?"

"But it's really him," Oliver insisted. "I heard them talking."

"Another Librarian?" Gatsby put his face in his hand. "That's just great. I don't need this right now."

"What does he mean, 'another one?'" Oliver asked.

"We've had a lot of people claiming to be the Librarian." Pride explained. "But it's never been the real one."

"That's because there isn't a real one," Gatsby said. "Now where's that lunch?"

The boy looked at Pride. "What's he talking about?"

"He's a myth, kid," Gatsby said.

"You don't know that." Fahrenheit made the argument but didn't sound convinced.

"Oh, please. He's a boogeyman dreamt up by Invictus and you know it. The Librarian is just his excuse to have his forces constantly shaking us down without looking like a complete Nazi."

"If he's not real, why did you name the Resistance after him?" the kid asked. "Why do you tell people he's going to come one day and save us? Why are you lying to everyone?!"

"We're not lying," Gatsby said. "We're using him as a symbol, just like Invictus does, but we're doing it for good. And the more Invictus paints him as an enemy of Alasis, the bigger a hero he becomes for us. People need a symbol, kid. They need something to believe in, even if that something is complete bullshit."

"He's real," Oliver said. "And I saw him at Charlie's Arm. He's here to save us all."

Gatsby laughed and turned to Fahrenheit. "Great job on the propaganda, Fahr. It looks like your stories are really sinking in."

"He's real," Oliver repeated.

"Listen to yourself, kid," Gatsby said. "You can't really believe it. Even if the Librarian was real you can't possibly swallow all the stories about him."

"Of course I can."

"You believe that one man fought off a whole city of plant creatures all by himself?"

"He wasn't by himself. He had three bears helping him."

Gatsby laughed. "Right, I forgot about the bears. That was a nice touch, Fahr."

"I just published what I heard," Fahrenheit said.

"Okay, kid. So was he a bear-training plant fighter or a knight in a magic kingdom? Or a fighter of crocodile-man monsters? Or the leader of countless rebellions? Or rescuer of lost children?"

It did sound difficult to believe. But, even if he was wrong, Oliver wasn't about to let Gatsby be right. "He could be all those things."

"Oh," Gatsby laid the sarcasm on thick. "Of course he could be all of those things. I don't know why I doubted it. How could I be such an idiot?"

"I don't know," Oliver spat back at him. "Practice?"

Pride didn't even try to hide her smile this time and Fahrenheit laughed out loud.

Gatsby's expression turned from mockery to anger. "Listen, you little shit. I suggest you get out of here before—"

"Gatsby," Fahrenheit interrupted. "You're threatening a kid, man."

"So?"

"So, it makes you look like an *asshole*," Fahrenheit explained slowly, with extra emphasis on "asshole." It was the slowest and most drawn-out of all the words.

Gatsby huffed. "Fine. I'll lay it out simple then. Even if the Librarian is real, it doesn't make a bit of difference for three reasons. One, no one could pull off the things they say he did. Two, no one would be a big enough idiot to get messed up in that much stuff to begin with. And, three, no one would be dumb enough to come here and help us. We're on our own. This is all up to us."

"But—"

"No but, kid. I'm done with this. Pride, get him out of here."

Pride led Oliver back through the crappy door into the hallway. There she lowered her voice. "Don't pay any attention to him."

Oliver wanted to say he didn't, but it still hurt to be called a liar. "Do you think the Librarian is real?"

"I do," she said in a sweet tone that didn't sound nearly as condescending as it was. "I think the Librarian is real. And I think he's coming to help us."

"But, Gatsby."

"Gatsby has a hard time seeing past himself," she said. "He can't imagine a man capable of such great things because he's not capable of them himself."

"I think it's him, Pride. I really think it's the Librarian."

"I know you do. And I hope you're right."

"So what do we do now?"

She thought for a moment and said, "Why don't you head home and get some rest. I'll check it out when we're done here."

"Yeah, gotta get that slogan just right."

She rolled her eyes. "I know, right? Gatsby seems to think leading people is more about symbols and chants and uniforms than actually leading. I can guarantee that's not what Invictus does all day."

# 6

Being a tyrant wasn't all beheadings and big speeches. Terrifying the people and keeping the underlings in line was certainly part of it, but an empire did not run on grand gestures alone. It took subtlety to pacify a populace. And getting the tiny details just right could go a long way in preventing an uprising. The right color cape could make his Legionaries more intimidating. A proper phrase could reassure his citizens that he had their best interests at heart. Even when he really didn't. The proper festival or performance could quell unrest much like the circuses of old.

These decisions were an important part of ruling. But that didn't mean they weren't boring. He had zoned out more than a few times already.

"...and that's the grand finale!" the young woman said.

A silence followed. The silence was the only thing that made him realize the presentation was over. He had drifted and now realized that the whole room was staring at him, waiting for his response.

He didn't stammer. He remained silent. These idiots would think he was lost in deep thought and not desperately trying to remember what they were talking about in the first place. Not enough people appreciated the power of a good long pause, and that was to his advantage.

Just after it caused panic but a moment before it became terrifying, he filled the silence. "That all sounds fine."

The young woman and her associate let out such sighs of relief that one would think they had been pardoned. And they may have; he couldn't remember what he'd threatened this particular pair with at this point. He had someone else to remember those things for him. Either way, the world had been lifted from their shoulders and they smiled broadly. The woman clapped once and said, "Wonderful. When people watch this race they won't have a worry in the world."

The race. Of course they were talking about the Niagara Regatta. He knew if he waited long enough it would come to him. They had held the event for several years now and it proved to be a popular distraction for the people of Niagara Falls. They spent weeks building rafts and boats in hopes of winning the grand prize. Which was food, or something. Maybe clothes. He couldn't remember. Races such as this usually occurred in the warmer months, but he insisted they hold it as winter loomed since he thought it was funnier when people fell in. Plus, people got restless this time of year. The citizens of Alasis, not to mention their extended empire, were getting irritable. This distraction was exactly what they needed. People would come from all over his empire to see it.

"And what do you think of the name?" The woman's associate asked.

Ah, dammit. He had missed that too. "Say it again."

The assistant put on his best scary voice. "Niagara Regatta 7: Revenge of the Falls."

"Yes. I like it even better the second time I hear it." He didn't really care one way or the other. Invictus waved the pair out of the room. "Make it happen."

The couple quickly gathered their presentation materials and rushed from the room full of excitement and an energy that can only come from not being summarily executed. It was how most people left Invictus's presence.

They passed through the door and another man strode in full of confidence. He wore a big grin on his face and kept it there while he set up an easel with several presentation boards. He took a deep breath, pointed a finger at Invictus and said, "You're human garbage."

Invictus shot him.

The Praetor stepped next to Invictus's throne and waved at two guards to dispose of the body.

"Who the hell was that?" Invictus asked.

"Your head of sanitation, Great Lord Invictus. I believe he was here to present the new cleanliness campaign."

"Oh," Invictus set the gun down. "So that was his opening?"

"I believe so. I think he was going for a shame tactic to get people to dispose of their trash properly."

"Oh," Invictus watched them drag the body from his courtroom. "That's not bad, actually. I think shame is a great motivator."

The Praetor stepped across the room to the easel and turned the first presentation board around. It read, "You're human garbage...if you don't toss your trash."

"I like it."

The Praetor thumbed through the other boards. He stopped about halfway through the stack. "Oh this is cute."

"What's cute?" Invictus asked.

"Yeah, he had a cute little raccoon mascot and everything." The Praetor turned the board to reveal a cartoon raccoon named the Trash Panda. The critter was pointing an accusatory finger at the viewer under a caption bubble containing the slogan. "It looks like that was the little guy's catchphrase."

Invictus nodded his approval. "A judgmental critter. I like it. Approve it."

"Feel bad for shooting him?" the Praetor asked.

"Meh." Invictus shrugged. "The only thing I'm feeling right now is boredom. I'm bored. I tire of these trivial meetings."

The Praetor pointed to the body as it was hurled out the window of the tower. "I'm sure he would tell you that sanitation isn't trivial. If you hadn't shot him dead."

"We've got bigger problems than litter." Invictus stood up and walked over to a bar. He poured himself a drink and moved over to the window. He pointed to the outside world. "There's an army somewhere out there. Just waiting. One day they'll be foolish enough to come out of their little hole. And they'll be stupid enough to think they still run things. We must find them and crush them before they emerge."

"We're looking, Great Lord Invictus. We—"

Invictus threw his glass against the wall. "Look harder! We have the advantage now. There's no telling what they took with them when they went into hiding. That army could be our undoing."

He stared out the window. The damned government had no idea what kind of world they left behind. He would be more than happy to show them once they emerged. But he would rather drag them out of their hole and show them. It would be best to wipe them out before they tried to reclaim the country.

"Did you get anything out of the last spy?" he asked.

"No, Great Lord Invictus," the Praetor said with a shake of his head. "Just a surprising amount of blood."

"Do you think that's funny?"

"I thought it was clever."

"Since you're such a good judge of humor, let me ask you this. How funny do you think it would be if I threw you out the window?"

"Less so, Great Lord Invictus," the Praetor said with a hard swallow.

The Great Lord let the threat hang in the air, but the truth was he was getting tired of throwing people out the window. It was still fun to listen to their screams and laugh at the ones that flapped their arms as if they were trying to fly, of course, but judging people, sentencing people, executing people—it was all becoming routine. He needed something to free him from his rut. He needed some excitement. "Is that fishing ship almost ready?"

The Praetor perked up. This he had an answer for. "Yes, Great Lord Invictus. The salvage operation is almost complete and we'll be ready to send it over in a couple of days."

"And who will we be making an example of this time?"

The Praetor's confidence disappeared once more. "No one."

"No one?"

"Not as of yet, Great Lord Invictus."

Invictus looked out the window of Skylon Tower. From here he could see 8,000 square miles of his domain. "In all of my empire you can't find someone that you think deserves to be tied to a ship and sent over the Falls?"

"It's been pretty quiet lately, Great Lord Invictus."

Invictus sighed and looked out the window. He now regretted throwing that morning's attacker out the window. He hadn't been thinking clearly. He chocked it up to working too hard. He knew he had been pushing himself lately, but what choice did he have? The populace wasn't going to threaten itself. Still, he wasn't about to let this opportunity go to waste. "Maybe, instead of standing here being a complete disappointment to me, you should be out there trying to find someone."

"Who?"

"Oh I don't know. Off the top of my head I'd say some of the Resistance members that are constantly working to undermine my authority!"

"Yes, Great Lord Invictus." The Praetor snapped to attention. "Uh, which one?"

He could throw the Praetor out the window. Easily. But it would mean the headache of finding a new one. "I beg your pardon?"

"Well, there's just so many now. There's the Liberty Belles, the Niagara Falls Liberteens and the Bushwackers?"

"I haven't heard of the last one."

"To be honest we're not sure if they are a resistance group or a band that hasn't had any gigs yet."

Invictus considered this for a moment. "Kill them to be sure."

"There's a new group trying to bring back hashtags, Great Lord Invictus."

"Why haven't I been told of this?"

"So far they haven't really done anything. They just keep scribbling '#Resistance' up all over the place."

"What do they want?"

The Praetor shrugged. "No one knows, Great Lord Invictus."

"Another group of fools that think they can run an empire better than me. Tell me, how would they do things any different?"

"They haven't really done anything else. Just the graffiti. We're not even sure they're serious."

"Well then maybe we should focus on the resistance group that is doing things. Bring me the head of the Bookkeepers."

"But they're just a bunch of nerds?"

Invictus grabbed the man by the cape and swung him toward the window. "They are organized nerds. They have inspired hundreds. It may seem lame to you but their organized protests, their symbols, their codes are the most immediate threat to your comfortable life. The most immediate threat next to me, that is."

The Praetor groveled well. "I'll find them, Great Lord Invictus."

"Do not underestimate them." He took a step closer to the open window. "All it ever takes is a push, Praetor. A gentle nudge can change everything."

"I understand, Great Lord Invictus." The Praetor didn't pee himself and that was disappointing. Invictus thought it was funny when they peed themselves. And he didn't have to clean it up. He had someone to do that for him.

"I hope you understand," Invictus continued. "Because if that damned Librarian ever shows up here, that's all the push they'll need. He will rally them to action. They will follow him into war and I'll make sure that you're the first casualty. They must be destroyed before he gets here!"

# 7

Joshua let the door close silently behind him as Lord Stanley went to take a leak on Jim Carrey's Riddler. The wax figure didn't mind nor appreciate the attention and took the leak in stride. Joshua left the dog to shake things off and moved farther into the museum past dozens of historic and celebrity replicas.

The museum was just one of the many shots fired in the great Wax Wars that had plagued the area years before the world ended. Such a conflict was the only thing that could explain the existence of so many wax-based attractions lining each side of the river.

There were, of course, the standard wax museum trappings to begin with, but as the war went on the combatants were forced to develop new strategies and tactics. A movie-themed facility appeared but did little to change the battlefield. A rock-focused museum made, if even for a moment, a John Oates figure a very real possibility. The horror-themed museum chose terror as their weapon of wax. However, in a missed opportunity, they never considered a John Oates figure for their menacing menagerie. And across the river in New York, the history museum threatened to bore everyone to death by mixing wax with a healthy dose of learning. There was no telling for certain when the hostilities ceased, but it appeared to be sometime in the mid '90s, as one could easily tell the artist behind the Forrest Gump figure had totally phoned it in.

Like everything else in the city, the museums had been scoured and looted for anything of value. As such, they looked completely untouched by the apocalypse with the exception of the growing yellow stain on Jim Carrey's leg. This complete lack of interest in the museum made it an ideal safehouse on Invictus's side of the river.

The others were already gathered around the DeLorean when Joshua arrived. An older man was poring over a map he had laid out across the hood while an Old English Sheepdog lay at his feet. Another man sat behind the wheel of the car dressed as Batman, screaming "Great Scott" and making engine sounds.

The grizzled man rolled his eyes and took a seat on the park bench next to old Forrest.

Joshua cleared his throat to get their attention.

The man in the DeLorean spun around and reached for his gun. The movement woke a Blue Heeler in the passenger seat that sprung up, quickly assessed the situation and went back to sleep. Once Batman recognized the two men, he set the gun in the passenger seat and asked "Well? How did it go?"

"About how we expected," Joshua said as he shoved Taylor Swift into a fountain and took a seat on the ledge of the water feature.

"Prick said no," the man on the bench added.

"So did you, Lucas." The older man never looked up from the papers on the car's hood. "So did Josh. I would have, too. Everyone says no at first."

"I didn't," said the man behind the wheel.

"No," said Lucas, tossing an arm over the back of the bench. "You're definitely the follower type."

"He'll come around," the man with the maps said. "Just like the rest of us. Isn't that right, Brittany?"

The Sheepdog looked up at the sound of her name, realized the question was rhetorical and went back to sleep.

"Oh, because we're all the same, aren't we, Eli?" Lucas suddenly realized he was snuggling with Tom Hanks and drew his arm back.

"It's the nature of a solitary warrior to remain solitary," Eli said. "Don't you agree?"

"First of all, duh. Second of all, I'm nothing like you do-gooders," Lucas said and punched Forrest for emphasis.

Joshua laughed. It was partly at the display of toughness but mostly at the comment.

"Something funny, Canuck?" Lucas asked, the question a thinly veiled threat.

"Yeah. Your tough guy act is hilarious. You're just like the rest of us whether you want to admit it or not. Just like us, you chose to spend the apocalypse putting your life on the line to help other people."

"For money, genius. You suckers do it for free, because you're too stupid to charge for it. Especially Connor."

"I especially don't do it for the money?" Connor asked from behind the wheel. "How does that make sense?"

"No, I'm saying you're especially stupid," Lucas clarified.

Eli pulled a pair of reading glasses from his face and stood up from behind the maps. "So what are you doing here now, Lucas? There's no money in revenge."

"This time—"

"It's personal," the three men finished the statement for him.

Lucas pointed at each of them. "Screw all of you."

"How many times was it personal out there in the wasteland, Lucas?" Joshua asked. "From everything I've heard about you, you were always working for the underdog. Does the losing side pay better?"

"Sometimes," Lucas said and looked at the figure next to him.

"What about the time you saved the village full of children whose parents had been wiped out by the adults-only virus?" Eli asked.

"What about it?"

"Did they pay you in candy?"

"No. They—"

"Maybe they just gave you a bunch of homemade thank-you cards to hang on your fridge," Connor said.

"Don't be stupid. I'm not going to charge a bunch of kids."

Joshua was next. "What about that time you delivered the medical supplies to the colony suffering from Purlpedemia?"

"You want me to charge people for bringing them a box of Kleenex?"

"I heard that box of Kleenex was a truckload of a rare vaccine captured from a hostile band of satanic cult members."

"Same difference," Lucas said with a wave of his hand.

"What about—" Connor started.

"What about what!" Lucas shouted and punched Forrest Gump so hard he dropped his box of chocolates. "What's your point?"

"The point is," Joshua said, "you're not such a bad guy after all. You'd set a price, finish the job and then, at the end of it all, you'd tell them to keep their money. More times than not."

"Those are just rumors," he said and hit Forrest once more. The figure's hand fell off and dropped to the floor. "You can't believe everything you hear. Is everything they say about you true? The stories about you in Portland have to be exaggerated, right?"

The Canadian didn't answer the question. "It doesn't matter. We've spent the last few weeks together and I can see right through you. You may not like it, Lucas, but you're a good person."

"Yeah, yeah, yeah," Lucas mocked. "I'm the merc with a heart of gold, you're the polite post-apocalyptic warrior and Eli's the wise old wanderer. I get it. Whoopdeefuckingdoo, what a team are we."

"Don't forget me," Connor said from behind the wheel of the DeLorean.

"But you're just so forgettable," Lucas said.

"So do you want to quit?" Joshua asked. "Are you going to try this alone? You see how well it worked out for that guy this morning. He cleared the bridge and got thrown from Skylon."

"That guy was an idiot," Lucas said. "I'm not."

"Joshua is right. We need to stick together," Eli said as he stepped to the center of the room. "What's your call going to be, Lucas?"

Lucas looked around the room at each of the post-apocalyptic warriors and then down at his feet. "Invictus must die."

"What did he do to you anyway?" asked Connor.

"Fuck you, kid," Lucas replied. "That's what he did to me."

"Oh, so mysterious," Connor mocked. Normally it would have been a weak reply, but it probably hurt more coming from Batman.

"That's awfully funny coming from 'The Stranger,'" Lucas said. "Could you have picked a dumber name?"

"It's not dumb," Connor said flatly. "It's who I am."

"It's pretty dumb," Lucas fired back.

"It's no dumber than Eli's," Connor said.

Eli went back to his maps. "Leave me out of this."

"Eli is The Man With No Name," Lucas said. "That's completely different."

"It is not," Connor protested as he pulled off the Batman mask.

"It's totally different," Lucas insisted. "For one, it's way cooler."

"I'm not sure this is helping," Joshua said.

"Can it, Molson," Lucas said. "How do we even know this guy, this Stranger, is who he claims to be?"

"I don't know. He's a stranger to me," Joshua said. "That should count for something."

"Thank you, Josh," Connor said.

"Well I've never heard of you," Lucas said.

"Oh no?" Connor walked toward the center of the room. "You never heard of the Stranger of Stab Wound Pass? The Arbor Day Stranger? The Stranger of the Fallen Tower?"

"Sure," Lucas said. "I heard of all those guys."

"They're all the same guy!" Connor spat. "They're all me."

"How do I know it wasn't just some guy?"

"It was. I'm that some guy. I'm the Stranger."

"Well that is some piss poor marketing, pal."

"Like The Mercenary is any better," Connor said and turned with a dramatic flair of Batman's cape.

"I'm not The Mercenary! I'm a mercenary. And people know what that is. It's not some nebulous title."

"Look, we all chose to remain anonymous." Eli put out his hands to break up the argument and tried to bring some peace to the room. He pointed to Connor. "Some just more anonymous than others. But that doesn't matter, because as much as you hate to admit it, Lucas, we are the same. The same path brought us here.

"We woke up one day and the world was on fire. And we saw it as our job to put it out. In doing so we helped a great many people. And we made more than a few enemies. But none so great as Invictus. And we all recognize that. He is the growth that has stopped the world from healing. He's tortured the world as it's struggled to recover and he's tortured us personally. He put a bounty on our heads. He had our loved ones murdered. He's tracked us across the country because we dared to stand against him. This evil must be removed for the world to move on."

"And I get to kill him," Lucas said.

"We talked about this," Connor said. "I get to kill him. I had dibs."

"Dibs?" Lucas laughed. "Are you fucking kidding me with this? We're not playing kids' games here, kid. When the time comes, I'm taking him down."

"That has not been decided, Lucas," Eli said. "We all have a solid claim to the title of executioner."

"Oh now we hear from the old folks."

"They say to beware old men in a profession where men usually die young," Joshua said.

"THEY say a lot of things," Lucas admitted. "But THEY are all dead. Probably because THEY were stupid to begin with. I'm willing to work with you three to get to Invictus. But when the time comes to kill that bastard, you all had better stay out of my way."

"Is that a threat?" Connor asked.

"Yes, it's a threat, moron! What did you think it was?"

Connor stammered. "I...I thought it was a threat."

"Well good for you," Lucas whined. "And that was sarcasm to be clear. I'm sure you're no stranger to that. Invictus is mine and he's going to suffer for every wrong he's done to me."

"This isn't about torture." Eli raised his voice. He didn't do that often. "It has to be about justice."

"Sometime justice screams," Lucas whispered.

"I never heard about justice screaming," Connor argued.

"Oh? You've heard that justice is blind, right?"

"Yeah, that I've heard."

"Well justice is going to scream when I gouge his fucking eyes out." Lucas mimicked the gouging of justice's eyes. His thumbs moved slowly and the expression on his face was one of delight. He finished the pantomime, wiped off his thumbs and looked back at Connor. "You have no idea what he's done to me."

"That's because you won't tell us!" Connor shouted.

"Enough!" the Canadian yelled. "This really isn't helping."

Lucas laughed. "Tell me you don't want to be the one to put a bullet in that bastard's head, Canuck."

"I don't care. As long as Invictus is dead and his influence is removed from this world, I don't care who does it."

"How very polite of you. You people really are so friendly. It's sickening."

"Friendly has its limits, Lucas. Now let's get back to the plan."

"We need more people," Eli said.

Lucas didn't argue that. "We need that stupid army."

Eli sighed. "I think we have to count the Resistance out. They won't listen to us."

There was no argument with this. Each of them had gone before the town's Resistance and each had been sent away. Joshua sat back down on the fountain and took a deep breath. "Maybe the new guy will have better luck."

# 8

———

When attempting to contact an underground resistance force, one has several options. Perhaps the most common is hanging around the more disgruntled citizens and sharing in their complaints. This method took time and often several drinks before one could let it slip that they, too, "wished something could be done." There would be some hesitation on the disgruntled citizen's part before they would cautiously lead you out a back door or, rarely, through a secret door in a bookcase to meet with the faction in question.

This had its perils. Many times, one was truly being led through a back door for a thorough mugging or merciless beating. Of course, since one was most likely drunk by this point, it made them easier to mug or beat. This happened less with secret bookcase doors. This is why one hoped for the secret bookcase door. Few mugging and beatings happened in bookcases.

The other risk one took with mouthing off at the bar was that the counter-resistance forces were usually on to this approach and were more often lying in wait for people trying to contact the resistance than the resistance themselves. If that happened, one usually had to kill the counter-resistance agent to get the attention of the undercover resistance agent and it was just really a lot of wasted time that could be better spent planning an assault.

A second method for contacting a would-be rebellion was to eavesdrop all over town until you identified a resistance member and approached them. This was shaky at best, as it was difficult to build a relationship on trust when you introduced yourself with the phrase, "I couldn't help but overhear your secret conversation... etcetera," because nobody likes a Nosey Nelly.

It was for these reasons that Jerry chose the third approach to contacting a resistance movement. He walked up to one of the Alasis Legionaries and punched him in the face. As luck would have it, it was the Legionary that had frisked him earlier in the day, so Jerry enjoyed the sucker punch more than he had expected. His fist made a satisfying smack when it hit the soldier's face, and the man's helmet made an amusing clang when it hit the brick wall behind him. Either hit ensured that the guard was going to wake with a ringing headache.

His partner was on the whistle before the Legionary hit the ground. The wail would bring more soldiers, but that was a crucial element in the plan. Hitting one or two was certainly enough to get arrested. But it was hardly enough to cause a scene. And a scene was required.

The guard dropped his whistle and leveled his rifle at Jerry.

Before he could shout Halt, Jerry had stripped him of the weapon, pulled the helmet over the soldier's eyes, and smacked him in the head with the rifle.

Finally lashing out felt good. His rage had been building for weeks and the restraint he had been using was frustrating. Having to take the soldier's abuse earlier in the day had pushed the limits of his willpower. This fight was exactly what he had needed. He'd known it would be a satisfying release when he finally got the chance to strike out, but he hadn't expected it to be so much fun. The soldier's costumes made it so.

The Librarian stepped behind the blinded guard as he struggled to pull his helmet from his head. Jerry waited for the helmet to hit the ground before he pulled on the guard's cape and brought the man stumbling back into his fist.

Summoned by the whistle, three other guards raced to the scene. They were firing their rifles in the air and demanding that Jerry get down on the ground. This was good. But not good enough. Taking out two guards and then getting arrested would get him nowhere except a jail cell. He needed to get people talking about what he had done.

He kicked the fallen helmet from the ground into the air. The polished metal caught the light just right before it hit the soldier's gun and caused a burst of wild fire. This got him his first round of cheers from the bystanders on the street. But it also got him shot at. Jerry dove for cover behind a nearby shanty as the other two guards opened fire.

This whole plan was more art than science. Punch a guard. Get arrested. Take out three or four and you were going to get yourself shot. This was where he was in the process. These weren't warning shots. Bullets tore through the plywood home and bounced off the surface of the old parking lot. It was easy at this point in the plan to think you had gone too far when, in fact, you hadn't gone far enough.

There was a certain level of anger and frustration beyond bloodlust that he had to reach. It was the same level of mad that turned swearing into angry gibberish. It was simple enough to get someone to want to kill you. It was something else entirely to get them so mad that they couldn't even pull the trigger. Where they would rather torture than kill. That was the level of pissed off he was shooting for.

He doubled back through the shantytown as the trio of guards raced around the corner after him.

The commander held up a hand and barked at the other two, "Wait here."

The two subordinates stood shoulder to shoulder with their guns trained ahead of them as their commander moved through the shantytown's street. They watched as he peered in the hovels the citizens of Alasis called homes with rapt attention. Their focus made it fairly easy to tie their capes together.

A large crowd had gathered now and, to their credit, they were able to hold their giggles until Jerry had the capes tied together in a solid knot. Their laughter finally erupted and the two guards spun to see what was so funny.

Jerry dashed off, but not so fast as to miss the two men smash into one another and realize their predicament. The crowd cheered as the two soldiers collapsed to the ground, each blaming the other for the situation they found themselves in.

The crowd followed him through the shantytown now, cheering him on in anticipation of his next move. They made it more difficult to maneuver. Hands patted him on the back as he tried to move through the crowd down the makeshift street.

The commander stepped out ahead of him and Jerry turned to run. At first the crowd was too thick. He pushed against the wall of people and they began to part for him. They stepped aside more quickly toward the back and he assumed he would soon have an opening. Unfortunately, the parting of the crowd was at the behest of the two other soldiers he had left in a bind. They had figured out their wardrobe situation and didn't look at all pleased.

He tried to break through the crowd to the right, but the first guard he had attacked was there. He was back on his feet and extremely pissed off. The soldiers began tossing people out of the way while screaming insults and threats at the thinning crowd.

The people moved under threat but were shouting at the Legionaries.

There were the normal boos and hisses, but other shouts rang out.

"Let him go."

"Leave him alone."

"You always were an asshole, Mangler."

"Set him free."

It wasn't long before Jerry was surrounded. He didn't try to run or fight. The fervor of the crowd was right where he wanted it, so he sat down on the pavement and waited patiently.

His original victim raised his weapon to fire. The crowd roared and took a collective step forward. Under threat it had thinned to let the soldiers in, but the spectators hadn't gone anywhere and the crowd rematerialized behind the guard. The man was red with embarrassment and rage as his finger moved toward the trigger.

But before he could pull the trigger, another soldier caught his attention and directed it toward the crowd.

They grew quiet, but to a man and woman their conviction showed on their faces. If the Legionary pulled the trigger, they wouldn't make it back to their side of the river alive. There would be no execution today.

The Legionary withdrew his finger from the trigger and lowered the barrel of the rifle.

Jerry smiled at the guard to aggravate him more. Even over the cheers of the crowd, he could hear the man growling at him.

"Seize him," the commander barked, and Jerry was yanked to his feet by two of the subordinate soldiers. They bound his hands behind him with zip ties and shoved him through the crowd.

The people of the city cheered. It was a victory for them. They could claim that they had saved a life that day even though they knew the soldiers would probably just march the prisoner into an alley a few blocks away and put a bullet in his head. But in this moment, they had saved a man.

The Legionaries marched Jerry down the street. Initially the crowd followed, but the farther the group moved from their homes, the more people peeled off until the mob shrank to a gathering, the gathering to a group and the group to one guy with not enough sense to realize he was all alone. That guy finally panicked and ran, leaving the Librarian alone with the guards.

Even they started to reduce in number until it was just the two he had encountered that morning.

They shoved him down the street. Jerry tripped several times and received a kick in the ribs for each stumble.

"You think we should take him to Invictus?" asked one.

"I'd rather just kill him here," said the one Jerry had sucker punched.

"They need someone to ride the Falls, you know?"

"He can't ride them if he's already dead," the Legionary replied while surveying the street. The would-be witnesses had fled. He pointed to an alley. "In there."

He fell once more on the way to the alley and was dragged behind a dumpster. They pulled him to his feet and forced him up against a wall.

"I warned you," the first soldier said.

"He did warn you," the second guard agreed.

"You should have listened."

"You really should have listened." The second guard didn't seem to have much of his own to add to the conversation.

"Shut up."

"Shut up," the second guard said.

"Not him. You."

"Oh," The second guard replied, and shut up.

"All right," the Legionary drew his pistol and thumbed off the safety. "Hold him."

"Wait, what?"

"Hold him against the wall. I don't want him to move out of the way."

"What? You think he can dodge bullets?"

"He can make a run for it. Hold him still."

"While you shoot?"

"I won't hit you."

"Not on purpose. What about a ricochet?"

"It won't ricochet."

"Oh now you're Mr. Physics?"

"Don't be such a coward."

"I'm not being a coward. What about the blood? I don't want this guy's brains all over me."

"Why are you being such a baby about this? It's not like it's the first time we've executed a guy."

"I'm not worried about killing him. I'm worried about cleaning blood out of my clothes!'"

"Oh my God, you are such a wuss."

"How about you hold him and I kill him? How about that, Mangler?"

"No."

"Why?"

"Because I'm in charge."

"No, it's because you know I'm right and you don't want blood all over you."

Normally, this plan called for a fair amount of stalling. Often it took time for word to get back to the resistance group, so some witty banter or subtle subterfuge was required to distract the would-be killers until the rescue attempt took place. But these two morons saved him the trouble by continuing to bicker until the Resistance made their move.

A rock bounced off the one called Mangler's head with a delightful clang, denting the helmet and successfully stealing his attention from the argument. Both guards turned to face the new threat and saw several men in ski masks at the end of the alley and more rocks being hurled their direction.

The Legionaries shouted several warnings while seeking cover and struggling to return fire. They opened up with their rifles and the Resistance members sought a safe place of their own. The encounter hadn't lasted long. But it was long enough for another Resistance member to signal Jerry from the other end of the alleyway. He raced unnoticed from the wall and met the woman in the mask.

"This way," she said and ran down the alley.

Jerry followed the woman as she wound her way through boarded-up buildings, broken fences, narrow passageways and debris-filled streets. He would have found keeping up with her easier if she cut him free, but his hands remained bound behind his back.

He stumbled several times and received no help in getting back to his feet. The only words of encouragement from the woman were, "C'mon, asshole. I'm not getting caught because of you."

"This would be easier if my hands weren't tied."

She gave no response and refused to slow her pace. He was begging once more to be cut free when she held up a finger to silence him. She had stopped at the edge of the street and was peering around the corner. A moment later she visibly relaxed and said, "I think they're gone. And you're an idiot. What the hell were you thinking?"

"I was thinking I wanted to talk to you."

"You don't even know who I am."

"I mean talk to the Resistance."

"And this was the best you could come up with?"

"I had a couple of other plans," he shrugged. "Not as good as this one though."

"You're lucky you're not dead."

"I had a way out if you hadn't shown. Could you untie me now, please?"

"You're an idiot."

"Yes, you've said that."

"You made yourself a target. An enemy of the state. They'll be looking for you now."

"They were already looking for me."

"So were we, dumbass. We were about to make contact when you attacked the guards."

"Oh, I didn't know that," Jerry said. "Why were you looking for me?"

"You were in Charlie's Arm this morning, right?"

"Is that the bar?"

She nodded.

"Yes, I was there this—"

"We were just about to approach you. Then you started that fight like a moron."

Well now he did feel dumb. Before he could say anything—not that he knew what to say—she looked over his shoulder and spoke.

"He says he wanted to talk to us." She wasn't talking to him.

Before he could see who she was talking to, the bag was over his head and he couldn't see a thing. This wasn't how it usually worked.

## 9

The Coyote pulled up to Charlie's Arm on the Coy-O-Te late in the afternoon. He killed the motorcycle's engine, stepped from the bike and looked around. The bar itself looked like the town—run down and dangerous. It was probably filled with troublemakers and tough guys looking for a fight. Willie would have liked this place.

Just thinking about his friend agitated the ball of rage in his stomach. The familiar feeling had formed weeks ago and had confused him at first. Because he had been fed his friend strip by strip, he thought maybe the feeling was Willie being angry at him. Coy didn't necessarily believe in ghosts, but he didn't necessarily not believe in them either, and he had assumed that anger and dread and frustration may be what a haunting felt like if that ghost was haunting a person's belly. After a few days he knew that it was his own rage causing the feeling because he was certain by then that Willie had passed.

Now that he knew it wasn't his friend causing the discomfort, he welcomed this feeling. He drew power from it. Coy had been a bit of a scoundrel, he would admit, but he was a nice enough guy really. Mostly harmless, if you wanted to put it on a scale. But, from this anger, he became The Coyote. And no one was going to fuck with The Coyote. He was filled with righteous anger and driven to kill the man responsible for his friend's death and embarrassing end. Nothing would stop him. No one would get in his way. He was living rage. And to prove it he put on Christopher's stupid hat, pulled a box from his bike and walked toward the bar.

The bouncer sat outside the entrance. He was the width of the door and nearly as tall. The man's arms were impossibly thick and, from The Coyote's point of view, he was all chest. He would be hell in a fight.

The bouncer made no move to stop The Coyote from entering the bar, but as he passed the giant reached out and lifted the hat from Coy's head and placed it on his own.

Coy would have pretended not to notice. Hell, Coy may not have noticed at all, but The Coyote would not be slighted. He set the box down, turned and nodded to the hat. "That's my hat."

The bouncer grunted and stood up from his stool. He folded his arms and loomed over the smaller man. Even his voice sounded like it could kick his ass. "What hat?"

Coy knew the man knew damned well what hat. He was playing him. Coy would have let it slide. The man was one of the biggest he'd ever seen and Coy would have been terrified to even talk to him, much less press the issue. But he wasn't Coy. "The one on your big, fat, ugly head."

The bouncer didn't seem to like one word of that. He uncrossed his arms and put a finger in The Coyote's chest. "Listen you little—"

Coy snapped the finger and drove his boot through the giant's right knee. The bouncer screamed, dropped to the ground and screamed again when his shattered kneecap hit the sidewalk.

The Coyote plucked the hat from the bouncer's head and picked up the bouncer's wooden stool.

"Take the biggest guy in the world, shatter his knee and he'll drop like a stone." The Coyote broke the stool over the bouncer's head and laid the man out cold. "I figured all bouncers knew their Road House."

The Coyote placed the hat back on his head, opened the door and stepped into Charlie's Arm.

The place was dimly lit by a host of neon signs for beer brands that didn't exist anymore. It was packed with men and women who were already halfway to tomorrow's hangover. The noise from the crowd was a combination of false bravado, lousy pickup lines and the distinct sound of someone hustling at pool. It smelled like spilt beer, stale cigarettes and poor choices. He really liked it.

He had grown up in places just like this one and the nostalgia hit him pretty hard. He hadn't seen a place like this since before the shit hit the fan, and the memories came pouring over him. It felt like home.

They were serving that fancy beer that always ended in letters or time. He never knew what they meant, but beer was beer and since he hadn't seen a Lone Star in years he ordered whatever they had from the attractive lady bartender.

Coy set the box on the bar and rested on a stool. He watched her pour the drink. She had long dark hair that looked like it had recently been washed. Dirty hair had never been a deal breaker for him but only now did he appreciate how much better shampoo made a woman look. She wasn't trying to hide her figure like so many girls did out in the wasteland. The world may have changed a whole hell of a lot, but the service industry still relied on tips.

She set the beer on the bar and nodded to his hat. "That's some hat."

The Coyote smiled and nodded. He didn't agree, but maybe that's why Christopher wore it all along.

"It could get you into some trouble around here."

Coy's smile grew. He was counting on it. "I'm looking for work. Know where any can be had?"

"What kind of work?"

"I figure Alasis could use a new bounty hunter. Since they seem to be missing theirs." The Coyote ran his fingers along the brim of the hat and winked at the bartender.

The bartender backed away and Coy assumed he had used the

wrong wink. He had intended to use the "you get my meaning" one but realized it could have been the "want to show me what you look like without pants?" wink instead. He was about to explain that he wanted the bartender to remain in her pants when he realized it wasn't the wink the woman was backing away from.

"I said, you really blew it this time, Christopher." The statement was said as if it had been said before—probably while Coy was worrying about the wink.

A thick and calloused hand landed on his shoulder. The unwelcomed touch agitated the ball of rage in his stomach.

"I guess you aren't quite the badass you think you are," the voice at the other end of the hand said.

The Coyote turned. The man wasn't as big as the bouncer, but he was big enough that the Dalton quote about knees popped into his mind again. This one wasn't alone. There were two more men with him. They were half the other's size but twice as ugly. The scars on their faces said they weren't unfamiliar with a fight.

The biggest one realized his error but felt no shame in it. "I thought you were someone else."

"You probably thought that because of the hat." The Coyote lifted his beer and took a sip.

"Yeah, I know a guy that wore one just like it."

"Knew a guy. You knew a guy," he said with a smile. "Named Christopher."

The man nodded. "That's him."

"Well, that's why you thought you recognized it. It was his hat. But I killed him. And now it's my hat."

The three men were skeptical. Coy could tell that even the woman was giving him doubtful looks from behind the bar.

The biggest of the bunch laughed. "Bullshit. You didn't kill him. He was a little punk, but he was way too smart and slippery. There's no way a little bitch like you could have killed him."

"Is that so?" The Coyote asked.

The bartender set three beers on the bar and each man in the gang took one. The biggest took a long drink, but never took his eyes off of Coy. He finally pulled it from his lips and wiped the foam away with the back of his hand. "You know what I think?"

"If you had more toes you could count higher?" Coy asked. It was something Willie had said. As he remembered it, the knot drew tighter in his belly.

"I think you bought a second stupid hat and made up this whole story to impress a bunch of losers."

"Not quite. I came here to take his place."

This made all of them laugh.

"What's your name?"

"The Coyote," he said it low and with a rasp. They laughed even harder. They started calling friends over to join in the laughter.

"And you think people are going to believe you just because you're wearing a stupid hat?"

"Not really," The Coyote replied.

"That's what I thought."

"That's why I've also got his head in that box on the bar."

"Bullshit," one of the others said.

"Yeah, that's bullshit," the big one agreed. "Let's see it."

The Coyote shook his head. "No. I'm pretty sure you're not the losers I need to impress."

The big man reached for the box and The Coyote's hand shot out. He grabbed the big guy by the wrist and knocked it away.

"Reach for it again," The Coyote said, "and I'll kill you."

"You're one crazy son of a bitch."

"You don't know crazy." Coy had disappeared completely now. Only The Coyote stood before the man. He growled low and slow. "Not unless you'd been forced to eat Willie fried up as bacon."

The sudden shift in Coy's demeanor caught the trio off guard. His words hadn't helped.

"What's he talking about, man?" one of the smaller ones asked.

"Forget this guy," the other added as he began to inch away. "Please."

Even the big one's expression had become less callous and a

little more cautious. "I'm not sure what you're saying, little fella. I don't know how to respond to that."

"It's not something I recommend," The Coyote continued as if they had said nothing. "It makes you a completely different person. Couple of weeks ago, you touch my stuff and I can't say I would've done much of anything. I would have tried to talk you out of it maybe. But, now, you reach for my stuff again and you'll come back short a hand."

There was fear in the big man's eyes. But there was also a bruised ego to defend. The Coyote could see him weighing the two emotions. Pride finally won out and the big man reached for the box.

The Bowie knife flashed neon red, yellow and green reflections as it cut through the air. It turned solid red as it cut through the man's hand.

The man pulled back his stump, screaming with a pain and fear he had never known. He turned to his friend for help and covered his friend's face with blood as it pumped from his arm.

The other member of the trio rushed forward and caught the blade in his belly. The Coyote plunged the blade deep and dragged it out slow before stabbing several more times. Every plunge of the knife fueled his anger further.

The other man had wiped the blood from his eyes and charged into the fight.

The Coyote stepped to one side and pinned the man between the bar and the blade. He didn't die quietly.

The knife dripped with blood and The Coyote turned to face the big man once more. It was then that he realized the man had more than just the two friends. Several of the bar's patrons had stood from their tables. The two men playing pool had stopped and stepped forward with their cues at the ready. The entire bar rushed him and the rage inside him exploded. It burned and made every decision for him. It told him when to stab, to duck, to drive a man's head through the jukebox glass. It made his every move faster and more powerful. These were things Coy could never have done. The Coyote was in charge now.

He snapped a man's arm and drove a broken pool cue through another's eye. It wasn't revenge. But it was another step on the road to justice for Willie. For Coy.

The fight didn't die down until The Coyote ran out of people to stab. He let many limp away with nothing more than a few cuts. But many didn't. Coy still held the blood-red Bowie knife in his hand when he sat back down at the bar and resumed drinking his beer.

The bartender stood up slowly from her hiding place beneath the bar and surveyed the damage.

"The Legionaries are coming!" Came a shout from near the door.

Coy paid it no mind and enjoyed his beer. It was no Lone Star, but it wasn't half bad.

"They're coming for you," the bartender said.

Coy leaned over the bar and refilled his beer from the tap. He sat back down and took another long drink. "I think I'll wait for them right here."

# 10

---

At some point he had been put on a boat. Or shoved in a washing machine. He had been tossed violently about and splashed with the coldest water he had ever known. The hood over his head had become soaked, making it difficult to breathe, though he couldn't tell if it was the wet or the cold that made it so. Even with some overdramatic gasping, he got little sympathy from his new friends and was forced to roll his head around until the fabric fell from his mouth.

They were near the Falls, that much he knew. The roar was deafening. But the noise coming from the natural wonder was so loud he couldn't say exactly how close they had been. They could have been right under them or a mile downstream. He didn't know.

There was also no telling how long the tossing and soaking had gone on, but he knew it was getting dark. What little light had passed through the hood was now fading. Between the wet, the cold and the blindness he was starting to wonder if he really needed the Resistance. He coughed up a mouthful of frigid water and swore because he knew that he did. Invictus was too well established, too well guarded for Jerry to take on alone.

The rocking finally stopped. Or, rather, he was thrown from the rocking boat on to solid ground. They led him inside somewhere equally cold and down a hallway. It was tight. He could sense the closeness of the air. A heavy door shut behind him and the sound of the Falls were dampened. But not by much.

An escort held him by each elbow and guided him through a labyrinth of turns across uneven floors, up and down stairs, and through a few puddles until they finally shoved him backward into a waiting chair.

It hurt when they pulled the hood off. The wet fabric caught on his face and wrenched his head back. The lights hurt, too. Several powerful work lights were mounted on stands and pointed in his direction, blasting him in the face. He had to squint to stop the pain but enjoyed the heat they were putting off.

"What do you want?" The voice was straining to sound more intimidating than it was, as if it was trying to reach lower tones than it was capable of. The question ended with a cough.

Jerry shifted in his seat, trying to lean forward and take the pressure off his arms. The zip ties were digging into his wrists and he could feel that his skin was on the verge of bleeding. Repositioning did little to alleviate the discomfort and he hung his head to get out of the light.

The floor was covered with cables that snaked around the room. He made a show of shifting his weight in the chair and worked his foot under one of the bundles. "I wanted to see you."

"Well, you've seen us." This statement also ended with a cough.

Jerry sighed and pulled on the cables with his foot. Two of the pole lights fell to the ground. One shattered, the other turned its blinding rays elsewhere and he could finally see again. There were three of them in the room. A woman, that he assumed was the one that pulled him from the streets, a slender man of average height that was doing his best to hide his averageness behind a hipster beard, and a large black man that smirked when the lights fell.

"Now I've seen you," Jerry said.

"Dammit," the bearded man said. It was the voice that had been doing the coughing. "Fahrenheit, get the hood back on him."

"Don't use my name, man," the large man said.

If they had asked Jerry, the big guy had the better interrogator voice. It was warm and friendly, but deep and could easily be turned cruel. It seemed obvious, really. When things didn't make sense it usually came down to politics. Chances were the smaller guy liked to be in charge.

"It's a codename, stupid, it doesn't matter." Another cough.

"Fine, Gatsby," Fahrenheit shot back with a fair amount of satisfaction.

"Don't use my name!" Gatsby growled in that stupid voice and the coughing fit took over.

"Stop using that stupid voice," the woman said. "You're going to hurt yourself."

Gatsby finally stopped coughing and switched to a much less intimidating voice. "Put the hood back on."

Fahrenheit laughed. "He's already seen you, man. I told you the lights were a dumb idea."

"They weren't dumb. They were— Next time we'll run the cords along the wall. That way the prisoner can't do...this."

"Both of you knock it off," the woman snapped. Both men stopped arguing and she hadn't had to do anything to her voice. She addressed Jerry next. "What do you want? Why are you in Alasis?"

"I'm here to kill Invictus," Jerry said.

"Oh, you are?" Gatsby stepped closed and leaned in. He was right in Jerry's face and he let out a raspy whisper. "Well, join the club, buddy."

Jerry was confused by the man's delivery of the line. He may have been attempting sarcasm, but it came out as an invitation. "Is that all it takes?" Jerry asked.

"Is that all what takes?" Gatsby asked.

"Joining the club."

He turned to the woman. "What's he talking about?"

"Do you even listen to yourself when you talk?" the man they called Fahrenheit asked.

"What?"

"You said join the club, dumbass," the woman said. "And you did it in your stupid tough-guy voice so it sounded sincere instead of sarcastic."

"I did not."

Fahrenheit backed her up. "You totally did, man."

Jerry joined the others. "You did."

The woman turned to Jerry. "No, that's not all it takes. First of all, who are you?"

Here it was. He'd been running from his reputation forever. It had been a bane on his existence for years. It had caused more suffering than he ever would have imagined. It was about time it did some good. He looked the woman in the eye and said, "I'm the Librarian."

The name hung in the room for a moment. You could almost hear the weight it carried. Then everyone laughed.

"Bullshit," Gatsby laughed. "Good try, though."

"Yeah, I've got to give you credit," Fahrenheit said. "Most guys that try this crap at least look the part. But you really went for it."

"I am the Librarian," Jerry insisted.

"Do you have any idea how many people we've had waltz in here claiming to be the Librarian?" Gatsby asked.

The woman answered for him. "You're the third one this month."

"And we sent them all packing," Gatsby said.

"But they weren't really him...I mean me. I'm me."

"Oh, I'm sorry," Gatsby said. His sarcasm was much clearer this time. "We didn't realize you were the really real Librarian. We didn't realize you were THE Librarian who single-handedly brought down an Alasis Death Truck."

"Well, it wasn't single-handedly, but yeah."

"And you were the man that liberated the Kingdom of the Seven Peaks?" Fahrenheit asked.

"Yes. That was me."

"And you were THE Librarian who fought the Man-Beast of Manatauk to a standstill with his bare hands?" the woman asked.

"Well, no. I've never even been to Wisconsin."

"Well then. I guess you're not THE Librarian after all," Gatsby said and spit on the ground.

"Man, I've asked you to quit spitting in here."

"Oh, shut up, Fahr. It's already wet."

"Yeah, but with water. No one wants to walk around in your spit."

Jerry had to raise his voice to be heard. "I did rescue a child from a Gatorman in New Orleans."

"Now you're just making things up." Gatsby was done with the conversation.

"It doesn't matter what you've heard, or what you believe. I am the man they call the Librarian. And even if I wasn't, what does it matter?"

"It matters a whole lot," Fahrenheit said.

"Does it? You say you've had three people in a month claiming to be the Librarian. And you turned them all away? Three men willing to fight the injustice of Alasis and you sent them packing. Why not welcome them in? You'd be all the stronger for it. What kind of resistance turns away help?"

"I'll tell you exactly what kind of resistance it is," Gatsby shouted. "It's our resistance and we'll do with it what we like."

Jerry sagged in his chair. "I was afraid of that."

"Afraid of what?" Gatsby asked.

"You're exactly the kind of resistance that doesn't resist shit."

Gatsby grew visibly angry at this and shot a look at the woman. She gave a nearly imperceptible shrug while Fahrenheit tried to hide a chuckle. It was clear this man thought of himself as the leader of this group. It was also clear that he was wrong.

Jerry pressed it, looking directly at the man with the beard. "I've seen this before. You gather in secret. You give yourselves codenames and signals and mantras. But you never do a thing. You stand around telling each other how brave you are and pat yourselves on the back for your sacrifice, but you're risking nothing."

"We saved your ass." Gatsby's voice was full of rage now. He raced across the room and put a finger in Jerry's face. "If not for us, you'd be dead in an alleyway or a helpless prisoner in Invictus's dungeon."

Jerry leaned back with a sigh and placed his hands behind his head. "Whatever would I have done without you?"

Gatsby backed away quickly. "He's free. Fahrenheit, tie him up!"

"Why, man? I think it's obvious he'll just get free again."

"You're the worst head of security!"

Fahrenheit yelled back. "If he wanted to cause problems, he would have. Hear him out."

"I will not hear him out. I will not risk what we've built here for some lying, piece of shit outsider."

"I'm not lying!" Jerry said.

"You are. You know how I know? The Librarian isn't real," whined Gatsby. "Don't you get it? He's a symbol. Nothing more. He's not our leader. He's not our savior. He's a mascot to get the people to rally to our cause."

"And what is your cause, Gatsby?" Jerry asked.

"Our cause is freedom."

"Is it? Because I think your cause is you. That's why you'll never stand up to Invictus. You need him. Without him you're nothing. Without him you'd have to be your own man instead of his antithesis and you couldn't handle that."

The girl was trying not to smile. Fahrenheit was trying not to laugh.

Gatsby didn't notice. His focus was solely on the man insulting him. "You don't have any idea who I am."

"And neither do you," Jerry said.

Gatsby pulled a revolver from his waistband and pointed it at Jerry's forehead.

"Gatsby—" Fahrenheit began.

"Shut up, Fahrenheit." Gatsby muttered.

Jerry leaned into the barrel. "You're not a resistance. You're a fad. You've probably got a bunch of chants and jars full of your own urine, but you don't have the balls to really fight."

Gatsby pulled back the hammer on the revolver and stared dead into the Librarian's eyes.

Fahrenheit lost it and began to laugh so hard he wheezed. "He knows about your strategic piss reserve, Gat."

Jerry stared back across the barrel of the gun. Gatsby was a coward. He'd shoot a man in the back but not while looking him in the eye.

"Put the gun away, Gatsby," the woman said.

"No."

"Now!"

Gatsby looked at the woman and back to Jerry. He released the hammer and lowered the pistol.

Jerry nodded his thanks to the woman and then looked at Fahrenheit. "I'd like to leave now. Who has my hood?"

The ride back was darker and colder than before. It even seemed a little rougher. They helped him ashore and led him inside. It wasn't warm, but it was out of the wind and the wet.

"You can take off the hood," the woman said.

She stared at him for a quiet moment, then turned to leave. She stopped at the door. "You're right about him. About Gatsby."

He knew he was right. But he wasn't happy about it. He just nodded quietly.

"But you're not right about us." She opened the door and left him standing alone in the dark.

# 11

Coy didn't have a lot of job-hunting experience. Work had never appealed to him and, if he was being honest, the idea of an interview had always made him nervous. The thought of so many questions being thrown at him at once made him uncomfortable. His palms would sweat. His heart would race. He would get confused and forget everything he knew. He just knew it. It was the same whenever he watched Jeopardy.

Now that he had taken the initiative to meet the leader of Alasis and demand employment, he was surprisingly calm. The box under his arm gave him some of that confidence. But he was smart enough to know that it wasn't all coming from the severed head. Severed heads didn't have powers like that. It was because The Coyote didn't get nervous. The Coyote didn't worry about what people might say or what they might think of him. The Coyote didn't worry if people thought he was stupid and wasting their time by interviewing for some job. Coy would be a wreck but not The Coyote.

Hell, The Coyote wasn't even claustrophobic like Coy. For example, right now he was stuffed in an elevator with five guards and he wasn't the least bit panicky, even though with so many men in such a small space they would surely run out of air. The Coyote remained calm but Coy would have been freaking out about how if he needed to get out of there these others would be in his way. He'd try to get through but he wouldn't be able to, and the harder he tried the more he would be pushed back, not being able to go where he wanted to, needed to, when all he wanted was to be out where the air wasn't so thick and hot and close. The Coyote spun away from the cluster of men and stared out the back of the glass elevator at the wide, open space unfolding hundreds of feet below him. It was an amazing view with nothing to get in the way but this thin, very breakable glass. Coy swallowed hard and was thankful that The Coyote wasn't afraid of heights like he was.

"Is it much farther to the top?" Coy asked.

He received only a single grunt in response.

"That's what I thought."

An eternity—or twenty seconds—later, the doors opened and Coy fought the urge to push his way through. The guards took their time getting out of the car and then commanded him to exit.

He repositioned the box under his arm. It was comforting to have something to hold. They had taken his guns and his knife. They had even taken the keys to the Coy-O-Te. But he had refused to hand over the box.

Another half dozen guards lined the hallway. Dressed in shining armor, they stood at attention, unmoving except for their eyes. All had turned to him.

The Coyote studied the men who studied him. The armor may have looked scary, but The Coyote knew it would slow them down if it came to a real fight. The helmets would limit their visibility and impair their hearing. And the capes were the dumbest part of all. How did they not trip on those things?

They led him into a round room where he saw more men and more capes and what could only be described as a throne. In the throne sat Invictus, draped in a massive golden cape and armor polished so finely that Coy could see The Coyote in it. The man did not look up until one of the guards announced, "This is the man, Great Lord Invictus."

The Great Lord rose from his seat. The golden cape fell into place behind him and made him seem twice as large as he was. He crossed the room and studied Coy from behind the visor of his polished helmet. Only the man's eyes were visible. The rest of his face was covered by a skeletal mouth and nose. This was the man that ruled the world. Coy had every reason to be afraid. But for some reason, he wasn't. It was probably the cape.

The man said nothing for at least a minute as he sized up Coy.

And Coy knew how it looked. He wasn't big. He didn't look tough. But he was covered in the blood of a dozen men and he hoped that would go some way toward impressing the leader of Alasis. Though he had never had to impress someone in a cape before and he wondered if the rules were different.

"This man killed a dozen men?" Invictus asked.

"Yes, Great Lord Invictus," the soldier said. "And the bouncer. And he's the biggest son of a bitch you've ever seen."

"Is that so?"

"Yes, Great Lord Invictus. They called him the Doorway. Because he was the size of a doorway."

"Then why wasn't he working for me?" Invictus asked.

The soldier swallowed hard and tried to talk his way past the question. "This man also claims to have killed Mr. Christopher."

"That's a bold claim," Invictus said. "What proof do you have?"

The Coyote smiled and tipped Mr. Christopher's hat.

Invictus laughed. It was a horrific sound through the metal skull. He pulled the hat off Coy's head and flung it out the open window. "You're going to need more than a stupid hat. You could have gotten that anywhere."

The Coyote smiled, stepped forward and opened the lid of the box.

Invictus's eyes grew bigger as he recognized the head of what was once his most feared bounty hunter. He didn't look so scary now. Creepy, Coy thought, what with his tongue hanging out and his eyes all rolled back, but hardly scary.

"I couldn't have gotten this just anywhere," The Coyote said.

Invictus laughed and pointed at the box. He addressed the soldier that had led Coy into the room. "Now, this is the kind of violence that gets my attention."

"I thought it might," The Coyote said.

"I am the Great Lord Invictus," he bellowed. "And who are you that brings me the head of my own man?"

"Mr. Invictus, I—"

"Great Lord," he corrected.

"Mr. Lord, I—"

"Great Lord Invictus." He added some rage to his voice for impact. "Do you want someone to write it down for you?"

"No. I–"

"Would that even help?"

"Great Lord Invictus..."

His eyes looked pleased and he nodded. "Go on."

"They call me The Coyote."

"The Coyote? That's lame." Invictus turned to his men and laughed. "Did you call him that?"

"No sir," the soldier said. "It's the first time we've heard it."

"And what do you think?" asked Invictus.

"It's lame," said the soldier.

"That's what I thought," Invictus agreed with a laugh. "What do you want, Coyote?"

"The Coyote," Coy said. Why couldn't people get that right?

Invictus laughed. "Correct me again and I'll have you thrown out the window."

It wasn't that difficult. Lots of things had a first name of *The*. The Eagles. The The. Coy got lost in this train of thought, searching for a third example, and forgot to even blink.

Invictus didn't seem to appreciate this stoic response. The man grunted and turned to his men. "Maybe I should have them throw you out anyway. You killed my man. You brought his head to me in a box. That's not typically a behavior that gets rewarded."

Invictus was an imposing figure. He looked a lot like a cross between Skeletor and a robot. But he wasn't afraid. Coy would have been. But The Coyote only felt rage. Coy wondered if that was the secret to never being afraid. To just hate everything so damn much that there wasn't room for fear or doubt. In all his wondering, Coy lost track of the conversation. He wasn't even sure what Invictus had said. The best he could do was just stare intently until the man spoke again and try to catch up as best he could.

"What do you think of that?"

Coy wasn't sure what "that" was exactly, but Invictus had waved toward the window when he said it. Except there was no window. And they were pretty high up. It seemed dangerous. "I think you should close that window. Someone could fall."

The guards tensed up when he said this. He wasn't sure why. It was a fairly obvious problem. Birds could get in. Maybe even bugs. He didn't know how high bugs could fly though. Their wings weren't so big, so maybe bugs weren't a problem. But most probably birds. Maybe Invictus could fly! Maybe that's why he wore a cape and he needed the window open to get into the building. No. That was stupid. It was probably a launching pad.

Invictus finally broke the silence with a laugh. Though it didn't sound like he found anything particularly funny. Willie used to do that. He had called it sarcasm.

Invictus turned and walked back to his throne. He spun quickly and sent his cape into the air. He sat quickly and the fabric settled around him. It was a hell of a way to sit down.

"Tell me what you want, Coyote."

This was it. Coy would have choked and chickened out. Coy would have muttered "nothing" and made up some excuse to leave the room. He would have probably said he had to go to the bathroom. But The Coyote took a bold step forward and declared his desire. "I want a job."

"A job," Invictus said with a nod. "Did you have any particular role in mind?"

Coy pointed to the soldier standing next to the Great Lord. "Well, what's that guy do?"

Invictus laughed. It was genuine this time. "That takes a lot of guts."

"So?" The Coyote said. "I've got as much guts as that guy."

"This man is my Praetor. He is my administrator. My Confidant. And his position is for life. He will be my Praetor until he dies in my service or until I push him out the window."

"You two sound pretty serious."

This made the Praetor reach for his gun.

"Calm down, Predator," The Coyote said. "I don't want your job. I don't have any confindanting in me. Besides, I don't think I could wear a cape all day. I want Christoph's old job."

Invictus went silent. His eye twitched. Invictus was 'musing things,' as Willie used to say. The Coyote took a deep breath. The thought of Coy's old friend tightened the knot in his stomach and enflamed the rage.

Invictus finally spoke. "You really killed him? You didn't just find his body and cut his head off?"

"I did."

He wasn't convinced. "How did you kill him?"

"Slowly," The Coyote said with a smile.

At first Invictus and the guards laughed. But The Coyote made it very clear with his gaze that he wasn't kidding.

Invictus stifled the laughs. "Now, why would you do that?"

"Because," The Coyote said as he took two steps toward the throne. "He made me eat Willie."

The entire throne room burst into laughter. There were a few comments from the guards to one another about how they owed one another for a bet they had made. But The Coyote didn't let the good times get far.

"They cut him up into strips and told me he was bacon!" He shouted. "But it wasn't bacon. It was Willie."

The laughter stopped and Invictus gave him an inquisitive look. "You met the Skinners."

That feeling in his stomach flared up like gasoline on a campfire. "I did."

"Did you kill them, too?" Invictus asked.

"No." That thought enraged him even more but instead of the anger growing hotter it turned cold and stopped altogether. Now he felt nothing. "I didn't get the chance. That Library guy killed them. He denied me the revenge I deserve. But I'll get it. I'll get my revenge."

"That's why you're here?" Invictus asked. "Revenge?"

The Coyote nodded. He looked around the room at the army of guards and finally let his gaze return to the man on the throne. "I aim to kill the man that started all of this. The man that, if not for him, Willie wouldn't have been made into bacon."

Invictus remained silent for a moment. He was musing again. Maybe even mulling. But he came to a decision quickly. "You're a special kind of idiot, Coyote. The kind of idiot I find useful. You want Mr. Christopher's old job? You've got it."

"Good." It was Coy's first real job. He should have felt proud of himself for acing the interview, but all he felt was one step closer to getting his revenge.

"Before you start, however, do you even know what Mr. Christopher did for me?"

Coy shook his head. "Not the particulars."

"He made problems go away. And the Librarian is a problem. But I have other problems, too. Much closer to home." He pointed out the window.

Coy followed the gesture to the missing glass. "I don't do windows."

"Not the window, you moron. The city. My city. Everything you see is mine. And I take care of what's mine. I take care of all those people down there. I keep them safe from the horrors of the wasteland. I feed them. I keep the lights on for them so they feel safe in the night.

"But there are some down there that are ungrateful. They want to overthrow me and cast me out. They want to seize power for themselves."

"Why don't you just tell them to leave? That's what I'd do."

Invictus stood and shouted, "Because I don't know who they are, you dolt! They hide from me. They hide their identities. They meet in secret."

"Okay. You don't need to holler. You made it sound like you knew who they were."

"I don't, but you're going to find out."

The Coyote laughed. "If you don't know who they are how will I? I just got here."

"You're going to find them. You're going to tear the city apart until you find them or I'll have you killed."

Coy wanted to run. The Coyote made him stay.

"But you're going to like this," Invictus said with a much calmer tone as he sat back down. "They call themselves the Bookkeepers. And the Librarian is their hero. His traitorous actions against Alasis have inspired them. They treat him like he is their savior and it's become a really big problem for me.

"I want you to find them and bring them to me. If you do this, I will give you an army to hunt down the Librarian and you will finally have your revenge."

## 12

Charlie's Arm was busted in a dozen places. The jukebox was broken, the pool table was out of order and the staff was doing its best to clean up the blood with a mop and bucket. But the beer was still cold, so Jerry drank.

He didn't ask what happened. He didn't care enough to ask. But in passing he had gathered most of the story. A stranger had come in and the locals didn't have enough sense to leave him alone. He'd ended up pulling a giant knife and cutting everyone up while screaming something about bacon. It wasn't exactly typical, but it wasn't that unusual.

Now more than ever, the world was full of crazy people. Jerry often wondered if it was the new world that had driven them all mad or if it took a fair amount of crazy to survive after the apocalypse. Maybe he was crazy himself.

Chewy dropped her snout in his lap and he scratched the dog's head. He wanted to say something to her but realized that might be an admission of how crazy he was. He set another beer on the floor for the dog. She'd been locked up in the Day's Inn for most of the day and deserved it.

He took a drink from his own glass and figured the odds of him being crazy were pretty good. A sane person wouldn't have done the things he had done. A sane man would have kept his head down instead of wandering around the perilous wasteland, getting embroiled in other people's messes. Maybe it had been the right thing to do, but it certainly wasn't the smart thing. Smart didn't get involved. Smart didn't get Erica killed. But being smart meant he never would have met her in the first place. If he'd never met her, she most likely would have died on the way to New Hope. But she wouldn't have died on the side of the road in Missouri. He shook his head. His thinking was getting circular. Or maybe he was just drunk. There was only one way to be sure. He ordered another drink. This was quickly followed by, "Make it two."

A man sat down on the barstool next to him and smiled. "Must have been a hell of a fight, huh?" he said, surveying the damage in the bar.

Jerry grunted his response. He was in no mood for a conversation.

Apparently the man next to him didn't speak grunt and continued with the small talk. "I wonder if it was the same guy that caused all the problems in town today."

"If you don't mind, pal. I'm trying to get drunk before the band goes on. And I'm kind of running out of time."

"You looked determined about something," the man said. "I figured you could use some company."

"I'm not looking for company."

"Sometimes, company finds you."

Jerry agreed with another grunt.

The man smiled broadly and thanked the bartender for the beer. He took a drink and said, "I know who you are."

Liv cast a sideways glance at Jerry and he saw her tense up. There was no telling how she'd react if he'd been identified and they came for him now. Her sense of self-preservation would tell her to do nothing. And it would be the smart thing to do. But she might even surprise herself.

He ignored her look and stared deep into his beer. Jerry said into his glass, "Well that's a relief because no one else seems to believe me."

"You're me," the man said and took a drink.

Liv breathed a sigh of relief and stepped away from the pair.

"That's not really where I was expecting you'd take that," Jerry said. "And quite frankly, you're going to a much weirder place."

The man smiled at that, but it wasn't reassuring. He set his drink down and continued. "I can tell your story just by looking at you, because it's mine."

"Well then there's no reason to tell it," Jerry said with a smile as he raised his glass in a mock toast. "But I doubt that's going to stop you."

It didn't.

"I was pretty average before the world ended. I wasn't famous. I wasn't rich or powerful. My golf game wasn't too bad, but nothing too exceptional. I had a bit of a slice I was working on. Just like everyone else."

"Yeah, I often get nostalgic for my slice."

"My point is, I was boring."

"You still are, if it makes you feel any better."

"There was nothing about me that made me a candidate for this new world. It was just chance that I survived. I didn't bug out or have anywhere to go. I wasn't prepared. I was in the middle of a business trip when all the bombs started dropping. I was caught on the road with no home to return to. So what did I do?"

"I don't care," replied Jerry.

"Nothing. I pulled over on the side of the road and did nothing for six months."

"I'll bet you really had to pee when that six months was over."

The man wasn't listening. He was lost in his own story. "I found an abandoned farmhouse. I have no idea where the owners were. I don't know where they went. Maybe they were the Bizzaro me. Maybe they were in the city while I was on the road.

"I felt like a burglar for the first couple of weeks. I kept expecting them to come home and shoot me for trespassing, but after a while I realized they were as dead as everyone else and I began to help myself to what was in the house. They had food and supplies enough for me to live on comfortably for quite a while.

"Survival was my only thought. I didn't look for anybody. I didn't try to contact anybody. One day I saw a group of people on the road. And you know what I did?"

"Bored them with this story?"

"I hid. I hid and let them pass. I made no effort to contact them or help them for fear that they would put me in jeopardy. And I could have probably lived there in that farmhouse forever."

"Yet, here you are."

"About a week later, one of those people came back. Just one. A woman. She was beaten and filthy. She could barely walk down that road. I couldn't ignore her this time and I brought her into the house and helped her as best I could. You should have seen the terror in her eyes when I first approached her. I had never seen such fear.

"The entire group had been jumped by raiders a few days up the road. Several were killed. Others taken as slaves. She was the only one that got away. Maybe if I hadn't hid from them, maybe if I would have reached out and invited them in, it never would have happened. I was ashamed of my actions and I did everything I could to make it up to her. I promised to keep her safe."

"But..." Jerry helped him transition.

"But then the raiders showed up looking for her. And that's when something inside me snapped. I decided right then and there that I wasn't going to hide any longer. I could no longer ignore the injustice that had overtaken the world."

The man grew quiet and took a long drink. He stared at the back of the bar, but he wasn't looking there. He was looking back in time. When he spoke again there was a haunted quality in his voice like he was telling a ghost story.

"I'm not proud of what I did to those men. They deserved every bit of it, but I'm not proud. I wasn't thinking clearly. I acted out of blind rage."

Jerry understood. He always told himself he was doing good but sometimes good looked pretty fucking cruel. He knew the feeling all too well and felt he had to say something. "You did what you had to do to protect her."

"Nope. She died in the fighting." He slid the empty beer glass away. "I tore those men up but it still wasn't enough to keep her safe. She died in my arms. In agony. In pain. I buried her in the dirt and I left. I came out of hiding and confronted evil and injustice head on. Ever since then I've done my best to help people. And I'll bet your story isn't any different."

"It's a lot shorter."

He laughed at the comment. "You're no different than me. Sure, I've got a few years on you, but that just puts me in the unique position to offer some advice."

The man went on before Jerry could decline.

"It's a lonely life we've chosen, this post-apocalyptic nomadic thing. Sometimes we think we're the only ones that seem to know the difference between right and wrong anymore."

"The definitions got a lot more flexible. Didn't they?"

"They did. But right and wrong still matter. Even if it's not a popular outlook anymore, it's definitely a necessary one. But it can be a lonely outlook.

"In some ways we think it's smart to stay alone. By insulating ourselves, we think we're protecting people but we're just hurting ourselves. A man needs friends."

Jerry looked at Chewy, who looked back at him like she wanted another beer.

"You've had enough, girl."

"That's a nice dog."

"She's the best."

"See?" he chuckled. "You and I are the same."

"Hardly."

The front door of the bar opened and a flood of silence entered. Several soldiers stood in the doorway surveying the room.

"Do you think they're looking for you or me?" the older man asked.

"It's usually me," Jerry said and set the glass on the bar.

"Well, I guess you could fight them. Though you seem to have made good on your goal to get drunk. Or—"

"Or we can fight them together as kindred spirits?" Jerry said. "And bond over a brawl? Just like that?"

"Or we could sneak out the back and I can show you that you're not as alone as you think you are. That's what I was going to say."

Part of Jerry wanted the fight. His meeting with the Bookkeepers had pushed him beyond reason. He had let his optimism get the best of him in thinking that they would be the answer to his problems. Discovering that they were a resistance in name only had been the final blow. He really wanted to hit something.

But the old man was right. He was in no condition to fight. Even Chewy looked a little tipsy. He stood, dropped a gold coin on the bar, and followed the man out the back door into the alley.

# 13
---

She was dripping wet and freezing cold when she got back to their headquarters. It's not like she needed any more motivation to overthrow the corrupt and tyrannical government of Alasis, but never having to set foot in their ridiculous secret headquarters ever again could certainly be added to the list of reasons.

The meeting was already underway when she returned from dropping off the latest in a long line of fraudulent Librarians. Gatsby was talking, Fahrenheit was ignoring, and the others sat around the round table feigning different degrees of interest. Pride took her seat and listened long enough to know that the leadership council was talking about nothing important as usual.

Gatsby wasn't wrong when he said that they weren't waiting for the Librarian to come in and rescue them. They wouldn't know him if they saw him, but it was true that the stories of the man known by that name inspired the Resistance. When news about the Texas town of New Hope first reached them, they had begun to organize and plan. It wasn't the first time someone had stood up to Invictus and his forces. But it was the first time someone had stood up to them and lived. Allegedly.

Separating myth and fact were all but impossible in a world where people were so disconnected. Stories took on a life of their own, and people were so desperate to be accepted by strangers that they were more than happy to embellish any tale if it made for a better tell.

As much as everyone wanted to believe that a blow had been struck against their oppressor, they had been trained by disappointment to never get their hopes up.

But when other reports of this nomadic hero began to surface, some people started to believe. *Could it really be true?* turned to *it could happen.* An alliance Alasis held with a kingdom out west was shattered by someone they claimed was the Librarian. He had brought the king to his knees and liberated the people. Next to Alasis, the Colorado city was one of the greatest powers in the new land. And if this man could bring change to the West, there was hope he could bring it east.

More rumors came in about heroics in the Deep South, the Northwest, south of what was once the border. There was no way all of the stories could be true. But it didn't matter. People began to believe. The stories were impossible, but the Resistance seized onto that flicker of hope and stoked it with more stories and promises and rumors that he was coming to Alasis. Rumors that he was going to overthrow Invictus and free the people living under his rule.

It didn't matter if the Librarian was real. He had already served his purpose. The whispers had grown to an organized system of communication. Signals and codes now flew freely across the city and into the wastes, where allies lay in wait for that one command that would bring everyone to arms. He had united them in spirit and served to help them form an identity and a purpose they could all rally behind. He didn't have to be real.

But she wanted to believe he was.

She shook her head free of the idea. Even if the Librarian was real, the chances of the stranger being him were next to nothing. Countless men had wandered into town claiming to be the legendary warrior and exactly zero had turned out to be telling the truth. They wanted access to their army, their cause. They wanted to lead the Bookkeepers against Invictus for their own ends and glory.

She didn't blame them for trying. Invictus and his army had caused misery across a large portion of the country. From Alasis, their network stretched out across the wasteland. They killed, raped, pillaged, looted, burned, and obliterated thousands in their quest for power. There was no doubt that Invictus and his underlings were at the top of countless enemies' lists. They'd make up any story to get their revenge. Why would this man be any different?

But there was something about this one. First of all, he didn't approach them with the claim. Oliver had overheard a conversation at Charlie's. The man hadn't said a thing. Also, the others had protested when called on their identity. They had crafted stories and gone on forever trying to convince the Bookkeeper leadership they were the Librarian. They had agreed to every claim anyone had ever heard about him. This man denied some of the stories. In the end he didn't seem to care if they believed him or not. He just wanted to help take down Invictus. And they had turned him away.

With the latest pretender gone, the council now turned their attention back to bickering about flags and slogans and government positions. They discussed these things as forgone conclusions, skipping over the fact that they still had to seize power from the greatest villain the post-apocalyptic world had ever known. That part, they treated as a mere formality. It was merely step one in a much larger plan. That plan was written on the whiteboard.

Typee was an older man and was polite enough to raise his hand before he spoke. Once acknowledged, he pointed to one of the bullet points on the board and said, "I want to talk about elections again."

"What's to talk about?" Gatsby asked. "We'll have them. Six months after we take power. Just like we agreed."

"Just like *you* agreed," Fahrenheit corrected.

"Look, it's going to take at least six months to transition," Gatsby said. "The people wouldn't accept a change in leadership twice in less time. But a call for elections will be my first—"

"You?" Omoo, Typee's wife, laughed.

"Yes, me," Gatsby said. "We decided this."

"When did WE decide this?" Typee asked.

"I volunteered as interim leader and there were no arguments."

"We all laughed at you," Fahrenheit said.

"A laugh isn't a no, Fahrenheit." Gatsby explained. "We were pretty clear on the voting procedure."

"We all thought you were kidding," Omoo said.

"About being the interim leader?" Gatsby sounded hurt. He probably was. That was the price of not being self-aware. "Why would I be kidding?"

"How could you be serious?" Fahrenheit asked.

Gatsby gasped and searched the room for an ally. "You're with me on this, right, Pride?"

She heard her name and snapped back into focus. "What?"

"There you go," Gatsby said with a small clap. "Pride is with me and you all respect Pride's opinion, right?"

Typee pulled his glasses from his face and pinched his nose. "I don't play these games, kid."

"Are you saying you don't respect Pride's opinion?"

"I'm done here," Typee said, and stood to leave. Omoo stood with him.

"Wait, we can table the leadership discussion for later. The more pressing issue is the uniforms."

"You're kidding me, right?" Fahrenheit asked.

"No, I think it would make a lot more sense to repurpose the Legionary uniforms rather than create our own."

"They're symbols of oppression and evil," Omoo said, reluctantly sitting back down. She gestured for Typee to join her.

"But they're already-paid-for symbols of oppression and evil. Fiscally it would make a lot more sense."

There was a chorus of grumbles at the table but eventually they all agreed to keep the Legionary uniforms as long as they didn't have to wear the helmets.

"Good. We're saving money already," said Gatsby as he crossed an item off the board. "These are the kind of ideas our leadership is going to need."

As he called for the next issue, Pride realized she would rather have a mythic figure in charge of the revolution than Gatsby. What if this new stranger was The Librarian? Could he lead them? Could he inspire the group to action instead of going over all of these to-eventually-do lists? They had plans, but those plans had been in place for months. Would it take someone new to enact them? He probably wasn't the Librarian, but like the man had said, did it really matter?

She rolled her fingers across the card table they had dragged into the headquarters "war room." Could someone else lead them to victory? If victorious, would that leader give up power? Had any other revolution in history met around a floral-patterned card table with one wobbly leg?

"Pride?" Gatsby asked, as if he had asked it a couple of times already.

She stopped rapping the table and looked up. "What?"

"Is all of this boring you?" he said, and pointed to the board.

"Yes," she said.

Gatsby was taken aback by her honesty. "Yes, it's boring you?"

"Yes, it is boring me. All of this is boring me."

"Well." Gatsby was briefly at a loss for words. He found them quickly in the form of sarcasm. "I'm sorry we can't make our little revolution more exciting for you."

"What revolution?" she fired back with equal, if not greater, sarcasm. "All we do is plan."

"We need to be prepared!" he fired back.

"We couldn't be more prepared. Now you're, what, designing costumes? Last week we decided on the insignias of the letter senders. Before that we agreed that it would be bad to continue calling the Death Squads death squads. And, in a surprisingly productive meeting, we also agreed that skulls shouldn't be used on any of our banners going forward.

"We have everything in place to take down Invictus. We have people in the power plant. We have people behind the wall. We have people outside the city. We have everything figured out. Lelawala is ready. We have everything. But you're here talking about the most trivial things."

"This is not trivial. If we take power without—"

"If!" she stood up from the table. Her outburst surprised even her. "I didn't join this revolution for *IF*."

"Fine. I meant *when* we take power. The people won't accept us if we don't have the systems in place. They'll have questions and we need to have answers ready."

"Invictus didn't."

"Enough!" Gatsby pounded the table for effect. The wobbly leg had finally had enough, and it collapsed. He stared at it for a moment as the last few snacks slid onto the floor. "We are not Invictus, Pride."

"Clearly. He stepped right in and took control. He didn't have a plan or soundbites approved by committee. I'm surprised you haven't run them all by focus groups."

This sparked a thought in Gatsby's mind and he turned to write on the whiteboard.

Pride stormed across the room and yanked the dry erase marker from his hand. She threw it across the room.

Gatsby held up the marker cap. "That's just great, Pride. Now it's going to dry out."

She grabbed the cap and threw it to the ground. "Invictus took over and we let him. He turned on the power and we gave him more. He built Alasis as he went on the backs of everyone we loved. We finally have the means to take back our freedom and all you want to do is plan and throw pee on him."

"That's only phase one!" Gatsby yelled.

"That guy was right."

"What guy?" Fahrenheit asked.

"The man claiming to be the Librarian. He was right. We're all talk. All plans. No action. And every day we talk about a new graffiti tag or protest chant, Invictus hurts more people."

"Are you questioning my leadership, Pride? Because I don't need to remind you that this whole thing was my idea."

"Yeah, well, it wasn't Armstrong's idea to go to the moon, was it?"

"And you're Armstrong in this wonderful analogy?"

"It's certainly not you."

Silence followed.

"I'm a little confused by the analogy," Typee said. "The moon was Kennedy's idea."

"Yeah, that would still make Gatsby President." Fahrenheit said.

"The point is," she said, "Even if he was the first one to think 'Gee, it really sucks living under a bloodthirsty tyrant,' it doesn't mean he's the best one to lead us. Right?"

Pride looked around the table at the other members of the leadership council, hoping for their support. They each did their best not to make eye contact with her. They had no love for Gatsby, but his leadership meant they'd never have to commit. They could continue to plan and feel good about being all seditious without ever putting their plan into action. Their silence angered her more. "What if the Librarian were here? Would you follow him? So far he's the only one who's had the balls to stand up for what's right."

"The Librarian isn't real," Typee sighed.

"What if he was? What if they weren't just stories and he was here right now saying, 'fight'? Would that get you to act?"

Silence was their answer.

"Every day people are suffering," she pleaded.

"Duh," said Gatsby, and sat back down in his chair.

"Would the Librarian—"

"We're not the Librarian!" Gatsby shouted.

Pride looked around the table once more and hung her head.

"That's obvious," she said, and stormed out of the room. She slammed the door behind her and leaned against it. Her mind raced with options and she finally landed on a crazy one. If they wouldn't take action, she'd find someone who would.

## 14

It was snowing now. The bitterly cold wind and wet sobered him up quickly but it did little to improve the canoe ride across the Niagara. The water was choppy, and they paddled hard just to fight the crests and the headwind.

Chewy lay as flat as she could in the middle of the craft, doing her best to stay away from any splashes that made it over the gunwale. It wasn't working, and the occasional shift in the wind filled his nose with the smell of wet dog.

The man who called himself Eli was trusting enough to give Jerry the back of the canoe, so Jerry could keep an eye on his newfound friend without fear of being shot in the back. Of course, they both had to worry about being shot from any number of directions if they were spotted by any of Alasis's patrol boats.

They paddled furiously for what felt like an hour and managed to stay clear of the boats by hiding in the darkness and the swells. They made the far shore wetter and colder than he had ever been and stashed the canoe in a scraggly clump of bushes a good distance up the bank.

Jerry shivered uncontrollably, and he could feel the cuffs of his jeans freezing solid, but he hadn't been shot and that was a pleasant surprise. He rubbed Chewy's fur to get the excess water out and spoke to Eli. "That was easier than I thought."

"It's just a river," Eli said as he pulled the last piece of camouflage into place. "Getting across isn't the trick."

The trick was the military presence. Guards were everywhere as the pair made their way slowly and quietly into the center of town. Even in the dimly lit streets, Jerry could see the many different-colored capes hanging from their armor. Surely they all had their place in Invictus's order, but Jerry couldn't tell one from the other.

They ducked and ran and scurried and dove for cover to avoid the sentries, and the more they did, the less it made sense to be here. Jerry finally had an opportunity to bring up the subject when they dashed inside an old souvenir store. "This side of the river doesn't seem the most practical place to hide."

"It's a the-place-they'd-least-expect kind of thing," Eli said with an eye on the street. "They've been tearing up the other side looking for the Resistance. As trite as it sounds, hiding under their noses is the safest option right now. That side is the enemy. This side is home and they feel pretty secure behind that wall, so they tend to let their guard down."

They ducked behind the counter as a flashlight's beam swept the store. The patrol moved on as the two men dashed back into the street.

More guards and more sneaking followed. The well-lit streets made the trek more perilous. There was no lack of shadows, but Jerry couldn't remember ever sneaking through such a brightly lit town. Nowhere left on Earth had access to the kind of power Alasis did. The falls began generating electricity more than a hundred years ago and nothing was going to stop them any time soon.

They wound through alleyways, ducked behind cars and hid in the storefronts of abandoned tourist traps and Tim Horton's. Eli finally held up a hand and whispered, "That's where we're headed."

Jerry looked across the street and sighed. "Your top-secret safe house is in a wax museum?"

"Pretty brilliant, right?"

"How is it brilliant?"

"Let's say we do get spotted and someone tells the guards we're in the wax museum." Eli smiled. "This place is lousy with them. They'd still have to check seven different places and we'd have plenty of time to escape."

Jerry grew concerned. He was always concerned to some extent. Most everyone who survived the end of the world was always concerned about something. There were mutants and superbugs and roving clouds of toxic gas. Being concerned was a general feeling most people learned to live with. But this was a specific kind of concern that told him he may end up paddling back across a river all by himself. "You're not crazy, are you, Eli?"

"I don't think so. But in a world gone mad, how would I know?"

"Fair point."

"No, I'm not crazy." Eli slapped Jerry on the arm. "No crazier than you are."

They waited several minutes before they felt it safe to cross the street and entered the building as quietly as possible. Once inside, Eli took a deep breath and dropped the hushed tones he'd been using since they stepped foot on shore. "Phew. It feels good to be back home."

Some people are creeped out by wax museums. And that's understandable. With lifeless eyes staring from poorly sculpted figures, it can sometimes look like a person was entombed in wax rather than sculpted from it. These eerie looks gave many people a feeling of being watched or haunted. It made their skin crawl and caused them to look over their shoulder more than normal. And that was with the lights on. If they ever saw it with the lights out, they'd piss themselves.

The low light and shadows even made the Mary Poppins figure look scary. The motionless figures lined the entire length of the entryway, and Jerry began to feel like he was being watched. It was as if the figures were just waiting for a command to lurch forward and attack like a host of zombie celebrities. He knew it was an irrational fear, but the gallery made distinguishing real threats and imagined ones difficult. Even if the figures didn't come to life, any number of enemies could be hiding in their ranks.

Chewy had bolted instantly into a world of new and bizarre smells. She ran from figure to figure, sniffing each one only briefly and then running on to the next. It wasn't until she stopped and pissed on Jim Carrey's Riddler that Jerry began to relax.

"This way," Eli called from the end of the hallway. "Let me introduce you to the guys."

Jerry followed Eli into a much larger room. A silent water fountain was at its center. Taylor Swift was floating in the middle and a one-handed Tom Hanks sat on the far side.

Jerry instantly recognized the two men he had tangled with earlier. The other one was dressed like Batman minus the Dark Knight's cowl. He wasn't much older than twenty.

Chewy recognized the men as well and began to growl. This woke Lord Stanley from his slumber while another dog leapt out of Doc Brown's time machine and rushed to the encounter.

The grizzled man laughed. "Well, well, well. Look what Eli dragged in."

Eli cleared his throat and spoke up. "Everyone, I'd like you to meet Jerry."

The other man called Lord Stanley to heel and waved. "Glad you changed your mind."

"I told you that you weren't alone," Eli said. "We've got a whole room full of post-apocalyptic nomadic warriors, just like you."

"Don't lump me in with you nuts," said the grizzled man.

Eli chuckled. "This is Lucas. And he doesn't like to be considered the hero type."

"We met this morning," Jerry said with a sarcastic smile.

Lucas returned a cold stare.

"They call him the Soldier," Eli said. "He's a wasteland mercenary. He likes to claim he fought for the money instead of what was right."

"Money is always right," Lucas replied.

"So what are you doing here?" Jerry asked, and before the man could answer, he added, "Let me guess. This time it's personal?"

Lucas wasn't amused, but a series of chuckles rolled around the room.

"You think you're funny?" Lucas asked, and pulled back his jacket to reveal his gun.

Jerry smiled back. "I've heard stories about The Soldier. And in not one did he demand a cent for helping people. People think 'This time, it's personal' is your catchphrase."

The room laughed harder.

"I don't see why that's any cause to laugh!" Lucas scolded his teammates.

"Take it easy, Luke." Jerry said. "All I'm trying to say is you're better liked than you'd like to be."

Eli continued with the introductions. "This is Joshua. He's a road warrior out of Canada. You may have heard some people call him the Mad Max with Manners."

Joshua waved. "Nice to meet you. Formally."

"And the kid sitting in the car over there is Connor."

Connor stepped out of the car and crossed the room. He stuck out his hand. "They call me the Stranger. You've probably heard of me."

"Did anyone ever actually call you that?" Lucas asked.

"What?" Connor said. "No, it's not like people said, Hi, The Stranger. But it's how I'm known."

"You're known as the Stranger?" Lucas said with a sneer. "Exactly how everyone describes everyone they don't actually know."

"What? No, I'm The Stranger. It's different."

"It's dumb," Lucas said.

"It's part of my mythos. The man with no name."

"Eli's The-Man-With-No-Name," Joshua said.

"Yeah, but metaphorically."

"Are you sure you know what a metaphor is?" Lucas asked.

The Stranger sighed. "We've been over this."

"Yeah, and we've talked about this and I'm still not convinced," Lucas said.

"Look, it's simple. When people say a stranger helped them out, chances are, that was probably me."

Lucas rolled his eyes. "And isn't that convenient?"

"You heard about the time The Stranger saved Hope Falls?"

"Yeah," Lucas said, but it sounded more like, "Sooo?"

"That was me! And there was the time that stranger saved the slave down in New Dawn from a dozen men. And half of them had chainsaw arms."

"What's your point?"

"Me again!"

"It's you every time, huh?" Joshua said with a smile.

"This is ridiculous, guys," Connor pleaded. "We've been over this. It's part of the game. We all chose names to protect our anonymity. Like, Jerry here. What did you call yourself?"

"I never called myself anything."

"And do people know who you are?" Lucas asked.

Jerry thought back to the Resistance meeting. They had no idea who he was. Even when he told them. "No."

"There you go!" Connor slapped Jerry on the back. "Now let's all eat."

Dinner was served in the Western diorama. They had replaced the prop campfire with an actual campfire and set to work cooking a canned-food dinner of questionable vintage, but if Jerry had ever tasted a bad baked bean, he never knew it.

"Who'd they send after you?" Joshua asked. "Was it Darius?"

"That piece of shit," Connor said, and spit on the ground.

"Hate that motherfucker," Lucas said through a mouthful of beans.

"I don't know who that is," Jerry said.

"He's one of Invictus's men," Eli explained. "Tough son of a bitch. He's got a scar across his neck where someone cut his throat. It still didn't kill him."

Lucas took over. "He's Invictus's attack dog. Head of his Legio X."

Jerry shook his head. "I don't know anyone like that. They sent a guy named Mr. Christopher after me."

"Oh," Eli said with somber tone. "That son of a bitch."

"Who's Christopher?" Lucas asked. "Another Legio?"

"No," Eli said. "He's worse."

"Worse?" Lucas chuckled. "Worse than Darius?"

"Much worse," Connor assured him. "Cold. Ruthless. Calculating. Some say that even Invictus is afraid of him."

"I don't see how he could be worse than Darius," Lucas muttered.

"Darius deals with Alasis's problems as they arise," Eli said. "Christopher hunts them down."

"He gets paid by the head," Connor added.

Joshua had been digesting the conversation quietly. He finally spoke to Jerry. "Who are you?"

"I told you, my name is Jerry."

"That is bullshit," Joshua said as he set down his plate of beans. "Jerry doesn't get the attention of Mr. Christopher."

"The mouth on you, Bieber," Lucas said. "I thought you people were supposed to be polite."

"Shut up, Lucas," he said, and turned back to Jerry. "What do people call you?"

Jerry looked around the campfire. It had grown quiet and they were all leaning in, waiting for a response. He might as well tell them. No one believed him anyway.

"They call me the Librarian."

It's an odd thing when silence gets quieter. Nobody moved. Even the fire stopped crackling for a moment.

The vacuum of sound was quickly replaced with laughter. Lucas's laugh had a tint of cruelty to it. Connor's seemed rather overdramatic. Joshua did his best to stifle his quickly and politely, and Eli just let it fly.

"Man oh man," Connor said. "Everyone wants to be the Librarian."

"Is that so?" asked Jerry.

"In this town anyway," Lucas said, wiping a tear from his eye. "I was the Librarian once."

"Me too," Joshua said.

"Why's that?" Jerry asked.

"The Resistance, man. They're just waiting for that guy to show up, so I figured, I tell them I'm the Librarian, lead them to victory. Invictus is dead and justice is served."

"Me too," said Connor.

"That was my plan," Lucas said.

They all looked to Eli, who eventually admitted, "Yeah I tried it too."

No wonder they hadn't believed him. If everyone that came to town claimed to be him, how could he expect them to believe he was actually him? Based on Gatsby's reply, however, he doubted it would have made much of a difference.

"Well, I told them that as well," Jerry said, and returned to his meal.

They all got another laugh out of this.

"Did you meet that prick, Gatsby?" Lucas asked.

Jerry nodded.

"Man, what a douche. I wanted to punch that bastard in the face so bad." This spurred on more laughter as everyone agreed that Gatsby was a douche.

"Did you meet the woman?" Joshua asked. "I think they called her Pride."

Jerry nodded, but added, "I didn't get her name."

"I don't care what they call her," Lucas said. "She was hot."

Everyone agreed with boyish enthusiasm.

"Don't you think so, Librarian?" Connor asked, using finger quotes to mock Jerry's claim to the moniker.

Was she hot? Jerry thought back to the meeting with the Resistance, and more specifically that moment on the shore when she dropped him off. He hadn't noticed it before, but she was attractive. Beauty standards had changed dramatically since the bombs went off, but Pride rose above those standards on either side of the apocalypse. It hadn't occurred to him at the time, and even now it was an acknowledgment of a fact instead of recognition of lust. Memories of Erica quickly replaced the image of Pride and sorrow filled his heart. That sorrow fed the rage in his stomach and wiped all of the images from his mind. It was best not to think at all, so he just shrugged and said, "I guess so."

"You guess so," Lucas roared with laughter. "What the hell's the matter with you? Did the nukes get your dick?"

"I guess they must have, Lucas," Jerry said, and grew quiet.

They continued to laugh and talk about the woman until Eli raised a hand and quieted them all.

"Who was she?" The older man asked. There was a compassion in his voice that came less from kindness and more from a kinship of misery.

"My wife," he answered softly. It was the kind of reply that usually drew tears, but he had been cried out for days.

"Christopher?" Eli asked.

"The Skinners."

Joshua gasped, "My God. I'm sorry, Jerry."

"Did they..." Lucas began to ask and stopped himself.

"Did they what?" Jerry asked.

"Never...never mind," Lucas tried to take back the question.

"Did they what?" Jerry asked again. Louder this time.

"They're cannibals, man," Joshua said as matter-of-factly as such a statement could be made.

Jerry looked to each man. Lucas and Eli gave slight nods. Connor looked away. So, it could have been worse. Jerry set his plate down and answered, "No. They ran her through with a knife in front of me."

Joshua hung his head. "I'm sorry."

"You saw them do it?" Connor asked. "What did you do?"

"I killed the man. The woman was already dead in a car wreck."

Connor said nothing after that. No one did. The campfire crackled alone for quite some time.

Eli finally spoke. "They got my family."

"Mine too," Joshua said.

Connor raised his hand. "They killed my brother."

Lucas sighed, "Looks like we've all got a good reason for revenge."

"What's yours?" Connor asked.

"Fuck you. That's mine."

"Okay, tough guy, jeez," Connor said, and changed the subject. "Did you kill Christopher, too?"

Jerry shook his head. "Invictus is behind all of this. He's the one that has to die."

"Get in line, pal," Lucas said with a chuckle. "I get to kill him first."

"We need to work together, Lucas," Eli said.

"You can make all the plans you want as long as I get to pull the trigger," Lucas said.

"What's the plan?" Jerry asked.

"Well, the standard 'give a speech, raise an army and overthrow the tyrant' just won't work here. Invictus is too well dug in. He's too well organized. His men are too devoted. You've seen the stupid capes."

Jerry nodded.

"Do you know how hard it is to get a man to wear a cape?" Joshua asked. "And they're all doing it."

"He's got half of them speaking Latin, too," Lucas added.

"That's loyalty," Eli said. "We're talking way beyond take-a-bullet-for-you loyalty: going-out-in-public-with-a-cape-on loyalty. It's the kind of loyalty most despots only dream of."

"Where is he?" asked Jerry.

"He's at the casino surrounded by Legionaries, Praetorians, Centurions and other delusions of grandeur. Only an army will get him out."

"I still think my plan to sneak in makes more sense," Connor said.

"And we still think you're an idiot," Lucas said.

Joshua tried to be the peacemaker with a little logic. "He's right, Connor. Not the idiot part, but that sneaking in is all but impossible. He's in a fortress surrounded by hundreds of men, in a town with hundreds more. They're devoted. They're well armed, well trained. Power, safety, authority, luxury—with what he has to offer, he's got his pick of the best men the wasteland has ever known."

# 15

---

"Because I want a damn Bandit hat!" Coy screamed at the Legionary. "That's why!"

"The Great Lord Invictus ordered us to find the Resistance," the soldier shot back. "Not a Bandit hat."

Invictus had indeed ordered Coy to find the Resistance. He had also assigned a dozen men to help him. And every one of them was in some stupid metal helmet with a broom on top. Invictus himself had that shiny skullface helmet, so it was clear to Coy, despite his short time in Alasis, that hats meant something and he wasn't going to be left out.

The Coyote ran his finger along the handle of the Bowie knife at his side. "And who did he say was in charge?"

The solider saw the threat but hardly seemed scared. Instead he seemed bothered by his new place on the Invictus org chart. He swallowed his anger and said, "You."

"That's right. And if I think the best way to find these Bookers is in a genuine 10x beaver fur felt hat like the one worn by Bo Darville, then that is the best way to find them."

"The Bookkeepers," the soldier said with a groan.

"Who?"

"They're called the Bookkeepers. Not the Bookers. You don't even know who we're looking for."

"I do. We're looking for a fat guy."

"Gatsby."

"A poo."

"Omoo."

"Teepee."

"Typee."

"Fuck you," The Coyote said. "They're stupid names anyway. Why the hell don't you use their real names? No one ever named their kid Teepee."

"Because we don't know their real names. They're codenames. They named themselves after literary characters."

"That's stupid."

"This coming from the guy that calls himself The Coyote?"

Coy shot him an evil look but let the insult slide. "So who's this Gatsby?"

"The Great Gatsby," the Legionary responded as if it was something Coy should know.

"You've got me looking for a damn magician?"

"He's not a...He's the leader of the Resistance."

"I thought that was The Librarian."

"No, he's their figurehead."

"So he is the head? So he's the leader."

The soldier put his face in his hand for a moment. Coy had noticed it was a common mannerism around here. "How did you even make it this far?"

"I don't know," Coy said. "Just awesome, I guess."

"The Great Gatsby was—"

"It doesn't matter!" Coy shouted. "I'll find him."

And he would. He would hunt down this magician and his Resistance, but he was going to do it his way.

"Invictus ordered me to do it. And we're going to do it my way. And my way is while wearing a Bandit hat! Understand?"

"You've already got Clint Eastwood's poncho. Isn't that—"

"No! It ain't!"

The soldier threw up his hands and turned away from the conversation. Coy was proud of himself. He couldn't recall a time he had straight-up won an argument before. He reveled in his victory for only a moment before looking up at the sign on the building. It was another wax museum. This town was lousy with them.

Under orders and veiled threats, the group had already searched several, and Coy had been one breath short of star struck every time. Some of his biggest heroes were featured in the displays, and they presented some pretty nice headwear options. Eddie Van Halen's wig, Robocop's visor, Arnie's sunglasses from when he played T2. But he wouldn't be any kind of leader unless they accomplished the objectives he had set forth, and the first objective was the Bandit's hat. To show that he was also flexible, he was open as to which movie it came from. And, honestly, at this point he'd even settle for a Hooper hat and just lie to the men about it since they didn't seem to know shit about Burt Reynolds.

"This just seems like a big waste of time," one of the other soldiers said when the order was given to enter the premises and locate the hat.

"Of course you'd say that. You've already got a hat." The Coyote rapped twice on the soldier's metal helmet.

The soldier pulled away at the thumping. "This is stupid."

"Oh, I get it," Coy said. "You're scared. You don't want to go in any more museums because you're afraid."

"I'm not afraid of a wax museum."

"Yeah right. Then why did you shoot that Ronald Reagan in the last one and say that he was looking at you funny?"

"That was you!"

"Not when I tell the story," The Coyote said with a rasp. "Now, if you're too scared to do what's necessary..."

"How is getting you a stupid hat necessary?" another soldier asked.

"I'll just do it myself." The Coyote took three giant steps

forward and kicked in the doors of the wax museum. He turned around and gave a look that said "See, it's not scary," and walked right in.

It was fucking scary. Coy had no idea who originally had the idea to make people out of wax, but they were a mean son of a bitch. With the lights out it was even worse. He put his hand on his gun and walked into the corridor.

The figures looked at him. He heard them talking about him and he had to remind himself that it was just his imagination.

Coy walked slowly down the corridor, giving a wary eye to President Clinton and his wife. He'd always liked that guy for the things he did in his office. But he didn't like the way he was looking at him now. Willy Wonka was asking for it, too. They all were. Each figure looked different, but they all had that same look in their eye, like they needed a soul and Coy's would do just fine.

Despite the looks, it was interesting to see what his heroes looked like up close. Sylvester Stallone was smaller than he imagined, and MiniMe was bigger. And he never would have guessed that Jim Carrey smelled like pee.

He was fairly confident The Bandit wouldn't be in the horror wing, so he happily skipped it altogether. He'd always told Willie he was a fan of scary movies. But that was a lie. Just a glimpse of Freddy Krueger sent his imagination into overdrive.

He heard the figures whispering about him. But he ignored them because he was smart enough to know they couldn't really talk. It was just his brain playing tricks on him. Coy and his brain had always had a contentious relationship at best. And, even though his brain would never tell him what exactly contentious meant, Coy was smart enough on his own to realize it wasn't a good thing. Maybe his brain was catching on that he didn't need it anymore. Because it was really playing tricks on him now.

He swore he saw James Bond move and heard Superman giggle. He was getting pissed at his brain now. Why was it so mean to him? What had he ever done to it? He had pretty much left it alone his entire life.

He had hoped that when he became The Coyote he would get a better brain than Coy's. But it seemed like he was stuck with what he had. He did his best to ignore it. When George Washington called him 'Cutie Pie,' he stopped and took a deep breath and repeated to himself several times, "The dollar bill guy did not just make a pass at you. That's just your imagination."

Convincing himself was getting harder and harder. The whispers were growing louder in his head. He started seeing movement everywhere. He finally stopped and screamed, "It's not real! None of you are real! You're just my stupid head being stupid!"

He meant every word and to prove it, he rushed into the Living Presidents' display, punched Trump in the face and kicked Obama in the balls. He knocked over Jimmy Carter, then raced across the room and tackled Brett Favre. He stood up and caught his breath.

"I told you it wasn't real," he said and really, truly believed it. Then Batman punched him in the face.

Coy grabbed his nose and stumbled backward as a fear rose within him. The figure was motionless now, but he couldn't deny what had happened. Coy wanted to run and scream and generally panic, but The Coyote wasn't having it.

The fear disappeared, and The Coyote marched up to Batman. The figure remained motionless as he eyed the Caped Crusader closely. It looked no different than the others. It smelled a bit, but The Riddler smelled like piss too, so The Coyote figured it must have something to do with the tights. He looked into Batman's eyes and spoke softly, "I'm not afraid of you, Batman. You're nothing but a wax figure. You're a statue. You're a dummy."

"I am the night!" screamed Batman, and planted a foot in The Coyote's chest.

The kick sent him reeling back across the corridor into Neil Armstrong, who in turn kicked him in the ass and sent him diving into Captain America. The Coyote grabbed the Sentinel of Liberty's shield from the statue and turned to face the Dark Knight. But the caped crusader was gone.

"Where are you, Batman?" The Coyote screamed. "Come back here and face me, you caped freak!"

There was no movement from the gallery, but a commotion arose behind him and he turned to face the threat.

His soldiers rushed into the room.

"We heard shouting," the captain said. "What happened?"

"Batman sucker punched me and Neil Armstrong kicked me in the ass."

"I'm sorry?" the guard asked.

"You heard me." The Coyote dropped the shield and drew his gun. "He disappeared somewhere in here. Now help me find him."

"Help you find Batman?" the guard chuckled at the question.

"Well he's not really Batman, you idiot." The Coyote said. "He's a wax figure of Batman."

The guards laughed at this.

"Just shut up and spread out."

The guards broke off into teams of two to search the museum. The commander stayed with Coy, and the two quietly made their way deeper into the museum.

Coy heard the whispers again.

"Did you hear that?" the captain asked quietly. "Whispering."

"Yeah, but don't worry. It's just my imagination."

"I'm hearing your imagination?"

"I've got a really good imagination," Coy said.

"Someone is hiding in here," the captain explained.

"No shit, Sherlock. I told you, it's Batman. And that Neil Armstrong fucker, too."

They moved into another gallery, and the captain spotted the space suit first. He bent over and picked up the suit and held it out to show Coy. "Do you know what this means?"

Coy took the outfit and threw it down on the floor in disgust. "Not what you think it does?"

"I really want you to tell me what I'm thinking."

"Well, you're thinking that it was the ghost of Neil Armstrong that kicked my ass. But that's just stupid because everyone knows that ghosts don't have feet. Obviously, it means it was just someone dressed up like Neil Armstrong. Someone's hiding in here."

Shouting and gunshots grabbed their attention, and the two men raced through the wax museum. Batman was standing over two fallen guards as several more surrounded him.

"I told you it was Batman!" The Coyote said, and started forward.

Batman, three other men and a couple of dogs moved about the troops, disarming and engaging the soldiers. Their metal armor clattered as they fell to the ground.

The captain pulled a whistle from around his neck and blew. The sound was deafening inside the walls of the museum, but the other guards quickly rallied to its sound and began to fire on the attackers at once.

With the element of surprise gone and with Neil Armstrong no longer on their side, the four men turned and ran for the exits.

## 16

The emergency exit was tucked away behind a diorama that featured dust-covered reproductions of three of the four Golden Girls. Jerry hit the door with his shoulder at full speed and exited into the alleyway behind the museum with Chewy at his heels.

Batman wasn't far behind them. Connor was trying to shed the costume as fast as he could while still running for his life. The cape, the cowl and the gauntlets went flying.

Jerry kept his pace even to make sure he wasn't leaving the kid behind. But once Bruce Wayne managed to struggle out of his tights, the younger man sprinted past him with little more than a wave.

Chewy loped along beside the Librarian as they ran through the back alleys of a half dozen abandoned sweet shops and souvenir stores. The pair quickly lost sight of Connor as the man rounded a corner and disappeared.

Jerry turned the corner to follow the Stranger and ran into a host of Legionaries as they stepped out onto the street. They were joking and chatting with one another and unaware of what was happening in their fair city. From Jerry's reaction, however, it was clear that he was up to no good, and they quickly reached for their guns.

Chewy gave the men a good barking, but that didn't stop them, so Jerry turned and ran as the soldiers chased after him.

They ran past a tattoo parlor, another wax museum and a place selling Cuban cigars to Americans under the impression that contraband was a flavor.

He crashed through the doors of an old sandwich shop and interrupted the meal of several more Legionaries.

Jerry and Chewy were able to make it through the back door before the men got to their feet and joined in the pursuit. He barred the door shut as best he could and heard the armored men crash into it. The barricade wouldn't hold long, but it gave him a chance to put some distance between himself and his pursuers.

The pair worked their way around the base of an old inn, and he envisioned it as a barracks filled with still more soldiers. They were everywhere this side of the river, and the risks of the hide-in-plain-sight plan were now evident. Of course, it did have its advantages.

Behind the old Ramada Inn, a pair of soldiers, convinced that they were alone on their side of the river, stood beside a pickup truck complaining to each other. The truck's tailpipe poured hot exhaust into the cold air and Jerry ran for it.

The two soldiers were engaged in conversation with their backs to the truck and didn't see him approaching. Jerry waved a gesture to Chewy that they both understood to mean "settle," and began to creep forward.

"So what are you saying?" one soldier asked. "You want to head back out into the wasteland?"

"No. Not that."

"You're never going to get it as good as it is here."

"All I'm saying is the man's tendency to hurl people out of windows makes me uncomfortable."

"You've got a nice house. Heat. You've got more than most

people. What's it bother you if someone gets thrown out a window every now and then?"

"So you're okay with his propensity for defenestration, provided you aren't cold at night?"

"You're such a nerd, Axeface."

"Oh, nice with the name calling, Dagger."

The handle and the door squeaked, but the guards couldn't hear the noise over their conversation. Jerry climbed into the driver's seat and signaled for Chewy to jump in the bed.

The guards were still arguing when he dropped the pickup into gear and pulled away, but it didn't take them long to react. A bullet cracked the rear window and he heard another slam into a body panel as he turned onto the street. Chewy was pretty comfortable in a truck, but she turned so fast that he heard her paws scrambling for traction in the unlined bed.

He looked in the mirror to make sure she was okay and then checked the cab for anything that might be helpful. There wasn't much except for a red blanket serving as a seat cover on the passenger side of the bench. Jerry pulled it free and draped it over his shoulders. Maybe if he were moving fast enough, it would be mistaken for a Legionary's cape and buy him a few minutes of not being shot at.

Working his way through the side streets of Niagara Falls, he doubled back to the wax district, hoping to find the others. There were even more soldiers on the streets now and they were actively searching for those causing the disturbance.

He made several passes around the area and saw no sign of his new friends. He assumed from the chaos on the streets that they had evaded their captors and he began to make his own plan. He had no idea what it was going to be.

Jerry turned south and began driving toward the casino Invictus called home. At the very least he could get a closer look at the defenses around the complex.

A pair of guards dashed across the street in front of him and he reflexively slammed on the brakes. The sentries shot him only a cursory glance as they hurried on their way. Jerry turned to follow them down the street and saw the reason for the rush. Connor had been cornered. The kid's back was against a wall and four Legionaries had him surrounded.

Jerry plowed into one of the guards with the truck. This drew the attention of the other three as he leapt out from behind the wheel. Chewy was over the edge of the bed before Jerry hit the ground and leapt at one of the men. She caught the soldier's cape in her teeth and pulled the man to the concrete before he could react.

Connor assessed the new situation quickly and sprang on the guard closest to him. The Stranger wrapped an arm under the soldier's chinstrap, pulled the man off-balance and walked him slowly back up against the wall while he choked.

The last guard swung at Jerry and missed as he ducked under the attack. He dodged more attacks as he studied the guard's armor, looking for a weak spot. He finally spotted an unprotected spot in the armor and drove a fist into the Legionary's back. Two more punches to the kidney took the fight out of the guard, and a kick to the helmet gave him time to see to Chewy's opponent.

That man had dropped his gun and had his hands over the back of his neck. He was also weeping. Good dog.

Connor and Jerry jumped into the truck's cab. A whistle later and Chewy had released her prisoner and leapt back into the bed. When they drove away, the contingent of soldiers made no effort to follow.

"Where are the others?" Connor asked.

"I didn't see them. Just you."

Conner pointed. "Head south. We'll be safe if we can cross to Chippawa."

"Safe?"

"Relatively speaking."

"What's there?"

"It's the southern border of the city."

The farther they got from the center of town, the more the

activity settled. What guards they did pass hardly gave the Alasis patrol vehicle a second glance. They drove slowly and stuck to the neighborhoods to keep a low profile.

Connor had been staring out the window for most of the drive when he suddenly said, "You really are the Librarian. Aren't you?"

Jerry dismissed it. He was tired of this stupid game. "Does it matter?"

"A lot of people think so."

"Not the ones that matter," Jerry said, as his frustration grew. "I spent the last few years running from my reputation. A myth built on half-truths and bullshit. It's caused me nothing but pain and suffering."

"It's given a lot of people hope."

"Not me. Never me. The one time I tried to embrace it, the one time I dared to hope that it would get me somewhere, it blew up in my face."

"The Resistance, you mean. They didn't believe you. I wonder why?"

"Because of you."

"Me?"

"You and everyone like you. You go around infatuated with building your legacy, your myth, as if popularity still counts for something in this mess of an afterworld. And you lie about damn near everything to build it."

"What are you talking about?"

"The Stranger. Rather convenient way to take credit for everything, isn't it?"

"I never lied. I—

"The slaves in New Dawn."

"What?"

"You rescued the slaves in New Dawn?"

"Yeah? So?"

"That was me. And there weren't a dozen men with chainsaw arms. There were two meth-heads with one knife between them."

Connor grew silent.

"The Stranger, hrmmph. Pretty convenient. You can claim to have been just about anywhere."

"I don't have to explain myself to you," Connor said, and turned back to the window.

"No, you don't. I get you. You're an idiot. The rest of us are trying to run from our reputations, but you're out there trying to get killed for one you don't even own. Let me ask you this? Do you take credit for your own failures? Or just others' successes?"

Connor didn't respond.

"Mistakes make a man quicker than victories, kid."

"Stop calling me kid. I'm no less capable than any of you."

"Maybe. But we'd never know it, now would we? What put it in your head to do this anyway? I was stupid and optimistic. I thought I could fix things. What's your excuse?"

"I didn't like the way the world looked when the dust cleared. I lost my parents. My grandparents saved my brother and me. They raised us, but we grew up starving and fighting for everything we had. We were getting by until Invictus's men came through town. The people there did their best to stand against him and he slaughtered half of them. My brother included. I watched the strong bully the weak, so when I was strong enough to punch back, I did.

"I needed something more to fight with than fists. I needed an image. No one trembles at the idea of an orphan. I've done good things, Jerry. I'm not a complete lie. But I guess I wouldn't blame you if you didn't trust me."

"Fair is fair," Jerry said. "You don't believe me and I don't believe you. Words failed us, so we'll have to go on actions. You fought well back there."

The rear window exploded. The cold air rushed in along with the sound of gunfire and roaring engines.

"Chewy? Are you okay?" Jerry risked a look over his shoulder to check on his friend and received a warm wet tongue across the face. "Hold on."

It was a mean thing to say to an animal with no hands, but

Chewy knew what he meant. She spread out her legs and lowered herself into the truck bed as Jerry sped up.

He cut hard around a corner and felt the back end of the pickup slide. Then he heard Chewy slide and shouted an apology. They raced down the street as the citizens of Alasis ran out onto their porches to see what was going on. Almost every one of them was armed and the neighborhood was soon filled with bullets.

Jerry cut right onto another residential street.

"No, this is a dead end," Connor shouted.

It wasn't technically a dead end, but it was a circle that didn't really go anywhere. He drove a complete loop and didn't realize it was over until he was passing some of his pursuers on the second lap.

He came up on a small Toyota and crashed into its rear. The push sent the car spinning into a yard where it struck a tree and came to a stop. By the third lap, he was in the lead again and the block was getting crowded.

"Cut right!" Connor shouted.

There was an offshoot from the circular road that obviously met a dead end in a growth of shrubs. Connor didn't wait for an argument. He yanked the wheel and stomped on the gas.

The small pickup truck crashed through the bushes. The occupants were tossed around, and Jerry had to fight to keep his ass in the driver's seat. When the truck finally settled they were in an open field that looked to have once been a city park.

"Go!" Connor shouted from the floorboards.

"You better not have hurt my dog!"

Chewy barked from the back of the truck. It sounded like a curse.

A moment later they passed a playground and found the walking path that led to the parking lot.

Their pursuers had followed them through the small hedgerow and were barreling across the park after them.

Jerry gave the little pickup all the gas he could, but tune-ups were few and far between in the apocalypse and he was sure it was operating on fewer cylinders than it had originally.

They reached the parkway and he turned south once more. Maybe they could get lucky and make it across the bridge at the southern gates.

They had just turned onto Portage Road when the tires blew. Two of them burst from either gunshots or fatigue, and the truck pulled hard to the right. Keeping it straight was a challenge, so he went with it and pulled into the parking lot of an aquarium called Marineland.

"Why are you stopping?" Connor yelled as Jerry jumped from the car.

"The car won't make it. We have a better chance on foot." Jerry called Chewy from the truck bed and the pair ran toward the entrance.

Contrary to what one might expect, the place was not a direct rip-off of SeaWorld. Even though its name sounded like they just flipped open a thesaurus, took the first alternative and whipped up a sign, the aquarium actually pre-dated its more famous cousin. The fact that the star of their show for years was named Kandu instead of Shamu was just lazy writing.

The whale's face and name were on everything from the signage on the walls to souvenir cups that littered the floor. The cartoon orca smiled broadly with a toothy grin that Jerry was pretty certain wasn't anatomically correct, but it did give Kandu the look of one of your more friendly killers.

Connor raced in the door behind him and they made their way farther into the aquarium. The complex wasn't large compared to most theme parks, but he knew it was big enough to hold at the very least a whale so hopefully it was big enough to shake their pursuers.

As they ran, Jerry was surprised to see parts of the aquarium were still operational. At first it was a mystery as to why a tyrant would waste resources on an amusement park. Once he saw that the main pool was filled with alligators instead of whales, it all made sense. What tyrant wouldn't want a gator execution pavilion that could seat several hundred at once?

"He's sick," Connor said.

"In his defense, I doubt many people are terrified of being eaten by dolphins."

The tale of the Marineland dolphins was like many from the end of the world—well meaning and tragic. Before Invictus but after the bombs, the people of Niagara Falls realized the animals at the park would starve and that something must be done. Things were getting desperate for the creatures and the town found inspiration in a sea lion named Jeff.

One of the original stars of the aquarium, Jeff had made a daring escape from the place in '63. The brave—or more likely ignorant—animal had made his way to the Niagara River and dove in. He was soon carried over the Falls themselves and disappeared. A reward was offered, and a frantic search ensued. Miraculously, Jeff was found a couple of days later 5 miles north, sunning himself on a rock with a teenaged kid named Tommy.

Once they were reminded of Jeff's story, the town had their solution. If a sea lion could survive the Niagara, so could the dolphins. One of man's greatest qualities is the ability to convince themselves of anything if they just stop thinking long enough. So they threw a party to see their flippered friends off, and into the water went the dolphins. Dolphins were mammals, after all. They weren't fish. They breathed air. What difference did it make what kind of water they were in?

Buoyancy was the difference. The dolphins could breathe just fine, but they couldn't swim for shit. They were less buoyant in the freshwater and everything was thrown off. Lida went over the Falls first. Upside down and backward. Marina was next. People swore they heard Echo chirping as he fell. The people rushed into the water to save the remaining two dolphins, so Tsunami and Sonar went over the Falls with a fair bit of company.

It was a sad day for everyone.

Gunshots rang out behind them and the two men turned to see

the soldiers blasting their way into the stadium. Connor ran left while Chewy and Jerry ran to the right, each circling around the pool while trying to stay below the stadium seats and doing what they could to shoot back.

It was chaos in the aquarium but as far as Jerry could tell, Connor was a terrible shot. Jerry struck one guard in the upper torso and kept the other rounds close enough to make them cautious. Connor wasn't even coming close and the guards were closing in on him with little fear.

He and Chewy reached the curve of the pool and took cover behind the concrete. He reloaded and risked a look over the pool's lip. Connor was halfway up a ladder that led to a catwalk over the auditorium.

"What the hell is he doing?" he asked Chewy.

The dog said nothing.

The Legionaries gathered at the base of the ladder and started shooting.

Jerry dropped two of them and sent the others diving for cover before they returned fire.

He ducked, slapped in a fresh magazine and rose to fire again.

The gator's breath hit him first as the massive reptile lunged for him. He sprang back before the jaws could snap shut on his face. There were reflexes and there was just plain flinching, and this was the latter. Jerry kicked back and fell to the ground.

By the time he got to his feet again, Connor was dangling from the catwalk over the tank full of gators screaming for help.

"Seriously? How did he do that?"

Chewy barked her reply.

The guards weren't backing down. Jerry bent down and pulled a pencil and a scrap of paper from his pocket. He scribbled a quick message.

"It looks like The Stranger and I are about to get caught." He tucked the paper in the dog's collar and pointed to the back of the stadium. "Go play Lassie, girl. Go get help."

Chewy barked and ran.

"If there's any to find," Jerry said to himself, and turned back to the problem at hand.

Connor was still dangling, the guards were still chasing and as soon as he went up his own ladder to save the kid, they would be surrounded.

He sighed and began to climb. Climbing a ladder one-handed was slow going, so he chose speed over defensive firing, hoping he would reach the top with as few bullet holes in him as possible. He was counting on a lot more missing. They hadn't hit anyone yet and Connor, dangling from the walkway, was hardly a tricky target.

He scrambled upward as fast as he could, and the bullets started flying. They were closer than he expected.

Over the shots he could hear Connor yelling for help and pleading with the guards to stop shooting. And surprisingly, they listened. The bullets stopped as he climbed onto the catwalk. A quick glance back down confirmed that he wouldn't be going back that way. Several guards had grouped around the ladder while two more began the climb.

They were climbing from the other side as well. He shot the top one off the ladder and watched as the Legionary took out the two that were climbing below him.

He reached Connor and reached for his hand. "Grab it!"

"I can't! I'll fall!"

"Grab my hand!"

"Pull me up!"

Jerry fired another shot to keep the guards at bay and set the gun on the walkway. He grabbed Connor by the collar and helped pull him up.

The kid was panicking, kicking his legs like wild to get back on solid ground. One kick sent Jerry's gun tumbling into the pool of gators below.

He swore and heaved the kid onto the platform. "You're good now. Get up."

The men that had followed him up the ladder were on the catwalk, and he leapt over the kid to confront them. The suspended platform was only about three feet wide and shuddered when he ran. He slid and took out the legs of the first Legionary he came to, who screamed his way into the pool below.

A roar rose up from the gator pit along with a clattering of armor. The armor might buy him some time, if he could keep the gators from drowning him first. In that case, however, the armor was on the gators' side.

He had the next guard in line back over the rail when the warning shot hit him in the shoulder. The impact spun him around. Connor was pinned to the platform with a rifle against his head and two more guards were crossing toward him.

Jerry dropped to his knees, put his hands behind his head and hoped that when they knocked him out he wouldn't fall in with the gators.

## 17

Night fell, and the bow of the aluminum boat crunched as it hit the shoreline. The three men disembarked as best as they could without getting wet. Eli pulled the craft out of the water. The cold from the hull penetrated his gloves and went straight to the bone.

The three men moved without a word up the shoreline and into the town with their dogs in tow. Ice hung from the sheepdog's fur and the old dog jingled as it followed along. Lord Stanley, bred to work the cold water of Newfoundland, had a spring in his step as he happily heeled at Joshua's side. Connor's Blue Heeler appeared the coldest of all and shivered as he walked at Lucas's feet.

Once they were a few blocks into the town, they felt comfortable enough to talk again.

"I don't like running away from a fight," Lucas said as he rubbed his hands briskly against one another.

"Don't think of it as running away," Joshua said. "Think of it as regrouping."

"That doesn't help." Lucas bent over and petted the Blue Heeler. The dog wagged in response but continued to shiver. It moved closer against Lucas's leg, and the man scratched at its head and asked himself, "What kind of asshole leaves his dog behind? What did he name it?"

"Heeler, I think."

"What kind of an asshole would leave Heeler behind?"

"It wouldn't have done anyone any good if we'd been caught," Eli said, and led them down a poorly lit street. Dying lights flickered and the licking flames from trash cans cast erratic shadows on the building walls.

They passed through a neighborhood and onto a broad avenue before crossing the street to an old theater with a tattered awning and black steel doors. Eli pulled the door opened and waved the party inside.

Inside, the setting improved. The tile floor was littered with debris, but at the end of the foyer was another set of doors with intact windows that promised to keep the wind off of the men for the night. Beyond the foyer they found an ornate wooden bar that stood as the centerpiece of a former music hall. And at the end of the room, an empty stage beckoned performers that would never show. Overturned dining tables were scattered around what had once been a dance floor, but there were more than enough chairs for the men to take a seat and assess their predicament.

"What do we do now?" Lucas asked.

"We'll be safe here for tonight," Eli said.

For all that had fallen apart in the theater, the acoustics still functioned perfectly, and the footsteps from the stage cracked around them. Out of the darkness of the black curtain stepped the woman from the Resistance.

The sheepdog barked and the three men jumped to their feet, pulling their guns as they did. Lucas kept her covered while the other two men checked their surroundings to ensure they weren't being ambushed.

"It's just me," the woman said. "I'm alone."

"Well, if it isn't the hot chick from the Bookkeepers," Lucas said.

"Well, if it isn't three little Librarians," she replied.

Lucas had no comeback. No matter how tough you pretended

to be, it was always difficult to get called out in a lie. And the harder you pretended, the harder the truth was to hear.

"What do you want, lady?" Eli asked as he holstered his weapon.

"I'm looking for the new guy. I'm sure you've seen him. He's a librarian, too." She walked calmly to the center of the stage and picked up a chair from the ground. She spun it around so the back faced the men and straddled the seat.

"I don't know what you're talking about," Joshua said.

"Yeah, no idea. Now why don't you go back to your little book club and keep doing nothing. We've got a war to fight."

"Oh, Lucas," she said with a smile. "Always so cranky."

Lucas was taken aback by her comment.

"How does she know you?" Joshua asked.

"She doesn't," Lucas replied.

"Lucas Dylan. AKA the Soldier. AKA the Wasteland Mercenary, the Merc with the Heart of Gold."

"Watch it!" Lucas said.

"You've spent years offering your services to the people of the apocalypse. But...always the poor ones. I'm not going to suggest you're not a very good soldier. But I do know you're not a very good businessman."

"And Elias Reynolds. How many times have you turned down the offer of a new home just to wander until you find yourself in trouble once again?"

Eli sat back down and folded his arms.

"Joshua Campbell and, of course, Lord Stanley. So polite. So helpful. The Savior of Sault St. Marie. The Martyr of Mississippi Mills. The Patriot of Pusey."

"Pusey?" Lucas laughed.

"Shut up, it's a place in Ontario," Joshua shot back.

"We know all of you," the woman said. "We may not be the best at revolting, but we've got our intelligence more than in order."

"So, you tell us. Who's the new guy?" Lucas asked.

"He's the Librarian," Pride said with a smile.

"Just like us," Eli said with a laugh.

"Yeah, we're all the Librarian. Isn't that right?" Lucas said with a fair amount of whimsy and sarcasm in his voice. "Because maybe the Librarian isn't a person after all. Maybe it's an idea that lives in all of us. It's our sense of honor. Our desire to do good. Deep down, we're all the Librarian. Is that what you're saying, lady?"

"No," Pride said. "He's really the Librarian."

"Yeah right."

"He is. And I need to find him."

"Well good luck," Joshua said, and sat down in his chair. "Invictus raided our little hideaway and last time we saw the new guy, he was running south."

"They raided the wax museum?" she asked.

Eli didn't respond. He could tell she had asked for no other reason than to reveal that she had known their location all along. He'd always hated games like that.

Lucas answered for him. "He and the kid got out, but we don't know where they went."

Pride sat up a little in her chair. "Who's the kid?"

"He's not a *kid* kid," Eli said. "But a younger guy."

"Everyone is younger than you, Eli."

"Shut up, Lucas." Eli looked back at the woman. It was all but imperceptible, but she was leaning farther forward in the chair than she had been. He continued, "Well, and here I thought you knew everything. His name is Connor. Claims to be known as the Stranger. He came to see you a couple of weeks ago."

Pride listened intently but gave no clue as to whether the information jogged her memory.

"Speaking of knowing everything," Joshua said, "what do you know about this new guy bossing around Invictus's men?"

"Who?" she asked, genuinely perplexed.

"From the way he was talking, he thought he was the new Christopher. He was bossing the troops around when they raided our hideout."

"We don't know who he is. He just recently showed up with Christopher's hat and head claiming to have killed him."

"So Christopher is dead?" Eli asked.

She nodded. "The Skinners, too."

"You can thank the new guy for the Skinners, but even he thought Christopher was still alive."

"They found his body in a Cracker Barrel."

"Like an actual cracker barrel?" Lucas asked.

"It amazes me you think you have a right to treat people like they're dumb," Joshua said.

"It could be an actual cracker barrel, cheese curd! It wouldn't be the worst place to hide a body."

"It wasn't an actual barrel," Pride explained with a sigh.

"Some guy kills Mr. Christopher, brings his head to town and takes his job and you don't know who he is?" Lucas laughed. "Then I guess your intelligence isn't as good as you think. You have no idea what's going on around you."

"Excuse me," a small child said as he brushed past Lucas, causing the mercenary to jump. The child giggled at the man's reaction and continued on to the stage.

"You pick the worst places to hide, Eli," Lucas snapped.

"What is it, Oliver?" Pride asked.

The child climbed up the stage and signaled for her to lean over. He whispered something in her ear and handed her a slip of paper.

"What's he saying?" Joshua asked.

Pride looked at the men. She chewed the inside of her cheek, perhaps mulling over how much she could tell them. She finally spoke. "Your friends have been captured."

"Where?"

"They caught them at the aquarium," the boy answered. "They're being taken to the tower now."

"That's enough, Oliver," Pride said and stood up. "We have to go."

"Wait!" Eli raised his voice. "What are you going to do?"

Pride looked at them again and Eli could see her weighing her options. Her answer wasn't what he expected. "That's our business."

"Oh get off of it, girlie," Lucas said. "You're not going to do anything. Your business is cowering in the shadows and waiting for Invictus to die of old age. You're the worst resistance in history."

"What we do is none of your concern, Lucas."

"Ooooh," he mocked. "Reminding me of your vast knowledge. Well, your fantastic intelligence network isn't going to stop the bad guy or save the good guys."

"You'd be surprised," she said, and let the phrase hang in the air.

"I'd be fucking flabbergasted."

"This is all insane." Joshua stood and approached the stage. "We are all here fighting for the same thing. We all want Invictus gone. We all want the people here to be free and the people out in the wasteland to live without the fear of Death Trucks coming to make paupers and slaves of them. We are offering to help. It would be foolish not to accept it."

"Every one of you lied to us," she sniped. "Trust has to be earned."

"Like getting your spies to keep tabs on us?" Lucas asked, pointing at the child next to her.

Pride looked at Oliver and back to the men. There was a certain concession in her expression, but she made no attempt to apologize. "It's not up to me. The council—"

"The council sucks," the boy shouted. "Gatsby sucks. All they ever do is talk."

"There you go, kid!" Lucas applauded.

"These men can help us," Oliver continued. "That one killed three guards by himself when they escaped."

"Which guy?" she asked.

"The ugly one," he answered, and pointed at Lucas.

"Hey, you brat!" Lucas suddenly wasn't a fan of the kid.

Oliver ignored the remark and continued his plea. "They can help us."

"We can't trust them," Pride said.

"Then don't trust us," Eli walked to the base of the stage. "Don't let us into your little do-nothing club. But we have the same goals here. We want Invictus gone as much as you do. That may be hard to understand. How could we hate him as much as you? You live here. You see his speeches. You may think he's just your problem. But there is a world outside this city. And he preys on them every day. There are few people out there that don't fear his trucks, his soldiers. He turns their homes into ruins, their loved ones into slaves. That's why we're here. Not to rob you of your cause but to end the suffering he oversees. Forget the Resistance. Honestly, none of us here really needs another nickname anyway. But let us help you stop this madman!"

Pride studied the men in front of the stage in complete silence. She eyed each of them individually and then sighed.

---

## 18

The Skylon tower was built in 1964 to offer a better view of one of nature's greatest wonders. It was later improved by adding two Starbucks and a 4D theater that featured a film about the Falls where viewers could appreciate the majesty and grandeur of the spectacle without having to step outside.

The tower's construction was financed by Charles Reese, the son of the man with all the peanut butter pieces. Despite this, the tower had never been referred to as the Tower That Peanut Butter Built despite it being tremendously fun to say.

For decades, the tower had provided the greatest view of the Falls and the surrounding area. Families rode to its great height and stood in awe of nature's wonder and 8,000 square miles of countryside. But an apocalypse changes everything, and now the tower served as the throne room of Great Lord Invictus. From there he ruled over all he surveyed. Everything in view was in his control. He even had binoculars installed so he could survey farther. His network of terror reached far beyond the visible territory into the wasteland.

Even now he smiled as a truck departed across the repaired Rainbow Bridge to spread his power and influence into the towns and communities that lay outside of his gates. He was in complete control. He was the ruler of whatever was left. He was going to get them to change the name of the Rainbow Bridge. It didn't fit his brand at all and would have to go.

"The prisoners, Great Lord Invictus," the Praetor announced.

Invictus turned away from the open window and watched as the two men, hooded and bound, were dragged across the room and cast at his feet.

He nodded his approval to the guards, and they forced the two men to their knees before him and ripped the hoods from their faces.

Invictus studied the two men. The younger one was terrified. Snot ran from his nose, and while it could have been allergies brought on by the hood, Invictus approved of the weak look on his face.

"Which one is it?" The great lord asked.

The guard responded by striking the Librarian between the shoulders with the butt of his rifle and knocking him forward on his face.

The prisoner grunted with the impact and struggled to get back upright.

"This is the Librarian?" Invictus asked.

"That's what he's been telling people." The guard struck the man once more and smiled at the grunt he had drawn from the prisoner.

Invictus bent down and smiled at his captive. "I'm not convinced. I want to show you something."

There was a fair amount of grabbing and jostling as both prisoners were wrestled to the ground. Some kicking occurred as the guards lashed ropes through the restraints on their ankles. The screaming started when the two men were hoisted up and dangled a few feet apart outside the tower window fifty stories above the ground.

The younger of the two all but wet himself as he dangled. He moved between kicking out of panic and complete stillness from fear of causing himself to fall. The other just hung there staring at the overlord.

"You probably have a lot of questions going through your mind right now," Invictus said. "How high am I? How long will it take my body to hit the ground? Will I be conscious when I land on the pile of bodies below me?"

Jerry pointed to the guard with his chin. "Mainly I'm just wondering if Dipshit there is any good at tying knots."

"Don't worry. You won't fall until I want you to fall." Invictus turned to the guard next to him. "Turn them around."

The process was not complicated. Pulleys, gears and a system of ropes were hardly necessary when one had a good poking stick. The guards prodded the prisoners until their backs were to the tower and they were looking out over the view the countless tourists had once paid good money to see.

"What you see is mine. All of it. Everywhere the light touches. Everywhere the shadows embrace. And beyond that? That's mine, too. Where there was chaos, I have brought order. I provide security. I provide food. I provide the power that keeps the world alive! And you shitty little wannabe heroes are threatening that."

He nodded to the guards, and the poking resumed.

"You inspire rebellion. You think you're doing good. But when people rebel, people get hurt. You are the cause of their suffering."

"You rape and murder and make slaves of your victims!" the Librarian shouted.

"A little bit," Invictus admitted. "To keep the peace. To keep order."

Jerry finished spinning and locked eyes with the overlord. "You should get out more. Your order is slipping away."

The Great Lord Invictus didn't display the rage that washed over him. He always found it more intimidating to deliver beatings while appearing calm. There was just something more frightening about it.

"Your empire is crumbling. You've lost your allies out west. Your trucks keep closer and closer to the city. Why? Are you afraid to venture into your own kingdom? You know as well as I do that your time here is coming to an end."

Invictus reached out and grabbed Jerry by his jacket collar. He pulled him closer until their faces were only inches apart and snarled. "I am the conduit for power in the world now."

He let the prisoner go and watched as he swung out over nothing. He turned away and began to pace the ledge near the open window. He recited:


Out of the night that covers me,
    Black as the pit from pole to pole,
    I thank whatever gods may be
    For my unconquerable soul.


In the fell clutch of circumstance
    I have not winced nor cried aloud.
    Under the bludgeonings of chance
    My head is bloody, but unbowed.


Beyond this place of wrath and tears
    Looms but the Horror of the shade,
    And yet the menace of the years
    Finds, and shall find me, unafraid.


It matters not how strait the gate,
    How charged with punishments the scroll,
    I am the master of my fate:
    I am the captain of my soul.


He had practiced the verse countless times in private and recited it just as many at times like this. It never failed to put the fear of God into his victims. He turned to face the prisoner once more and found him smiling. "What's so funny?"

"You don't even understand Invictus, Invictus."

"Oh no?"

"You think it's about being tough. You think it's about will over adversity. It's not about conquering everything. It's not about power."

"Educate me."

"'Because strait is the gate, and narrow is the way, which leadeth unto life, and few there be that find it.' It's from the Bible, bub. It's about faith in the face of adversity. It's about conviction. It's about doing what's right when the world is against you. And you know that there's not a part of what you're doing that's right."

Invictus could feel the guards around him tense up. They expected that to be the end of the conversation. One word from him, one gesture, and there would be another body on the pile at the base of the tower.

He turned to his Praetor. "It does sound like him. Pompous. I've heard he was basically a nerd."

"I had some time to read."

"Do you think it's him, Praetor?" Invictus asked.

The man shrugged.

"How about you?" he asked another soldier, and proceeded to take a quick survey of the room, with no one committing a solid answer.

The Great Lord finally turned to the man hanging out the window. "Is it him, Jonathon?"

"He thinks he is. And his name is Jerry. You should have seen him come back for me when I pretended to fall at the aquarium. Which, by the way, was the only way your guys were going to catch him. Maybe consider less armor for the troops and more calisthenics."

"I'll take it under advisement," Invictus said. "Bring them in."

Jerry turned and looked at the man dangling next to him. "So, it's not Connor."

"Sorry, Jer. My name is Jonathon Skinner. You killed my grandparents."

Jerry jerked and the distance between the two men closed suddenly. There was a crack as the Librarian's head shattered Jonathon's nose.

"You dick!" Jonathon cursed, but it sounded more like 'you mick!' because his nostrils had quickly filled with blood.

"You betrayed us all," Jerry growled.

"I bid mot. I mas neber on your smide, smo I coulbn't metray you. I mought you mere smose to be mart." He screamed at the guards. "Mull me bin!"

The guards began to respond but Invictus stopped them with a raised hand. "What if it's not him?"

"Kill himb anymay. I'll jus mork my way back imto the groub. They hab no idea I'mb faking."

Invictus nodded and the guards dragged Jonathon Skinner back into the tower and cut him free. He pinched his nose and pointed back out the window at Jerry. "Mop ma Mufker."

The guards looked to Invictus to see if they would indeed drop the fucker.

"No," Invictus said. "He rides the Falls. This city must see him die."

"Mis if mullshit!" Jonathon shouted, and pointed at Jerry hanging outside the window.

"Jonathon," Jerry said softly. "I owe you an apology."

"Mhat?"

"Your grandparents. It wasn't right. I wasn't myself. I was angry. Angrier than I've ever been. That doesn't make it right, but I hope you can understand. They took the person I loved most from me and I just went blank. I felt nothing. It's like it wasn't even me, like I was removed from my body and all I could do was watch. I did things I'm not proud of. I gouged out his eyes and listened to his screams. I can't even imagine the kind of suffering I caused. Yes, there's the immense pain, but can you imagine the frustration, the feeling of powerlessness that must come from being violently deprived of your sight. In a brief moment you would realize that your life is forever changed. That nothing could ever bring it back. That you'd never look upon your loved ones again. See their faces. See how they look back at you. See the love in their eyes. That's what I heard in his screams. It wasn't pain. It was loss. I took that from him and I'm sorry."

"Myou sum omf a mitch!" Jonathon screamed and rushed toward the window. He had no plan. He wanted blood.

Invictus's guards grabbed the young man and pushed him back from the window. The guards let him go, and he screamed and stomped then rushed the solider holding the end of the rope.

Jerry dropped from sight.

"Grab the rope!" Invictus shouted as the soldiers dove to the ground.

There was a clanging of armor and screams of rope burn as the men got a hold of the cable and stopped the prisoner's descent, while others tackled the young Skinner and pinned him to the ground.

"Pull him up!" Invictus ordered the guards, and turned to Jonathon. "What the hell was that?!"

"He's not Mibrarian! Kill hib!"

"You said it was him."

"How the mell mould I bow? I'b neber met the guy."

"Oh, now I get the deal with the window," Coy said, as he entered the throne room wearing a garish black cowboy hat. He walked across the room and nodded to Invictus. "That's a good idea, Mr. Great Lord."

Invictus took a deep breath. The Coyote was a moron. A frustration he didn't need right now. But maybe he had good news. "Did you catch them?"

"Not all of them. But I heard my men got two of them." Coy spotted Skinner on the floor and pointed at the kid. "That's one of them. What did you do? Throw the other one out the window?"

The guards were winded and starting to sweat, but one final pull brought their prisoner back into view outside the window.

Coy smiled and walked to the ledge. He put his hand on his hat and turned his head upside-down so he'd be eye-to-eye with the man hanging by his ankles. "Well, well, well. If it isn't the Library Guy."

Invictus pulled The Coyote out of the way and knelt before the prisoner with a grin of pure joy. "Ready the boat."

# 19

Potato sack. Pillowcase. Stitched-up sweatpants. By this point Jerry was getting pretty familiar with the different types of hoods used to blindfold a captive. He didn't really have a preference for material. Burlap and canvas tended to chafe more, but whatever it was they made sweatpants out of really held onto the smells of former prisoners. He found it was more the methodology of the hooder that really made a difference.

The guards in the tower were rough. The Resistance was the worst. The gentlest captors in town, surprisingly, were the prison guards. Admittedly, gentle was relative.

The hood came off quickly, but an effort was made to lift it straight up versus violently back or forward for that head-snapping effect kidnappers seemed to live for.

The view was shocking enough. It was a dungeon. Rock walls. Steel door. Wooden bucket. There was a pile of hay on the floor he had to assume was his bed.

He shrugged off the question of where one could find a dungeon in Niagara Falls. Tyrants were, almost without exception, a resourceful bunch. It had to take a remarkable imagination to consider yourself worthy of praise while considering others expendable. To hold with the conviction that you were best suited to decide what was best for others. And furthermore, that the pain and misery you inflicted on others was truly for the greater good.

It was a fantasy they all lived, and that creativity often extended to the physical constructs of their tyranny. Not everyone had access to alligators, bears and/or mutants. Shark tanks were almost completely unheard of away from the coast. Still, the despots of the apocalypse had adapted in surprising ways.

Tusk the Terrible's entire porcine motif had been built around the feral hogs of the Southwest and included a death pit filled with the massive 800-pound beasts. Victims of the Long Leg found themselves caged with vicious territorial ostriches with nowhere to run. But the worst had to be what legend had come to call the Furry Fury, where a prisoner was encased in a box with a thousand hungry hamsters. It was an embarrassingly adorable and brutal way to go.

But he had to give credit where credit was due. Between the scale and presentation of the gator pit, the tower throne room and the authentic dungeon, Invictus had the other warlords beat when it came to the tyrannical theme game.

He was also the most powerful warlord Jerry had come up against. But he was no less confused than the others. The man simultaneously wielded, manipulated, tortured and forced others to do his bidding while holding the belief that it was what was best for everyone. It wasn't a unique perspective. The world had lost perspective long before the end, when we started telling each other what we should believe. Not just debating or arguing, but holding in contempt and punishing others for thoughts that conflicted with our own. At the time there were differing opinions on how we had gotten here. Some claimed that mankind had grown more horrible over time. Others said mankind had always been horrible and the internet made that horrible nature visible. Still others argued that mankind was an offensive word and should not be allowed anymore, and accused anyone who used it of possessing some of humanity's most horrible traits. That didn't help things.

Thinking we knew what was in the hearts and minds of others was a slippery slope that hit bottom when the bombs fell.

Then came the war, and some of the survivors hoped that things would be put back into perspective. But blowing everything up just made things worse. People still hung onto the thought that they knew better than others. Entire tribes were built around these beliefs, and dissenters were either cast out into the wasteland or relegated to a lower class within the society. And as long as it worked for those in power, it continued. Right and wrong had become twisted and intertwined into an unrecognizable mess.

Jerry put his hand on the wall. The gray paint flaked from the sculpted foam into his hand. He sat down on his bale of hay and thought. Maybe he was the one who had it all twisted. Maybe it was the natural order of things for the strong to prey on the weak until there was enough to go around. Maybe he was interrupting the new natural selection by defending those that would otherwise fall.

And where had doing the right thing gotten him? He had saved a lot of people. He had stopped evil people from harming others. But Erica was dead. Maybe revenge was right after all. Maybe righteous anger wasn't as just as we'd all been led to believe. But the more he thought about her, the more it seemed right.

He had to stop thinking about her. He had to put her in the back of his mind and find a way out. Could he rely on his "friends" from the museum? Connor had betrayed him. Had the others been caught? And what about Chewy?

She was always clever enough to hide when the need arose and loyal enough to come through when it counted. But she was shit at picking locks, and he couldn't count on the assumption that his note had found anyone that would help.

"I'm here to see the prisoner." The voice came from around the corner and Jerry saw the guard nod in his direction.

Jerry had first met the hired gun named Coy in a steakhouse in Amarillo and had hated him ever since. He and his partner had chased and harassed and even momentarily abducted Jerry as he chased Mr. Christopher. This was the dumber of the pair, and he was surprised to have seen him in Invictus's tower.

Coy smiled and tipped his cowboy hat. "Do you remember me?"

"I think your name was Coy."

"That's right," Coy seemed genuinely excited to be recognized. "Well, that was right, but I'm not Coy anymore. I've changed. Now I'm The Coyote. Want to know why?"

"Not really."

Coy laughed at that and pulled up a chair in front of Jerry's cell. "Well, seein' as how you're locked away in here, I'm going to tell you anyway. But I think you'll like this story. You're in it."

Jerry leaned on the bars of his cell. "You know what I miss? The Geneva Convention."

"You see, Coy and Willie were the best of friends. They did everything together since they met in high school. They cut class together, got expelled together, they partied together. And everything was going just fine until the end of the world. And then, things got even better.

"You know what there were less of when the world blew up?"

"Hygiene standards?"

"People," Coy said. "Less cops. Less people telling you what to do. Less people complaining about how much noise you were making. No one bitching about you setting off fireworks in the middle of the night outside the La Quinta. Things were pretty good for old Willie and Coy. They had free reign of the world.

"So one day, the two best friends were sitting around Bomb City minding their own business, planning to have a few beers and maybe steal some shit or hit the trails and do sweet jumps on their dirt bikes. That's when this guy shows up, wearing a stupid hat and offering them a job. He says they can make some easy money if they just help catch this guy from the library."

Jerry grabbed the iron bars of his cell and did his best to twist them. "How'd that go over for them?"

Coy smiled. "It sounded easy enough. Bookworms are nerds. And Willie and Coy never met a nerd they couldn't wedgie, so they take the job and they're going to be rich and do some amazing things with the money."

"Maybe they should have spent less time daydreaming and focused on the job at hand."

Coy removed his hat and looked at the ground. His voice dropped. "Things got messed up along the way. There were a lot more people involved than they knew. Some pretty fucked up people. Cruel people. Crazy people. There were people dressed up like animals. But ole Willie and Coy thought they could outsmart them all. They were going to double cross everyone. But then they got caught."

"I'm just shocked that their brilliant plan didn't work."

Coy looked up at Jerry. His face had changed. His eyes were heavy on the verge of tears. "That's when Coy met the Skinners."

Jerry hung his head. This man had pursued him across the country, tried to kill or catch him several times, and still he felt for him because he now knew how the story was going to end.

"They were looking for the guy from the library, too. And the guy that had given Willie and Coy the job in the first place. They were all nice at first. They treated Coy kindly and even fed him some bacon. It had been a long time since Coy had had any bacon." Coy looked away, his eyes about to pour. When he looked back they had changed. They were cold and dry. "So he ate the bacon."

Coy stood up and turned away from the cell. "But it wasn't bacon. It was his friend. His only friend in the world."

"There aren't words for this, Coy. I'm truly sorry."

"Don't cry for Coy. Coy's dead. After he ate Willie, Coy couldn't live with himself. Friends, real friends, don't eat their friends. So Coy did the only thing he could think to do. He killed himself." Coy turned back around. "And ever since that day I became The Coyote. I changed. I'm smarter, meaner and better-looking than Coy ever was. And The Coyote only has one purpose in life. Revenge.

"I tracked down those bastard Skinners to make them pay for what they had done to Willie and Coy!" The Coyote grew enraged and kicked the chair across the dungeon. "But you know what?"

"They were already dead."

"They was already dead!"

"Because I killed them."

Coy rushed up to the cell door and put a finger in Jerry's face. "Because you killed them!"

"Because they killed my wife."

"Because they killed your wife!" Coy slammed his hat on the ground in a fit of rage and then snapped his eyes back to Jerry. "What?"

"They killed my wife, Coy. Christopher had taken her. I chased that bastard in the stupid hat halfway across the country. I fought a war. I fought you. I fought marauders and raiders and cannibals just to see her once more. And the moment she was finally back in my arms—the moment when we both believed that everything would be okay—that old man ran her through with a knife and took her from me." Jerry trailed off.

"Fuuuuuck." The Coyote backed away from the cell door. He looked more like Coy than his alter ego. "That is a total dick move!"

"I know."

"You must have been pissed right the hell off!"

"I was. I still am. It's not something you can forgive."

Coy picked up his hat, still shaking his head in disbelief. "And you probably thought the whole time that everything would be okay."

"I hoped it would."

"'Cause that's how it works right? And then just all of a sudden? Out of nowhere."

All Jerry could do was nod. Murder was often sudden and rarely expected. You didn't hear the click of a firing pin before the gunshot or the pop of a cork from a vial of poison. It just happened, and life had to change around it.

"I mean, shit, you couldn't write something that terrible."

Jerry hung his head and looked at his feet as the memories and the horrors came rushing back. He relived his revenge on Skinner and felt his hands tighten on the cell door as he remembered forcing his thumbs into the man's eyes. He heard the screams. He felt the neck snap in his hands. And it wasn't enough. He'd still wanted more. He wanted the world to know of his outrage. He wanted everyone to know that it had been unfair.

"You know?" Coy said softly. "I killed that Christopher guy."

"Good," Jerry said.

"Good?" The Coyote sounded as confused as his old self. "I figured you would have wanted to kill him."

He did. He wanted to kill them all. To kill every person responsible for his pain. But what's done was done. He looked back up and saw Coy in front of him, not this persona he had created in his own moments of rage. "As long as he's dead."

"But I took your revenge from you," Coy said. "Doesn't that piss you off?"

"As far as I'm concerned, there's only one person responsible for the death of my wife."

Coy remained silent. Jerry could see the gears turning and all but hear the hamsters running around in the man's head. Coy looked over at the dungeon guard. The Coyote looked back at Jerry. "Do you have any idea what they're going to do to you?"

"It sounds like I'm going for a ride."

The Coyote nodded. "Something like that. They call it riding the Falls because everything around here seems to have a name. They're going to tie you to a boat and send the boat over the Falls. If you live, you're innocent." The Coyote put the hat back on his head. "But I doubt they'll let that happen."

Jerry watched as The Coyote walked out of the dungeon and left him alone once again.

---

## 20

Standing sentry on the border between Wallacia and Transylvania, on a mountain most likely shrouded in mist, fog and werewolves, is Bran Castle. With its peaked spires and blood-red tiles, the palace has often been referred to as the home of the titular character from Bram Stoker's *Dracula*, despite bearing no resemblance to the home described in the book or being even remotely related to the character's inspiration, Vlad the Impaler. Right up until the end of the world, Bran Castle was kept in good repair and remained a spectacle of wonder and grandeur.

Another castle tried to lay claim to the house of Dracula. Despite its ghoulish outward appearance, however, it had difficulty convincing anyone of its authenticity since it shared space with Gags 'N' Giggles, Niagara Falls's premiere joke and magic shop.

Pride approached the castle and shivered. It wasn't the Castle Grayskull visage that served as the front door, or the fierce looking barbicans guarding drawbridges that didn't draw or cross anything —it was what was inside the building that gave her pause.

Within weeks of seizing power, Invictus had converted the wax dungeon and torture chamber into a very real dungeon and torture chamber. It had a romantic appeal that would be almost impossible for any tyrant to resist. If Invictus wasn't feeding his enemies to alligators or dropping them out a window, they were sent here to either await their punishment or wither away inside the evil façade of Dracula's Castle.

Pride walked by the wooden door, passed into the mouth of the giant skull and opened the glass doors to the dungeon that were still clearly labeled as having to remain unlocked during business hours. She closed the door silently behind her and looked around the lobby. The ticket window had been turned into a defensive gun nest, should anyone be foolish enough to attempt a rescue of the prisoners inside. No one had been foolish enough for a long, long time, so the guard manning the position snored away, kicked back in his seat with his feet up on the counter and his helmet cast carelessly aside.

The guard's dress was no different from his counterparts on the street, although she'd heard that there had once been an interest in dressing the guards like headsmen of old. Those who had drawn guard duty had issues with the decision, as the area grew frigidly cold in the winter, and wearing only leather pants and a hood would provide little protection from the elements. It also ran closer to the S&M motif that so many groups had adopted in the wasteland. It was more for the latter reason that the Great Lord Invictus dropped his insistence on the theatrics.

She watched the guard for a moment before moving silently through the lobby doors into what was once the start of the exhibit. The hallway was covered in cobwebs—at this point it was impossible to tell which ones were real and which ones were fake. The red eyes of bats glowed in the darkness like fading LEDs. Wax mannequins lined the hall in various states of disrepair. It was all fake, but ever since the purpose of the building had changed, even the fake decor took on a more ominous meaning than ever intended.

The hallway took her past several torture exhibits. Once filled with wax victims, the devices now sat empty but covered with real blood, and she wondered if the screams that seeped through the hidden speakers weren't just echoes of the dead still wailing out for mercy. Much like the cobwebs, no one knew anymore whether the caged skeletons were real or fake. So, wax or not, she did her best not to make eye contact.

At first blush, it seemed silly that any prisoner would be intimidated by a fake dungeon. But once one realized that it had been made very real, it would no doubt add to the unsettling feeling that the prisoner was literally stuck in a tourist trap.

At the end of the hallway was a large wooden door with an iron handle. Some local artisan had been commissioned to make the door appear authentic to the period. It looked and felt like the entrance to a dungeon of horrors. It was the banded iron that truly made it feel like you were in the Middle Ages. And you could see it really well under the glowing red of the exit sign above the door.

Pride reached for the handle. The prisoner would be inside.

"Who goes there!" asked a booming voice.

Pride screamed and turned to face the voice.

The guard looming over her jumped and screamed as well.

She fell back against the wall with a hand against her chest.

"Dammit, Jenny!" The guard had fallen into his own corner. He pushed himself off the wall. "You scared the crap out of me!"

"You scared me first!" she screamed.

The guard started laughing.

She slapped the guard playfully on the shoulder several times. "Shiv! You ass. I hate it when you do that."

"Serves you right. You could have given me a heart attack. You know I hate working here as it is. Why were you sneaking down the hall all quiet like that?"

"Just lost in thought, I guess."

"Did you happen to think of a way to get me promoted yet? You were going to help me get out of this stupid dungeon, 'member?"

"I remember," Jenny said. "I'm still working on it.

Shiv leaned around her and pulled the heavy wooden door open. It triggered a recorded horror-filled scream.

"I hate that scream," Shiv said with a sigh. "I'm starting to hate it more than the real ones."

He let her pass through the door into the holding area. It was better lit, as new lighting had been added for pragmatic reasons. There was a fine line between keeping the prisoner in a state of fear and making sure they were still in their cell.

"I heard we got a new one," she said, as she pulled off her jacket and hung it up on an extinguished torch attached to the wall.

"Yeah, but you don't need to worry about him much."

Pride walked up to the cell and saw Jerry looking back at her. He recognized her. She could see that. But, he didn't let on. He had to be wondering what she was doing here. A double agent. That much would be clear. But for which side? Was she a spy for the Resistance? Or for Invictus? "Why don't I need to worry, Shiv?"

"No one is supposed to open that door for anything. Not food. Not to change the bucket. Nothing."

"So we'll feed him through the bars."

Shiv shook his head. "Nothing goes in. Great Lord Invictus said so himself."

Pride turned back to the guard and put on her cutest pout. "That's disappointing. I've got a new recipe for gruel I wanted to try out."

The guard bent over and laughed. He slapped his knee "If that's what you call what you've been serving the prisoners, you can bring it to me. You treat these prisoners too nice, girl."

"Well, it is usually their last meal.

Shiv bent over and slapped his knee again to accentuate his laugh. "It would be for this one. He's going to ride the Falls."

"Really? That's the first time in a while." She looked back into the cell. Was it really him? "He must have really pissed Invictus off."

The guard smiled and looked around the room. He knew they were the only ones there, but Shiv liked to build drama. "Can you keep a secret?"

Pride smirked. "You know I can, Sheldon."

"Ixnay on the Eldonshay," Shiv said with a smile. He waved Pride over and lowered his voice to a whisper. "He's the Librarian."

Pride smiled like he was lying. "You don't believe that. Do you? Another one?"

"If the Great Lord Invictus tells me he is, he is. And Invictus is convinced. That's why he's riding the Falls instead of getting tossed back in the aquarium. Hell, he was up in the throne room. If he wasn't someone important, he would have been tossed right out."

"Then I guess you don't need me today," she said, and pulled her jacket from the wall.

"I'll always need you, Jenny," Shiv said with a playful wink that just came with being Sheldon.

She smiled back and walked closer to the guard. She whispered, "It's really him?"

Shiv nodded and sat down in a rickety wooden chair facing the cell door.

Pride had already decided that she didn't care if this man was really the Librarian. But if everyone else was convinced, it would be an easier story to sell to the Resistance. "If it's really him...that's an awful risk letting him ride the Falls. Don't you think?"

"Why?" Shiv asked.

"If he survives, he gets to go free."

Some people were just born with comedic timing. Shiv wasn't, and he held her stare for a moment longer than most people would before he started to chuckle.

Pride chuckled as well and slowly built it into a full-fledged laugh.

Shiv followed suit, and he burst into laughter just before he bent over to slap his knee.

Pride dropped her jacket over his head and brought the torch crashing down on Shiv's skull. The first strike did little but confuse him, and it wasn't until the fourth or fifth that the guard finally stopped moving and shouting. She pulled the keys from his belt and walked over to the cell.

"What are you doing here?" the prisoner asked.

"I work here," she said, and slipped the key into the rusty lock.

"Why are you doing this?"

The lock was giving her problems. She reached into her pocket and pulled out the slip of paper Oliver had found in the dog's collar. She handed it to him and went back to working on the lock. "I'm not sure if this was meant for me."

He looked at the paper and then back to her. "So you decided to believe me?"

"No," she said as the key finally turned. She opened the door. "I've decided it doesn't matter. I need a Librarian. Any Librarian. And you'll do."

"That's flattering," he said.

"I don't really care. If Invictus thinks you're him, we can convince the others. This tyrant's reign has to end." She pulled him out of the cell and led him through the dungeon's back door.

"What about Gatsby? Won't he be upset you're speeding things up? Going off plan?"

She stopped at the exit. "You were right about them. The council. They were never going to do anything. They truly hate Invictus, but I think they hate change more. They've been making plans forever and never taken any action."

"Are there any plans?" he asked. "Really?"

"Yes, really. There are lots of plans."

"Any good ones?"

"There's Lelawala."

## 21

Long before the first intrepid pioneer cast eyes on the majesty of the Niagara Falls and thought, "This place really needs a t-shirt stand," the Ongiara tribe inhabited the area despite a distinct lack of donut shops. Among the peaceful tribe there was none more beautiful than the maiden named Lelawala.

They say her beauty rivaled that of the Falls themselves and attracted the love of He-No, the God of Thunder. Her love for He-No was immeasurable, but not meant to be, as her father bequeathed her to the king of another tribe.

She refused and set out to find He-No, who lived and lurked in the cave beneath Horseshoe Falls. The wouldn't-be queen paddled onto the Niagara River in her quest to find her lover and was quickly swept away by the river's ferocious current. She and her canoe were swept over the Falls and sent plunging toward the rocks and rapids below.

But He-No, hearing his lover's scream, emerged from his cave behind the Falls and caught her before she could drown in the cold waters of the river. He took her back to his cave, where it is said their spirits still live. He-No, the God of Thunder, and Lelawala, the Maid of the Mist.

The young maiden's story had all but been forgotten after the end of the war. Mythical elopers with suicidal tendencies were hardly the first thing on anyone's mind when food and supplies became scarce. But it seemed a fitting codename for the plan that would see the Maid of the Mist IV plated in armor and sent up the Niagara River to once more defy a king.

The tour boat had spent its previous life taking passengers into the plunge pool beneath Horseshoe Falls to hear the thunder and feel the power of the Falls from within the mist itself. For more than 180 years, the Maid of the Mist IV and her sister ships had taken celebrities, royalty and Gorby as well as countless others upriver for a once in a lifetime experience.

Those before her had been retired and sent elsewhere to finish off their days. Some had been brought into service to continue their tours on calmer waters. Another had been sent to the Amazon where it plied the massive river doing the Lord's work in South America. But the Maid of the Mist IV had been in service the day it all ended, and in the chaos and confusion that often accompanies the end of the world she had been forgotten. Her send-off had consisted of nothing more than a snapped mooring line and a slow drift north down the Niagara until she finally came to rest on the shores of a dairy on Lake Ontario.

"I've only ever seen it in *Superman II*," Eli said. "I don't remember it looking like this."

The Maid of the Mist IV had been pulled up a creek where the Resistance had put torch and toil to the tour boat's hull. She was now painted flat black with the mouth of a demon on either side of her bow. Armor plate covered the decks and machine gun nests were positioned at six points around the ship.

"Meet Lelawala," Pride said as the four reunited warriors walked the shore in front of the boat.

"You can keep calling her that, lady," Lucas said. "But it says Bitch of the Mist on the side and I like that a whole lot better."

Pride groaned. "That was Herbert West's idea. We thought it

was a little too crude, but, since he's the head engineer, he painted it on there when no one was looking."

A hatch in the armor plating squeaked open and a head popped though the opening. A round face beneath a greasy ball cap asked, "Did you call me?"

"Everyone, this is Herbert."

"The best fabricator in the Resistance or elsewhere," he said. "I'll be right down."

The man disappeared and let the hatch slide shut with a scrape. Clattering and clanging made it easy for those on shore to guesstimate where he was inside the ship right up until he emerged on the shoreline. He shook every hand offered to him and repeated every name as it was given.

"Good to meet you all. I'm Herbert West."

"What's the matter, Herb?" Lucas asked. "No codename for you?"

"Herbert West is my codename," he said.

"That's a terrible codename."

"It's Lovecraftian," Jerry said.

"Well," Lucas said with a shrug, "I'm glad you like."

"He was a mad scientist."

"That's right," Herbert said. "And just like my namesake I've brought the bitch back from the dead. She wasn't in the best shape when we found her moored up on shore. But we got her floating and looking a whole lot better than her old self. She was already tough enough to brave the plunge pool, so we figured why not toughen her up a bit more and see if we can't sail her right up Invictus's asshole."

Pride groaned again and turned away.

"I'm sorry, Pride." Herbert pulled the baseball cap from his head. "I forgot I was in mixed company. I meant Invictus's butthole."

"That's not any better, Herb."

The mad scientist gave her a wry smile and threw a wink at Joshua.

"This is impressive work, Herb," Eli said as he put a hand on the hull. "How much do you have left to do?"

"Nothing. The Bitch has been ready to sail into history for a while. But it seems the plan is to just let her sit there until she falls apart again."

"We're here to change that," Joshua said.

"Yay!" Herbert said with a sarcastic cheer. "And just who are you guys anyway?"

"Bogus Librarians!" Gatsby shouted. He stormed up the shoreline with the Bookkeepers Council and several armed Resistance members in tow. The giant one they called Fahrenheit was right behind him but didn't join in Gatsby's raving. "Bullshit artists! Con men! Liars!"

"Oh," Lucas sang. "You say the nicest things."

"Fahrenheit, arrest these men," Gatsby said as soon as he got close.

"Arrest them?" Fahrenheit asked.

"Or take them prisoner or whatever."

"Leave them alone, Gatsby," Pride said as she stepped in front of the four men.

"Arrest her, too!" Gatsby screamed. "You're insane, Pride. You have finally lost it. What were you thinking showing them Lelawala?"

"Hey!" Lucas shouted. "That's Bitch of the Mist to you, buddy."

Gatsby glanced at the hull of the ship and pointed at the name. "I thought we talked about you removing that."

Herbert West shook his head as if he couldn't remember that particular conversation. "No. I remember you saying something about some people might think it's offensive."

"Exactly," Gatsby said.

"Well, I decided I didn't care what some sniveling shit of a nobody thinks."

"I want it removed!"

"I'm pretty sure I just explained that I don't care what you think."

Gatsby growled in frustration and turned his attention back to the four librarians. He waved Fahrenheit toward the group. "They've seen too much, here."

"So what? It doesn't change anything." Pride shot a look at Fahrenheit that made the large man stop in his tracks. "She's been ready for months. She's just been waiting for you to grow the balls to act. We have everything we need to take Invictus down. Just not the will to do it."

"You think it's that simple. Just ride across the river and kill him. It's that easy to you? You complain about all of our planning, but it matters. We can't just take him out. He has to face justice. And some really powerful dramatic justice. Judge. Jury. The whole show put on in front of the city. Otherwise we're just creating a vacuum. We need—"

Lucas raised his hand. "I'm sorry to interrupt your soliloquy, but this seemed like a good time to point out that you suck."

"Fuck you. You're a liar."

"In his defense," Joshua said, "I think you suck, too."

"You're all liars. No one cares what you think."

"I think it's safe to say it's unanimous on the whole sucking thing." Eli concluded.

Gatsby turned his rage back to Pride. "You've really screwed up this time, Pride. Now we have to kill these men. And you know how much I hate doing that."

"Oh, please, please try it, Skippy." Lucas crossed his arms in front of him, revealing the pistol in his hand.

To Gatsby's credit, he barely flinched when he saw the weapon and stammered for only a second before returning to the tough-guy persona. "That's your solution to everything, isn't it? Just shoot the problem till it goes away?"

"It's worked so far," Lucas said.

"All of history, really," Jerry added.

"Yeah, once shot, the problem rarely comes back," Joshua said.

"You're nothing but a bunch of wasteland thugs." Gatsby spit on the ground, most likely because he'd seen it done in movies. "Fahrenheit, seize them."

"'Seize them?'" Joshua laughed. "Wow, you sound just like Invictus."

Gatsby turned to the head of security. "Why aren't you seizing them?"

"I'm still not clear on what they've done," the big man answered.

Gatsby pointed at the boat. "They saw the Bitch!"

"Language, fella," Herbert West scolded the man.

"So? I've seen lots of boats," Fahrenheit said. "You want me to arrest myself?"

Gatsby grabbed at his hair. "Why isn't anyone listening to me?"

"Because the time for talk is over," Jerry said. "Because every sentence you speak and every word you utter is another innocent person beaten or killed."

Joshua leaned over to Eli and whispered, "Did he just transition into a rousing speech?"

"I think he did," Eli whispered back.

"That was pretty smooth."

"I've seen smoother," Lucas muttered.

Jerry continued. "You should be proud of the work you've done here, Gatsby. You all should. You've laid the groundwork of a solid revolt. You've set the foundation for a future you can all be proud of."

"Any idea where he's going with this bit?" Joshua asked.

"Just stroking the ego a little bit," Eli said, unconcerned. "Letting the guy save some face before he completely ousts him."

"That's a nice touch."

Lucas disagreed. "What's this 'foundation' bullshit? It's a little cliché."

"Yeah," Eli agreed. "But it's working."

Work had stopped on Lelawala. Resistance members had multiplied behind Gatsby and his council. Jerry had to speak up to be heard in the back.

"What you've all accomplished is nothing short of remarkable. But it's time to take the next step. It's time to take action."

"Invictus grows stronger every day," Gatsby protested.

"So he'll never be weaker than he is right now," Jerry retorted.

"Nice!" the three warriors agreed.

"This is working," Lucas said. "I'll be killing Invictus in no time."

"You mean I'll be killing him in no time." Joshua patted Lucas on the shoulder.

"We'll see."

"Now is the time to strike. You have the numbers. You have the element of surprise. But most importantly, you have the right to rise up and take your freedom back from that madman across the river. It's time to get on Lelawala and show that bastard what the Bitch can do."

Gatsby's whining was drowned out by the cheers and applause of the crowd.

Eli applauded and said to the other two warriors, "It's him."

Joshua clapped. "It really is."

Applause can't last forever, and the cheers slowly began to fade. Jerry nodded his appreciation to the crowd. Gatsby seized the lull to rush forward and get in Jerry's face. He screamed, "Who the hell do you think you are?!"

Fahrenheit pulled him back as Joshua and Lucas stepped up behind Jerry.

"Don't you know?" Joshua asked.

"He's the motherfucking Librarian!" Lucas shouted.

There was no shouting over the crowd now. Gatsby's protests were swallowed up by the noise and he was soon lost in the crowd as it rushed forward to greet the man they had all been waiting for.

Jerry shook hands and bumped fists for several minutes before he was able to find his way to the edge of the crowd. Pride stood with the other three warriors. "Have we got a plan?"

Joshua nodded. "They do have a plan."

"It's a terrible plan," Lucas said.

Pride snapped. "Do you have a better one?"

Lucas wore the confused look well. "Well, yeah."

## 22

On the shores beneath the Observation Tower, the racers gathered with their cobbled crafts. The rafts looked as rough as the racers themselves. Constructed from discarded barrels, coolers and anything else that would float, and lashed together with rope, wire and hope, the rafts were a clear indication of the desperation that possessed the entrants into the regatta.

The Niagara Regatta had been held several times since the formation of Alasis but had never resulted in a winner. There had been many deaths. Few technically drowned, while dozens succumbed to the frigid waters. Despite the risks and the odds being against them, the event had always drawn a mass of entrants. The reward of a life behind the gates was too much for most to ignore. And this year's crowd was one for the record books.

Hundreds of men and women stood by their shoddy watercrafts, ready to risk life and limb for one shot at the other side.

Snow was falling, and the seasonal ice had finally begun to form in the calmer waters along the shore. The participants tread cautiously out to the edge where the race would begin. Looking down through the sheet, they could see a structure that once served as the dock for tours into the mist. At the edge, they prepared their homemade watercrafts and waited for the official start.

"Safety" was provided by Alasis soldiers and their entire patrol fleet of jet boats. The former whitewater touring vessels had long ago been stripped of their passenger seating to provide a weapons platform for the Legionaries assigned to the craft. Despite their stated purpose, they had never once made an effort to save a life and had taken more than a few in their enforcement of the city's borders. Should any entrant approach the far shore, in an earnest attempt or in error, they would be sunk, shot or both.

*Carmina Burana* played through a network of loudspeakers that ran throughout the city, and the people turned their eyes across the river. It was all but impossible to see from the banks of the river, but they knew that the Great Lord Invictus was about to appear on the jumbo screens that lined the casino building. The music was the cue for those in town to find a government-approved viewing center and make themselves accounted for before the address began.

The music continued, and the racers crowded around the loudspeaker at the base of the tower. The music faded out and the Praetor's voice filled the air. "The Great Lord Invictus, Guardian of Alasis, Bringer of Peace, Provider of Power, welcomes you to the Imperial Niagara Regatta and wishes you luck in your efforts this day. Should there be a victor, they will be awarded passage beyond the gates, where they will receive the honor of serving in the army of the Great Lord Invictus and be rewarded accordingly. The course remains unchanged. You must pilot your craft downriver, pass under Whirlpool Rapids Bridge and through the rapids themselves. The first craft to arrive at Devil's Hole shall claim the prize. And now, the Great Lord Invictus."

"Go."

The racers scrambled at the sudden start. Men slipped on the ice as they tried to turn and run at the same time. The teams arrived at their crafts and hurriedly handled out paddles before hastily shoving their rafts into the river. Others scrambled to affix sails in hopes of catching the wind that howled through the gorge, driven by the Falls behind them.

The first leg of the race was the simplest. The current was swift, but the water was as calm as it was going to be, and it afforded the crews a chance to acclimate to the craft and develop a rhythm before the more dangerous parts of the course. Many of the rafts spun as the teams found the balance and coordination needed to navigate their homemade craft.

The patrol boats weren't helping. They darted between the racers, casting up wakes from the jet boats and tipping more than a couple crafts. The crews pulled themselves from the freezing water and set back to work in piloting their boats.

After ten minutes of this, the racers began to make progress. Crowds along the shoreline cheered for family members and friends as the rafts began to track with some sense of direction. By the time they were halfway to Whirlpool Rapids Bridge, most of the teams had gotten the hang of it.

The patrol boats continued to weave in and out of the contestants until the horn sounded. It sounded like ten freight trains. The sound overpowered the roar of the Falls and bounced along the canyon walls, causing confusion among the security boats. It sounded again as the guards quickly realized that it could not be coming from upstream.

The Bitch of the Mist appeared a minute later. She moved slowly at first but built considerable speed once free of the rapids' hold. Another blast from the horn signaled the Bookkeeper agents to cut the power to Alasis.

The security team reacted instantly, and two of the armed boats shot downstream to engage the intruder.

The horn blared again as the boats met. From the rafts, it was all that could be heard, though they could see the flashes of gunfire from all parties involved.

One of the patrol boats got too close, and a funnel of orange fire reached out from the Bitch's port side, enveloping the craft and crew in fire.

The crowd on the shoreline screamed with enthusiasm as the black ship powered forward and the security boat retreated. The other elements of Invictus's navy sped toward the ship. The machine guns mounted on the bow of each jet boat spat lead as they went. Soon they swarmed around the armored tour boat, firing at anything they could hit.

The Bitch shot back, and the circle the patrol had formed around her quickly shattered. Another jet boat went up in a blast of smoke and screams, while yet another began to sink as it was pulled into the swift of the rapids.

"All right," Jerry said to his crew on the raft. "Let's do this."

The order was echoed on every raft in the river, and the armada of trash and planks changed their course. The crews paddled with more vigor than before as they pulled themselves across the unguarded banks of Alasis.

"I told you it would work," Lucas shouted from a nearby raft.

Joshua paddled alongside with another raft full of Resistance members. "We haven't landed yet, MacArthur."

"Just keep paddling, Dudley. You're almost home."

Jerry glanced behind him. The entire regatta had turned into an amphibious assault. Eli, Pride and Fahrenheit each commanded a raft. Even Gatsby was barking out a speech meant to inspire his troops. They were twenty feet from the shore when one of the patrol boats realized what was happening and broke off from their attack.

"He's coming in fast!" Eli screamed.

Lucas dropped his paddle and opened a crate built into the center of his raft. The shoulder-fired rocket screamed across the river and exploded under the bow of the patrol boat. The Alasis craft flipped nose over tail and crashed back into the river upside down. The recoil from the round sent Lucas's raft drifting in a circle. He did his best to balance it as he got a 360 view of the assault.

"She's going down!" Lucas pointed out to the Resistance ship.

The Bitch was listing to one side now, but she fought on. Flames spouted into the air and the machine gun fire could be heard over the Falls. But the farther she leaned, the more her belly was exposed, and the patrol boats concentrated their fire there. It wasn't long before The Bitch had capsized completely.

"Do you think Herbert's going to be okay?" Joshua asked.

The Bitch of the Mist exploded, sending flaming debris across the water. Armor plating splashed down with cavernous *whunks* into the river, while burning embers of wood sprinkled down in stark contrast to the falling snow.

"No," Lucas answered.

With the Bitch sunk, the patrol boats came for the rafts.

Jerry's raft touched the shore first and he eagerly waved the soldiers onto dry land. More than half the rafts were within twenty feet of shore now. They would probably make it. The ones in the back, however, were falling victim to the jet boats. The patrols didn't even have to fire. A fast pass sent the crews tumbling into the river where the current quickly carried them away from their crafts. Those who tried to swim for shore were easy targets for the gunners.

Some of the Bookkeepers tried to fire back from shore, but the success of the assault depended on moving forward. They designated only a few men to fire on the patrol craft and gather the rest at the base of the hill.

"Up the hill!" Jerry shouted.

"To the tower!" Fahrenheit's voice was perfect for shouting over a war, and the men responded. They tore the rafts apart to reveal weapon stashes inside the barrels and beneath the boards. The wave of fighters rolled up the hill and into the streets of Alasis.

What resistance they encountered retreated quickly or fell to Bookkeeper gunfire. Legionaries ran as fast as their armor allowed them to as they fell back farther into town. This urged the Bookkeeper army on.

The force charged up Niagara Parkway. With the river on their left, it was only the right flank that could experience an ambush. An occasional shot was fired from the cover provided by the homes, but it was more of the fire and flee type than established positions.

The force split at Ontario Park. Pride and Fahrenheit led a small army up Ontario Avenue with Skylon Tower as their ultimate objective. The larger group continued on the parkway.

They marched unchallenged until they reached the Rainbow Bridge. The heavily defended toll plaza was key to taking the city. Their reinforcements numbered in the thousands across the river. All they needed was a way to cross.

The majority of the defense was pointed at the bridge, but the guards at the plaza reacted quickly to reposition the more portable pieces of artillery.

Rifle fire slowed their advance, and mortar shells soon began to rain down on the invading army and sent the rebels scrambling for cover in the woods along the road.

Behind their main force, Invictus's patrol trucks arrived. Light machine guns mounted in their beds began to make any movement across the streets a deadly race. Bookkeeper snipers fired from the woods and Jerry watched two of the trucks turn silent as their gunners fell.

Emboldened by the guns' silence, Joshua stepped out into the road to rally his men. "It's time to—"

Another burst of machine gun fire cut him off and sent his men back behind the trees. The fire had come from the former immigration services tower in the middle of the plaza.

Jerry shouted as he grabbed Gatsby by the shoulder and dragged him closer. "There's a nest up there!"

The Bookkepper knocked Jerry's hand away and snarled, "Well obviously!"

Intelligence had been the one thing the man could truly offer and now it was coming up short. "That wasn't there in the intel!"

Lucas screamed with frustration as he rushed into the street. Bullets tore at the asphalt around him, producing a cloud of dust. He slid to his knees and raised the rocket launcher to his shoulder.

The high-explosive projectile shot from the tube as the exhaust blew the cloud of dust apart.

"That's for my fucking dog!" Lucas shouted back to the trees.

"Your dog?" Jerry shouted. "You're here for a dog?!"

"Don't you judge me!" Lucas shouted. "You didn't know Snaps!"

Eli appeared next to Gatsby and shoved the man to the ground. He cast a finger at the smoking tower. "That wasn't in the intel!"

"We've covered that," Gatsby shouted back. "It's taken care of with the rocket guy there."

"Taken care of?! Josh is dead!" Eli spat as he shouted. "What else did your people miss?"

Gatsby jumped to his feet and put a finger in Eli's chest. "Don't question my people! They've dedicated their lives to the cause. They risked everything to tell us what we know."

"They don't know shit!"

"I don't know when they put that up there. Could have been this morning. It's not like it's hard to move a machine gun."

"There better not be any more surprises!"

"Or what, old man?" Gatsby made sure to speak loud enough that his men could hear him. "You wanted this! I told you that we needed to wait. That the time wasn't right."

"You would have waited forever," Jerry said. "And every day Invictus would have more hell waiting for you."

Another salvo of mortar rounds struck the street. Shrapnel and asphalt struck the army and sent the rest to cover.

"What could be worse than this?" Gatsby asked with a smugness that few could master.

"Worse Than This" exploded from Bird Kingdom. The building's windows shattered as three tanks rolled out into the street in front of the rebellion. What had once been the "world's largest free-flying indoor aviary" had apparently been converted into the Alasis Motor Pool.

"Where the hell did those come from!?" Gatsby shouted as the tanks turned their turrets toward the woods.

Jerry looked to the mercenary. "Lucas?"

Lucas dropped the rocket launcher. The now hollow tube made a fitting bonk when it hit the ground. The man just shrugged.

"Fall back!" Gatsby shouted. "Retreat!"

"No!" Jerry shouted, but it was too late. The literary-themed Resistance fighters were already booking it back downriver. Jerry tried to cancel the retreat but was drowned out by the tank guns.

Trees exploded and toppled around them.

"We have to go!" Lucas shouted.

"This is our only chance!" Jerry said, knowing it could have gone without saying.

"Our army is gone, man!"

"We'll think of something else," Eli said. "There's always another way."

"We should at least work our way through town. Help Fahrenheit and—"

"If this was waiting for us, what do you think is waiting for them?" Eli said.

"Then we have to warn them."

"Librarian." It was the only thing Jerry had ever heard him say calmly. "It's over."

A tank crashed through the tree line in front of them and separated the trio. Jerry fell back as the machine's treads tore up the ground where he had been standing. Mud and diesel filled his face until the vehicle had passed. What it left behind horrified him.

Lucas screamed at the body left behind. Crushed and bloodied, the voice of reason among the warriors' quartet was no more.

Over the gunfire and cannon rounds, he heard laughing. Lucas turned and saw the man they had known as Connor standing at the edge of the street. "I was tired of hearing his shit. Weren't you?"

Lucas drew and fired without a word.

Connor shrieked and grabbed at his leg as he collapsed to the ground.

Lucas was on the kid a moment later, bashing away at what only moments before had been a young face free of scars.

Abandoning reason, Jerry wanted to join in, but before he could stand he felt a hand on his shoulder. He turned with a fight in mind but saw a child at the end of the hand. He recognized the kid from the bar on the other side of the river.

"You need to come with me," the kid shouted.

"What are you— You're going to get yourself killed!"

"Pride said to get you out if things went bad. Come with me."

"Get out of here!" Jerry said and got to his feet. "I've got to do something."

"You're the Librarian. They can't catch you. They just can't."

A second tank crashed through the woods and barreled toward him. An army of men marched behind it.

It was lost. They had rushed Lucas and it would only be a matter of seconds before they spotted him.

Jerry scrambled out of the way and followed the kid down the hill to the shoreline. The child led him through the trees, under the Rainbow Bridge, always seeming to know when to duck, when to wait and when to run. They made their way upriver as the sounds of the war faded behind them.

## 23

---

The boy led him up the shore into the mist. The rocks, frozen and slick, were made passable only by the addition of a rope that had been driven into the cliff face sometime in the past. It was too loud to talk, and the mist was too thick to see. He lost sight of the boy several times and for minutes at a time.

The rope finally ended and he found the kid waiting in a small metal boat, waving him on. He got in and followed the boy's gestures to strap himself to the seat. It was going to be a rough ride.

They were tossed about violently as the kid maneuvered them out into the plunge pool. At one point the boat was all but upended. Sitting in the bow, he saw the kid rise almost directly above him, still tied to his seat. They settled back into the crest of a wave. The child seemed unfazed.

It was impossible to see where they were going. Wind drove the cold spray about them and clouded their path. The cold urged him to shut his eyes lest they freeze. He fought to keep them open and twisted his head to see where they were going.

Gusts of wind whipped the mist around in sheets, occasionally clearing a view farther downriver. That's when he saw their destination, the pile of derelict ships rusting in the middle of the plunge pool.

They were almost thrown onto the pile. As they neared, a wave lifted them up and crashed them into the hull before sliding back down into the water. It took several attempts before the boy secured a grappling to the pile and began to pull them in.

They lashed the boat to the ship and they crossed the slippery deck to a sealed hatch. It wasn't any warmer inside, but the wind stopped and he finally felt he could breathe again.

"This way," the boy said, and started down the uneven hallway.

"This seems a bit excessive, doesn't it?"

The boy didn't answer but led him through a hole in the hull to another ship and into a room where Chewy was waiting.

The dog barked and rushed to Jerry.

"Chewy! What are you doing here?"

"I brought her here," the boy said as he started a kerosene heater. He handed Jerry a blanket. "I didn't want her to be alone in the motel room."

It was the same room where he'd first met the Bookkeepers. The work lights had been righted and for the first time, Jerry actually saw the efforts of Gatsby's work. An entire shelf of glass jars lined the wall, each filled with different shades of pee.

The boy saw him looking at the shelf. "It's weird, right?"

"It's weird," Jerry said, and took the blanket. Then the two sat on the floor with the dog between them, soaking up the heat from the kerosene burners. They sat in silence, petting the dog.

There was only one thing to think about: Eli, Joshua, maybe Lucas and how many others were dead in the failed assault. Damn tanks. Damn Resistance. Where did they think they were going to go? As far as he knew, there wasn't an evacuation plan. It had been all or nothing to finally take down the tyrant. But he would be the first to admit he may not know everything. Where was Gatsby running?

They sat in silence for what felt like hours. He played the battle over and over in his mind. All they had to do was buy Fahrenheit and Pride the time they needed to take the tower.

"You're really him, aren't you?" the boy finally asked.

Jerry saw hope in the kid's eyes. Still. After what had happened. It was a perfect opportunity to say something reassuring, but all he could do was sigh and nod.

"I knew it," the kid said. "So what do we do now?"

"Nothing!" Gatsby snarled as he kicked open the door to the room. He had several armed men with him. Omoo and Typee walked in quietly with the group. Gatsby pointed at Jerry. "He's not going to do a damned thing except leave."

Chewy raced across the room and buried her head in Jerry's lap, making his rise to meet Gatsby awkward as he stumbled backward.

"What the hell was that up there! You called a retreat!"

"You're damn right I did. It was the only way to save my people."

"How? There was no way out. You just got them killed."

"The rafts, numbnuts. That was always the plan. Ride the rafts downriver."

"Through the rapids?" the boy asked. "That's suicide."

Gatsby hesitated. "We lost a lot of good people."

"You idiot," Jerry said. "You sacrificed them for your cowardice."

"I saved the Resistance!"

"You handed Invictus the war!" Jerry collapsed into his chair, exhausted. He should have known he was fighting the war on two fronts. Gatsby had been cowed but the little shit hadn't stopped being a problem.

Chewy did what she could to comfort him.

"What about Fahrenheit and Pride? Did they make it to the tower?"

"Oh they made it all right. In chains. Invictus dropped Fahrenheit twenty minutes ago. Pride is set to ride the falls. Along with that other idiot that caused this mess."

"Lucas?"

Gatsby shrugged. "If you say so. All of you piles of shit look the same to me."

Jerry stood up again. "We have to save them."

"We're not doing anything!" Gatsby shouted. "You don't make the decisions anymore. We tried listening to you and look what happened. We got our asses kicked. Fahrenheit's dead. Pride is captured. All of our planning, years of planning. Gone!"

"And your new plan is this? More hiding?"

"Invictus is tearing up the city looking for us," Omoo said. "We have to lie low."

"Forget that. We're getting out of here tonight," Gatsby said.

"You're giving up?" It sounded like a question. But it was an accusation.

"Giving up?" Gatsby laughed. "We were beaten. This wasn't a failure of strategy. It was an unbeatable foe. No one turned on us. No one betrayed us. Invictus is just too strong. And now he has tanks. We're better off running and hiding in the wasteland."

"He'll find you."

"No he won't."

"He found me," Jerry said. "He'll hunt you down. All of you. He will have his revenge. It doesn't matter what it costs him."

He could see that Gatsby knew it was the truth. "This is your fault."

"You gave up!"

"We couldn't win!"

"We could. And we still can. We have to stop that ship from going over. The people will see it. They'll rise up. There's more of us than there are of him."

"Stop it," Gatsby said calmly. "Just stop it. Your speeches didn't work on me before and they won't work on me now. We can't save them. It's a trap."

"Of course it's a trap," the Librarian said. "That's no reason not to go."

Gatsby grew flustered. It wasn't in a coward's mind to see possibility. "Maybe I should explain to you exactly what a trap is?"

"So they die?" Jerry said.

"So they die," Gatsby said.

"You're such a coward."

"So what if I am?"

"Cowards are why Invictus rules. How many times was there a chance to stop him in the past? Hundreds? Thousands? But the coward said no, 'the odds are too great' or 'he's too strong.' A knife. A bullet. That's all it would have taken. One brave moment to spare a thousand lives and a million nightmares. You're a coward. You refused to act. You held your people back. You are complicit in every murder under his rule."

Gatsby looked at the remaining members of the council. They refused to look back. This enraged him. "We were doing something."

"Planning isn't taking action." He dropped the blanket and looked at the kid. "I'll show you what doing something is."

The Librarian turned his back to Gatsby and took a step toward the door, and Gatsby waved for the others to block the exit. "You're not going anywhere."

"You don't want to do this, Gatsby. You've already lost one fight today."

"I'm going to finish this one."

Jerry didn't hear Gatsby draw the gun, but he heard the slide rake back.

"Chewy."

It was a startled scream at first, but Gatsby's cries turned to pain as Jerry heard the dog lunge and latch on to the man's wrist. He sprang at the nearest soldier, grabbed the barrel of the man's rifle and pulled him forward. His fist and the momentum twisted the guard's head sideways as Jerry turned and clubbed another with the rifle.

Typee and Omoo weren't foolish enough to stand in the way. They backed away from the door and waved Jerry through.

Gatsby grabbed him from behind and spun him around. He grabbed the rifle with both hands and shoved it against Jerry's chest. The force drove the Librarian against the wall. Blood flowed from Gatsby's wrist and curses spewed from his mouth. It was a pure animalistic rage that flashed in his eyes. He growled. "You ruined everything. This was my army. This was my resistance!"

Jerry let go of the barrel and reached out to his left. His hand found a shelf and a row of jars. Gatsby was screaming something foul when he shattered the jar on the man's face.

The shock hit him first. Then the pain. And then finally the realization that he was now covered in his own piss. The sound he made was *OofAarrfrghAhhhhhh*! And then crying.

Jerry stepped through the wooden door into the slanted hallway.

There was another guard waiting for him with his rifle leveled at Jerry.

The Librarian didn't raise his weapon. He just stared at the man and kept walking.

The guard pulled the rifle tighter to his shoulder and opened his mouth to start barking commands. But he didn't. He lowered the rifle a fraction of an inch and spoke. "Was that Gatsby screaming?"

The Librarian nodded.

"You going to go get her?"

He nodded again.

The guard lowered his gun and pulled an automatic from his waist. He handed it to Jerry as they passed in the hallway, and stepped aside.

He reached the hatch without further incident and began to work the latch when he heard the kid behind him.

"No, kid."

"I need to show you the way."

"No."

"They're on the boat now. They'll be sending them over soon. There isn't any time."

"No."

"There's a way up. I'll take you to it."

He looked back at the kid. The child was standing next to Chewy, patting the dog's head and sending her tail into all sorts of bliss. The kid had gotten him out of Alasis. Maybe it was the only way to get back in.

"I won't have to shoot anybody," the kid pleaded. "I promise. You won't be corrupting any youth. I swear."

They unlashed the boat and set it back in the water. He held Chewy tight as they motored to the American side of the river near the base of Bridal Falls. The trio stepped onto shore and the kid explained the path.

He pointed to a series of crumbling decks that lined the cliff's face. "They called it the Cave of the Winds. But there isn't a cave anymore so I don't know why. But there's an elevator at the top that takes you to Goat Island."

Jerry knew he could find the boat from there. He had seen it on his earlier trip through town. He also knew there was no way his friend could follow. The decks were crumbling and had collapsed in several places. If the elevator wasn't working, he would be forced up service ladders.

He bent down and scratched the dog's head where she liked it. Behind the ears, on top of her nose and the wrinkly skin on the side of her face. "Looks like it's just going to be me this time, girl."

The dog licked his hand.

"Stay with the kid, okay?"

Chewy barked. But there was no enthusiasm to it. She continued to bark as he began the climb.

## 24

---

By the time his climb was finished, Jerry emerged from the elevator shaft to dimming light in the sky. The Falls were lit in an array of colors with powerful floodlights. Across the river, he could see Invictus. The Great Lord was fifteen stories tall in full regalia on massive screens that hung from the side of the casino tower. His voice boomed everywhere on the island.

"—you dare rise against me. I have provided you with safety, food, warmth. Purpose. That you should take arms against me is folly, as those accused quickly learned."

The boat was on the far end of the mostly wooded island. Jerry dashed across the parking lot and ducked into the woods. The coming darkness would make it easier for him to remain unseen, but he would still have to be cautious. It was definitely a trap.

"As I have built this empire, we have recognized great traditions. It seems fitting that those that tried to bring down all that we have built should be forced to honor one of our greatest traditions."

The camera cut to the ship moored at the far end of the island. Pride, Lucas and several others were hooded and bound to the ship's rail.

"These traitors to our cause will ride the Falls to prove their innocence. If they survive the fall, they will have proven their worth. They will have served their sentence." The dictator couldn't help but laugh at the idea of anyone surviving.

It wasn't without precedent. Several people had gone over the Falls with nothing more than a prayer of surviving and walked away with little more than a scratch and the world's greatest tale to tell. Some had fallen in. Others had jumped with the hope of ending it all. One had attempted suicide only to find that he survived. Several years later he attempted to take the plunge again with the intent of finding fame. That time, however, it did kill him, proving that experience wasn't really a factor in living or dying.

One thing all of the survivors had in common was that not one of them had been lashed to a boat by a sadistic post-apocalyptic dictator. Not one.

In the history of Alasis, no one had yet to be found innocent in a trial by falling boat.

The camera cut back to Invictus. "Justice separates us from the animals in the wasteland, and everyone deserves to be tried. We still have room for more."

Jerry ducked into the woods and started running. The trap was on the boat. That's where Invictus wanted him. He wanted to show everyone the death of the Librarian. The city had pinned its hopes on the myth and if he could kill the man, the people would fall back in line.

He reached the improvised dock and kept running. It didn't look as if it was guarded. They expected him to rush right on. He'd spring the trap, but he was going to do it when he was ready. He kept running and didn't make for the shoreline until he was further upstream.

Invictus wasn't letting up on the rhetoric. The speakers continued to play his horrid voice as he went on about his greatness, how unappreciative the people were of his greatness, but how, in his greatness, he would give them all another chance—if the Librarian was delivered to him before the ship went over the Falls.

The water was freezing. Pain shot through his legs. He could feel each individual vein go cold. He ignored the pain. He ignored every signal his body gave him to get out of the water. As if he had a choice.

The current took him. It was too strong to fight. All he could do was go with it and direct himself as best he could. If he didn't aim just right, he'd be over the Falls in a matter of minutes.

The fishing trawler was moored at the outer edge of Three Sister Island and came up quicker than he expected. He hit the hull with a thud and began looking for something to grab onto. The current pushed him against the boat and he had to fight from being pulled under as he inched his way to one of the mooring lines. The rope was taut enough that he could hang from it and not cause any noticeable difference on the ship itself.

He told his hands to climb, but it took several seconds before his fingers got the message. Even his nerve endings were running on willpower at this point. Everything else was frozen. He eventually got his legs up on the rope and began the crawl.

His clothes weighed a ton. They had never felt so wet. He stripped his jacket off and let it fall into the river. It wasn't doing him any good at this point. He was shaking so badly that he now realized his plan was shit and he was just going to end up giving Invictus what he wanted.

Jerry stopped his ascent and focused. Rage had brought him this far. Maybe if he stoked the fire inside, it would warm him up. He knew enough about biology to know that wasn't how it worked but any motivation now, anything that released an endorphin or adrenalin or anything would be helpful.

He thought of Erica. He remembered her standing before him threatening to shoot him when they first met. He remembered her standing before him at the wedding ceremony in New Hope. He heard her voice. He felt her breath on his chest in memories more vivid than he had ever experienced. They'd had plans—dreams that would never be realized. They were simple dreams.

His hands were still cold. But they moved. He climbed the rope and pulled himself over the railing. He didn't even feel it when he hit the deck.

There was no rush of boots stomping towards him. No one yelled, "Seize him!" He stood up and shivered and looked around. He hadn't been spotted and that didn't seem possible.

Invictus was still ranting on the big screen. Night had fallen quickly, and his image cast an eerie glow over his side of the river.

It wouldn't be long before he was spotted. There were cameras mounted everywhere on the ship. There was surely a producer somewhere who had seen him climb aboard.

Pride and the others were just down the rail. Jerry drew a hunting knife and cut the woman free first.

She pulled the hood off herself. "Thank you, Lib–"

"It's Jerry."

"Thank you, Jerry."

He handed her a second knife and they worked to free the others. Lucas pulled off his hood, looking for a fight. Aside from that, he wasn't looking good.

"The Legionaries went pretty hard on him."

"That lying piece of shit Connor took a few sucker punches, too," Lucas added.

"We'll deal with him later," Jerry said, and put his hand on the man's shoulder. "Let's get everyone out of here."

"Aaah," Lucas said as he pulled away. "Your hand is freezing."

"I swam here."

"I thought you were supposed to be really smart or something."

The party made their way to the makeshift dock.

"Where do you think they're hiding?" Lucas asked.

"Other side of the bridge, probably."

"You only brought the one gun?"

"I told you I had to swim."

They reached the end of the dock and Invictus's voice filled the air around them. "I knew you wouldn't disappoint us."

Lights snapped on and filled the area around the boat. The Praetor stepped out from behind a tree with several other

Legionaries in tow. They aimed their weapons at the group and signaled for them to raise their hands.

"You called it," Lucas said.

"Well, it was obvious." Jerry raised the rifle above his head.

A door on the boat opened behind them and a cameraman backed out onto the deck. He hastily set up a shot and gave a hand cue toward the door.

Invictus, his armor shining, his cape flowing, stepped onto the deck. "I see the stories of your loyalty are true. That is admirable even if your choice of friends leaves something to be desired."

The Coyote stepped out onto the deck and tipped his cowboy hat at Jerry. The Skinner kid limped out behind them both.

"You're one to talk," Jerry shouted back.

"Hi there, Library Guy," Coy said with a wink.

"Do you ever take off that stupid hat?" Jerry asked.

"I take my hat off for one thing, one thing only."

Everyone winced.

"It's time for your trial, Librarian," Invictus said, his voice echoing in the loudspeakers on the island.

The Praetor ordered his men forward.

"Will you let the others go?" Jerry asked.

Invictus shrugged. "I could lie and say 'Yes.'"

Lucas looked up at the rifle in Jerry's hands. "Look. I've been doing some thinking."

"Good," Jerry said. "I'd say make it a habit."

"Well, when you're tied to a ship's rail with a hood over your head and you're about to be sent over Niagara Falls—it gives you a new perspective on things."

"Oh?"

The guards formed a line in front of the prisoners.

"Yeah. I think you should be the one that gets to kill Invictus."

"Are you sure about this?"

Lucas nodded slowly and looked back up at the gun. "Yeah. Just make sure and tell him Snaps sends his regards, okay?"

"I will, Lucas."

"Drop the gun," the Praetor ordered.

Jerry did, and Lucas caught it. The Praetor fell first. Two more soldiers were struck before the others decided to fall back to the trees.

Jerry spun and drew the pistol. His first shot struck Invictus in the temple and sent Coy and Skinner diving for cover.

Lucas looked over his shoulder as Invictus hit the ground. "You killed him? What about Snaps?!"

"I'm sorry. I—"

"You promised!"

"Not technically."

Invictus rolled over and got to his knees.

"He's not dead," Jerry shouted.

"Good," Lucas replied. "Go tell him about my dog."

Lucas pushed forward with the prisoners, firing just enough to keep the Legionaries' heads in the bushes.

Whoever was working the video feed was covering it all on the giant screens, cutting between the battle on shore and the chaos on the boat. They focused on Invictus long enough to reassure his subjects that he was not dead.

Jerry raced up the dock firing at anyone that dared poke their head up. He was out of bullets by the time he reached the boat. Invictus was still stumbling to his feet. There was a second bullet hole in the helmet now and blood ran down his face, but there was a clarity in his eyes that told Jerry the man wasn't out of the fight yet.

"Get hi—"

Jerry leapt and planted a boot in the tyrant's chest that sent him flying back into the cabin.

Skinner jumped out of his hiding place and tackled Jerry into a fishing net and pulled it down on top of him.

He barely felt the impact and realized that his body was either still numb from the swim or that the rage was really doing its thing now. Still, he was tangled in the net and the kid was raining blows on him at will, which couldn't be healthy.

The Coyote appeared beside the kid and the pair dragged the net to the open deck as Invictus stepped back out of the cabin. He had removed his helmet and Jerry could see where the bullet had grazed him. The tyrant bent over until their faces were inches apart.

"I should thank you really," he said softly, running his finger along the wound. "You've proven once again to these lowly peasants that I am bulletproof. You've made me twice as immortal in their eyes."

He stood up, found his helmet and tucked it under his arm. Then he signaled to the cameraman for his close-up. There was posturing before he nodded and the feed went live.

"Librarian. For your crimes you will be judged. For your betrayal, the Falls will surely find you guilty. You have sought to usurp the rule of the Great Lord Invictus. Now, as you face judgment, you must surely understand that order must rule over chaos, and only I am fit to bring order to the people of Alasis."

"I guess so," Jerry said, and nodded toward the casino screen. "It looks like they can't wait to congratulate you."

"Uh...Invictus," Skinner stammered.

"It's Great Lord In—" The Tyrant turned to scold Coy but noticed the screen. The battle on shore wasn't going well. The prisoners had picked up the soldiers' arms and pressed forward. It cut again and showed a crowd of hundreds crossing the bridge to Goat Island. And they didn't look like a happy mob.

Jerry found the edge of the net. "Looks like they forgot the pitchforks."

Invictus turned back to Skinner. "We're leaving."

Skinner nodded and the two moved toward the dock.

"Now hold on a second." The Coyote stood at the head of the dock with the Bowie knife in his hand. It was enough to slow the men. "I came to this city looking for revenge on the person responsible for the death of Coy's friend. I'm not leaving until I get it."

"Fine," Invictus said, waving for Coy to move. "Stay. Kill him. It's your death."

"You see, the problem is..." Jerry watched any vestige of Coy fade away as the psychopathic The Coyote held up the knife and smiled. "...it wasn't him."

This stopped Invictus in his tracks. "Of course it was him."

"Nope. They killed Willie because Christopher hired us. And you're the one that sent Christopher to find him. That means you're the one that started all this."

Invictus cast a finger at Jerry. "You told me he's the one that made you eat dick."

"It wasn't dick! It was Willie! I—" The Coyote stopped midsentence. "Oh, that's why everyone kept laughing at me."

Invictus rushed forward and tackled The Coyote against the ship's rail, nearly sending him into the river. Coy struggled to stay on board while the Tyrant drove fist after fist into the man's ribs.

During this time, two things happened. The cameraman quietly slipped off the boat, and Coy cut a mooring line that held the ship to the shore. And it happened to be the one that was doing most of the work.

The boat lurched into the stream as the other lines snapped free and the deck tilted.

Jerry pulled the net over his head and rolled free of its hold.

Skinner saw this and raced to stop him.

Jerry came up with an uppercut that snapped the kid's head back and sent him stumbling to the floor. Invictus was next. He crossed the rollicking deck, grabbed ahold of the tyrant's armor and sent him falling toward the other side of the boat.

He pulled Coy back from the brink of going over. "Thanks, Coy."

The Coyote faded and Coy looked up at him. "You're still not my favorite person. I'm still pissed you killed all them Skinners."

"Then have I got good news for you."

Once he was brought up to speed, The Coyote dashed across the deck and kicked Skinner in the ribs as he was trying to get to his feet. Many times. "Your. Fucking. Grand. Pa. Made. Me. Eat. Willie!"

Skinner caught the final kick and pulled Coy's legs out from underneath him. He hit the deck and the Bowie knife bounced out of his hand. Both men lunged for it, got a hand on the weapon and began to struggle for control of the blade.

Invictus came back with a metal gauntlet across Jerry's face. He grabbed the Librarian by the shirt and pulled him close. "You fool! You've doomed us all."

The armor was mostly cosmetic but hurt like hell to punch, so Jerry grabbed Invictus's arm and twisted it away from his throat.

Invictus struck with a right cross, rocking Jerry down the railing. "There is a war coming. And I was the only one strong enough to fight it."

"We'll manage it without you."

Invictus drew his fist back again. The ship struck a rock before he could launch the attack and threw both men to the ground. The sound of rending metal screeched as the current pulled the ship against the force of the stone.

Alasis had blown the channel near the Falls deeper, but Jerry figured it was still going to be a rough ride to the edge.

Coy screamed as the knife pierced his shoulder. Skinner drove it into the hilt and planned to pull it free, but The Coyote grabbed the kid's hand and held it in place as he tried to pull it free.

This insane action and the crazed look in the eyes beneath the garish cowboy hat caused him to let go and back away.

"You are sick."

The Coyote grinned as he pulled the knife from his shoulder. "This ain't nothing compared to you Skinner freaks."

"It's a new world, psycho." Skinner backed into a pile of fishing equipment and knocked it over. "The rules have changed. We do whatever it takes."

"Even turning people into bacon?"

"Sometimes. Usually it's a burger. People will tell you anything when you put their bits into a grinder." Skinner grabbed blindly at one of the wooden poles behind him and lunged at Coy with a grunt. He put his entire force into the swing.

The pole caught The Coyote on the shoulder and snapped. Wood rot had saved his life. And it ended Jonathon Skinner's.

He plunged the knife deep into the young man's stomach, twisted the blade and pulled it out. He did this several times as the color left Skinner's face and spilled across the deck.

The ship struck another rock, sending it spinning. The heaving deck sent Skinner crashing into the rail. Coy followed him with a clothesline and knocked him into the Niagara River. He lost sight of the body almost immediately as it was swallowed by the building whitewater ahead.

Jerry caught Invictus with a combination of blows that sent the man to his back. Getting up so many times with all that armor on had to be wearing him out.

"Hey Library Man!" They were going down the river sideways and Coy was standing on the bow pointing to the shore.

He followed the gesture and saw Lucas and several others running beside them. One of them threw a safety rope into the water and Jerry got the hint.

Coy was way ahead of him and dove into the rapids.

Jerry climbed up into the bow in time to see Coy grab the rope and watch the people on shore pulling him to safety. He put one foot on the bow to jump when another rock spun the bow toward the Falls.

He dropped down and ran along the rail, looking for the best place to make the leap. He reached the stern without finding it and realized this was his only chance. He dove out over the water.

Invictus grabbed his ankle and all but stopped his momentum. The safety line fell in the river behind him, well out of reach. He watched as his would-be saviors fell into the distance, then he turned around and headed back to the ship.

His only hope now was to survive the Falls.

# 25

The mooring line was almost literally a frozen rope, but he pulled himself out of the water and onto the deck of the ship.

Invictus was waiting with a club.

Jerry dropped out of the way and saw the metal pipe crash through the cabin window.

"You've ruined everything!"

Invictus swung again and once more Jerry dodged the strike.

"Why did you have to come here?"

With the third swing the club became entangled in a panel of nylon webbing and Jerry moved in with frozen fists.

"You brought me here!" He didn't even feel the punch but he heard it crack off the tyrant's face. "We were half a world away. All we wanted was to be left alone. And now this? We're both going over. But I'm going to be sure to kick your ass the whole way down."

The beating and lecturing went on until the boat dragged along the bottom of the riverbed and ground to a halt. The two men were thrown forward. Jerry hit the metal deck as Invictus stumbled toward the bow. He'd lost the club and his temper. He howled as he dove for Jerry with hands outstretched like the talons of a bird of prey.

A drum, cast about by the boat's perilous journey, rolled by his foot and he kicked it at the madman's leg.

Invictus tripped on the barrel but fell on top of Jerry anyway. He wasn't even using words now. Just grunts and strings of vowels that garbled in his throat.

Jerry felt the world growing dim as Invictus closed his hands around his throat. He struck back but couldn't find a way past the armor.

An invisible hand freed the ship from its perch and sent them downstream once more, but it did nothing to loosen Invictus's grip. He could barely feel the knife handle in his hand. If he somehow lived, he wondered how many fingers he'd lose to the cold. There was no tactile sensation left, just the pressure of the handle.

He thrust the blade under Invictus's arm between the armor on his chest and shoulder. Once, twice and a third time the blade plunged in clean and came out red. Blood ran down Jerry's hands. That, he could feel. The warmth felt almost unbearable.

Invictus screamed and rolled away from the fight. He stood, his hand under his arm, checking to see what his enemy had done. Given time, it would be enough to kill him. Before the realization could set in, Invictus's eyes grew wide and his face pale. He began to desperately claw at his armor, pulling the pieces from his body.

Jerry got to his feet and saw past the bow of the ship. They had almost run out of river.

Invictus stripped off his shin guards and turned to run.

But there was nowhere to run to. It was too late. Going over was the only thing that was going to happen.

Jerry grabbed Invictus by his cape and dragged him back into the fight.

"Let me go!" Invictus said between getting punched in the face. "We have to swim."

Panic had taken him completely. He wasn't even fighting back now, just doing his best to pull away and run from the inevitable.

"You don't get the easy way." Jerry laid into his opponent.

Kicking at his knees, punching him in the ribs—with most of the armor gone there were so many new places to choose from.

Beaten and bleeding out, Invictus collapsed to his knees.

Jerry pulled a length of rope from the deck and wrapped it around the dictator's neck. He pulled the man to his feet, gasping, and walked him toward the bow. "C'mon Great Lord. You don't want to miss this view."

They were just about at the bow when the ship reached the Falls and shuddered to a stop. The momentum threw the pair into the peaked railing at the front of the ship. Jerry leaned into the man as they both looked over the edge into the black mist below.

The current pushed at the boat, but it was ground into the edge and only the rear end lifted up, giving the pair a once-in-a-lifetime view of the plunge pool and mist below. Jerry idly wondered if Gatsby was still in the pile of boats below. Part of him—most of him —really hoped so. And he hoped they landed on it.

The back of the boat crashed back down, and he felt the hull slip closer to the edge.

The cameras were catching all of it. To his left, he could see that the monitors on the casino tower were focused on their faces. Jerry looked up and spotted the camera mounted on the bowsprit.

"Everyone's watching, Invictus." He had to scream to be heard over the Falls. "Everyone sees you for the coward you are."

Invictus grabbed the rail and tried to push away, but Jerry held him in place. "You're not the king of the world. You're a cancer. You're a stain in history that I'm about to wipe away. With you gone, the world will finally have a chance to heal."

Another surge raised the boat once more and set it back down with another slip of the hull.

"Here it comes, Invictus! Do you feel that?"

Invictus screamed and Jerry loosened the rope just to give the man more breath to scream with.

Another surge. Another push closer to the edge.

"You're going to die. And you're going to scream until your lungs are filled with water and rock."

Another swell. Another inch.

"For everyone you've wronged."

Another surge. The tearing of metal.

"For everyone killed in your name."

Jerry had to fight to stay in the boat with the next swell.

"For every slave you've taken! For every child you've murdered!"

Another swell. How long was this boat?

"For Eli's family!"

The current felt angrier now.

"For Joshua's wife!"

The swells were coming faster now, each one pushing the bow farther out into the abyss.

"For Snaps."

The boat sank in the river as if the water had retreated around it. Like it was reeling back for one final push. It even felt quieter.

Jerry leaned into Invictus's ear and whispered, "For Erica."

The river struck the rear of the boat with a slap that could be heard over the thunder of the Falls. The river rose around them and the ship lifted from its perch on the unseen rock. The boat lunged forward and Invictus screamed the whole way down.

Chewy sat on the shoreline under the observation tower, staring up at the Falls. Her ears were perked up and her head twisted constantly back and forth as if listening to something. Anything besides the sound of the Falls. She turned at the sound of approaching footsteps and stood up to meet them.

Lucas walked toward the Mastiff with a trio of dogs at his side. Lord Stanley wandered off to sniff at the water's edge. Brittany found a sunny spot to lie. But Heeler stayed faithfully at Lucas's heel.

"It's Chewy, right?"

Chewy barked at the sound of her name but did not approach.

"My name is Lucas. I was...I'm a friend of Jerry's."

Chewy barked louder at Jerry's name.

Lucas walked closer and sat down on the rocks next to the dog. She turned her head back toward the Falls and let him put a hand on her back.

"We've looked," he said. "We haven't found anything except that bastard's cape and torso."

Chewy sniffed at the air.

"We're not going to stop looking,—" he peeked. "Girl."

Chewy turned to look at the man.

"He deserves to be found. We owe him that."

She laid her head in his left hand and let out a sigh that made her jowls flap.

"I'm sorry you're alone. I know how that is." He scratched her and looked away. "I had a best friend once."

Chewy dug her head deeper into his lap as if she understood.

"I was thinking. Maybe you and I can be friends."

She didn't move her head, but looked up at him with big brown eyes and peaked, puppy-calendar-class eyebrows. She laid down next to him and they sat quietly looking at the Falls upstream.

"It was really him, wasn't it? He was really the Librarian. And he was everything they said he was. You don't know how rare that is these days." It grew difficult for him to speak so he sat quietly for a moment just patting the dog's head. He even found that spot behind the ear.

"He's a hero, you know. He was already a legend, but this just caps it. These people will never forget him. Neither will I. He saved them. He saved me. Hell, he may have saved everybody. With that bastard gone, things can get good again. The world is going to be okay."

Chewy barked and sat up fast enough to startle Lucas.

"What?"

She looked at him and barked louder.

"What is it, girl?"

She stood up, ran halfway to the river and stopped. She cocked her head and listened for a moment. Then she began to bark and bound. She spun around and barked once more at Lucas.

Lucas shrugged. "I don't have the English to Wookie thing down yet. What is it?"

Chewy barked at him one last time, could see that he would never understand and took off running downstream, barking and wagging her tail the whole way.

Lucas watched her disappear and did begin to understand.

There would be more rumors. There would be more myths and legends. And he hoped to God that every one of them would be true.

- THE END -

If you enjoyed the Duck & Cover books,
check out a different kind of apocalypse
in
JUNKERS

They stand between us and destruction.
And that's a stupid place to stand.

Check out the first 4 chapters now.

**Read the first 4 BONUS CHAPTERS
of JUNKERS now:**

Benjamin Wallace

Copyright © 2016 by Benjamin Wallace.
All rights reserved.

# Prelude

He hated walking. It went against everything he believed in. Physical exertion of any kind wasn't really his thing at all. He was completely against manual labor. It's why he became a farmer in the first place.

No lifting. No sweating. It was the farmer's life for him. All you had to do was sit back and watch the drones work.

On a bad day you might have to take the controls and pilot the drone yourself. That was about as bad as it got. He'd heard stories of some farmers having to go into the field to check on malfunctioning equipment, but until now, he'd never really believed it. He figured they were stories farmers passed around to scare off the masses from such a cushy job.

That's why, when the alarm first came up, he assumed it was the day shift pulling a prank on him. Those guys had a hard time telling the difference between being funny and being dicks. Even at that, this wasn't their best work.

A few keystrokes sent the drones to investigate and he kicked back to plot his revenge. The day shift foolishly left their food unguarded in the communal fridge overnight, and spiking their drink with some Nanolax would be a good start to the retaliation.

He figured they could laugh at him all they wanted as long as a million microbots kept them glued to a toilet.

A chirp indicated that the drone had arrived at the site of the alarm and found nothing. Nothing at all. The equipment that was sending the alarm wasn't even there. He set a search path and the drones began running the preset pattern.

He kicked back in his chair, much to the dismay of its springs, and put his feet up on the console.

Watching the cornstalks zoom past the fish-eyed lens had made him queasy. Every row was the same. Every stalk was identical. Every leaf and ear was pitched at the same angle. They had been designed that way to ensure maximum exposure to the sun, but the whole effect worked to lull him into a trance.

He spent an hour searching the cornfield for the missing machinery to no avail and was on the verge of passing out when a series of damaged stalks broke the monotony and provided the first clue as to what was happening. Seizing the controls, he piloted the drone back down the row then turned to follow the broken plants.

Something had crashed through the crop. Someone was making off with the equipment.

He sat forward in his chair and willed the drone to follow the trail. He smiled. This was no longer work, it was crime fighting. Capturing the thief on the camera was all it would take for the authorities to identify the culprits. But he would be the hero, and for the second time in his life he might even trend. He smiled at the thought of this story supplanting the old one in the feeds. Finally.

"'Never live it down' my ass," he muttered to himself as he pushed harder on the control pad.

Sweeping through the crops, he followed the busted stalks and fallen ears of corn. He wasn't a farmer anymore. He was a fighter jockey piloting the latest generation WarBird through enemy canyons. The whir of the rotors played through his monitor's speakers, but they weren't quite fitting to the mood so he made his own scramjet engine sounds until he reached the center of the cornfield and stopped the drone.

There it was. A shadow moving quickly between the plants. Each time the figure darted, another plant fell to the ground with the dry crack of firewood.

He chased after the shadow for two rows and turned right to follow. But there was nothing there. The trail of destruction had ended. He flipped the drone 180 degrees in a deft move he would have to recount to the reporters later.

For a brief instant, the figure filled the monitor. Then everything went dead.

The drone dropped from the air and landed with its camera pointed toward the night sky.

Corn swayed in and out of view through a cracked lens, but the machine no longer responded to his touch. He could hear nothing but the breeze.

"No!" he screamed as the headlines faded from his daydreams. He shot up with such speed that his chair sailed back across the room, spinning as it went. He didn't wait for it to stop. He pulled a denim coat from a hook by the door with one hand and a shotgun with the other as he dashed out the door into the night. He had to bring these evildoers to justice. He had to have another fifteen minutes—a better fifteen minutes—of fame. They could take whatever busted piece of farm equipment they wanted from the company, but they couldn't take that opportunity away from him.

The utility vehicle whirred into action. Knobby off-road tires skipped on the concrete before biting into the dirt with an unbreakable hold and catapulting him into the cornfield. A thousand acres separated him from his prey, but he wasn't going to let it get away. He kept the pedal to the floor.

The cart's suspension ate the uneven soil without complaint and kicked the looser earth into the air behind it as it went.

Much like the view through the drone, the rows of corn blended into a mesh of green silk as he zipped past. This time he accepted it. He kept his eyes forward and let his peripheral look for the trail. The broken stalks would be a sore thumb sticking out in the genetically engineered pattern.

They were. He stood on the brakes when he spotted them and turned the cart into the path. The ride grew rougher as he crossed the furrows and the cart threw him back and forth, left and right, but he pressed on and let the cart jostle him about until he found the downed drone.

The cart idled in complete silence as he stepped into the field. He was alone.

Breathing heavily from the excitement, he was startled by how loud his breath was in the middle of the night. He swallowed hard once to try to hold it back and exhaled slowly before approaching the fallen drone.

The device was peppered with holes. The rotors were shattered. Shot clean off. He bent to examine the wreckage more closely.

There was a snap and a nearby corn stalk fell.

He hurried back to the cart and grabbed the shotgun. He racked a shell into the chamber and turned back to the crop.

"Show yourself."

There was no response.

He took a cautious step away from the vehicle. "You're not supposed to be out here."

Again, there was no response. There was no sound at all.

He racked the shotgun. The unspent shell fell to the ground and he closed his eyes at his mistake. "You're trespassing. Do you know what that means?"

He bent down and grabbed the shell off the ground. "That means I can shoot you. Legally. That's what that means."

He plugged the shell back into the bottom of the gun.

"I don't want to shoot you." He so wanted to shoot them. He was terrified. But being the hero behind the trigger instead of the hero behind the camera was going to ensure him at least a half-day in the top fifty stories. Number one in the farm feeds for sure.

Another stalk cracked a few rows over and he dove into the corn. The leaves whipped at his face as he fought through the tight plantings and burst through into the furrowed earth.

He turned and saw the figure a few yards away.

The shotgun bucked in his hands as he fired from the hip. He felt the blast in his ears, then heard it, then watched sparks dance as the shot bounced harmlessly off the metal scarecrow rooted in the field.

The robot stood on spindly, telescopic legs that enabled it to set its head above the crop. Its straw hat flopped around, leaving only the lower half of its face visible.

"Good thing the news didn't see that." He chuckled to himself and fired at the lanky sentry again. "Damn thing scared me."

The scarecrow took the blast in silence.

Its eyes began to glow red.

"What are you... You're supposed to be offline at night."

The machine looked right at him. Hydraulics in the legs lowered the body into the cornfield. Then it took a step toward him.

He ran.

Against everything he stood for, he ran. He broke through the stalks and sent them falling to the ground as he scrambled back toward the cart.

He had only made it two rows when he heard the scarecrow's Gatling gun begin to whir.

# 1
_____

It was a bright cold day in September and the clock struck thirteen. Nothing in the office worked right.

Jake took out a long list entitled "Broken Shit" and added the clock to the bottom beneath everything else that needed his attention.

He scanned the list. This needed that. That needed this. This thing was making that noise. This was leaking something most likely hazardous. It went on.

The list had been shoved in and out of the drawer so many times that the paper itself was falling apart. There were more important things on the list than a broken clock, but none of it was going to get fixed without money. And to get money they needed a job.

He looked at the phone and willed it to ring. He willed at it for five minutes before giving up. He shoved the list back in the drawer, stood up and pulled the malfunctioning timepiece off the wall. He gave it one last look before tossing it in the trashcan. Even if the phone did ring and even if the job did actually pay, it's not like he was going to spend the money on a stupid clock.

Since the phone wasn't cooperating and he no longer had a clock to watch, there wasn't much reason to stay in the office. He did the books by moving the envelopes on the desk marked "FINAL NOTICE" to the trashcan and stepped into the shop to see if he could help with anything.

The first thing that hit him was the sound of work, clattering, clanging and some grunting, the crew pounding something into place somewhere in the back. It didn't sound like it was going well.

The next thing that hit him was the question of the day.

"Hey, Jake, do you think ankles are sexy?"

The man behind the question was kicked back in a chair, behind a book, with his feet up on a coffee table. His name was Mitch Pritchard, but since he was full of cybernetic parts and horrible ideas everyone on the team called him Glitch. Glitch had been big and strong before he started adding parts to himself. Now he was twice as wide as a person should be and whirred when he walked. He called these enhancements "oddmentations" because even though Glitch tried to sound smart, he really wasn't.

The ankle question rolled through Jake's head, trying to land in a place where it would make sense, but nothing stuck. "What?"

"Do you think ankles are sexy?" Glitch pulled up his pant leg and pointed at his own ankle like he was presenting Exhibit A.

Jake put his hands up between himself and the ankle. "I'd really rather you leave me out of your upgrades, Glitch."

The big man laughed and leaned forward. He held up the book and tried to explain himself. "I'm reading this book about the court of King Charles Vee Eye Eye and there was this woman named Agnes Sorel that started a fashion trend. She'd show up with her boobs all hanging out. That would be the modern equivalent of walking into the White House with your nipples saluting the President."

"Glitch..." he tried to interrupt, but he had lost the manmachine to either a vivid imagined scene or a hardly safe-for-work reference image on his optic implant.

"And then other women started doing it, too. They wore dresses with their boobs all hanging out. BUT, they always had their ankles covered because it was considered scandalous to show ankles. And I thought, I never thought the ankle was really hot, but I don't know, maybe I've just seen too many, you know? Like I've been overexposed to ankles and I became desensitized to their inherent sexiness. And then I thought, maybe we're really missing out on this ankle thing." His eyes wandered to a wall and a smile grew across his face. There was no telling what he was seeing.

"Glitch..."

The cyborg's attention snapped back to Jake. "Well what do you think?"

"I think, for the first time ever, reading has made someone dumber."

"Says you. But I could be onto something big with this ankle thing. It could be a big market." He leaned back in the chair and returned to his reading.

Jake shook his head, hoping any memory of the conversation would refuse to stick. Thankfully the thought was replaced by another. "Hey, Glitch?"

"Yeah, boss."

"What's everyone up to?"

"I don't know. Working or something."

"Do you think maybe you should help?"

"Nah." He pointed to a mechanical joint that served as his elbow. "You see that regulator? It's been giving me fits lately. If it acts up while I'm helping out, I hate to think of the damage it could do. I could kill somebody. But don't worry. I'm going to get it fixed."

"Yeah? And when is that?"

He shrugged and turned the page. "I'm waiting on a part."

"Everything around here is broken." Jake muttered, and walked away, leaving Glitch to his book and his assortment of dumb ideas.

The diamond plate stairs rattled beneath his feet as he descended into the garage. There was an alternating stream of clangs and curses coming from beneath a monstrous red, white and rusted truck. A pair of legs stuck out from beneath the vehicle and kicked with every grunt and stomped with every swear word as their owner beat at something on the Beast's underbelly.

The Beast was a 1974 Travelall from International Harvester. It was seventeen feet long, just as wide, and illegal in every state. Its operation required a host of special permits, certifications, and the blessing of the local constabulary. And you had to have a really good reason for driving it.

In their line of work they needed a vehicle that was off the grid. Almost half their business, when there was business, came from shutting down gridsmart cars that had become a little too smart for their own good. And since being connected to the city's traffic system made for a pretty ineffective and extremely unexciting chase, they needed the ability to move independently of the highway systems.

The Beast weighed more than two tons before their equipment was loaded. A massive 401 cubic-inch engine made it go, while drum brakes and hope made it stop. It didn't go extremely fast, but the machinist had managed to bore, beg and coax the massive V-8 into putting out over 500 foot-pounds of torque. It would move if it had to.

More swearing found its way from the floor and up through the open hood. The voice behind the curses was soft and sweet even if it was damning the truck's mother to horribly foul acts in hell and other uncomfortable locations.

Jake gave a gentle rap on the fender. "What's the matter with her now?"

"It's an ancient piece of shit held together with nothing but my genius and your empty promises. Guess which of those is broken."

"You know I'd never blame your genius, but what's wrong?"

Casters rolled against concrete and the machinist's legs disappeared under the truck. He heard the creeper spin and a moment later her head emerged from under the chrome bumper.

She wore coveralls and engine grease like other women wore

ermine and makeup. She had fine dark hair that she refused to keep short despite the safety hazard it caused to both herself and the people around her that she distracted with it.

"This thing is older than both of us put together," she said. "That's what's wrong with it. The patches are falling off the patches I patched the patches with. I need parts."

"Parts aren't cheap, Kat."

"No, but you certainly are."

"If I had it to give I would. But you know things have been slow. We all have to make do with what we have right now. You don't hear Mason complaining, do you?"

There was a red flash, a white spark, a quick dimming of the lights and a blue streak that ended with the word *sonofabitchinlittleprick* being shouted from the back of the shop.

Kat smiled, tilted her head and disappeared back under the truck.

Jake hurried to the back of the workshop. It smelled like a thunderstorm had rolled through which, he had to admit, was more pleasant than it usually smelled.

Mason stood back from a disassembled disrupter pack and alternated between waving his hand through the air and shoving it into his mouth. The man was in mid-suck on a finger when Jake rushed up.

"Mason, are you okay? What was that?"

He jumped up and down for a moment before shoving his hand between his thighs. Bent over, he pointed a damning finger with his free hand at the device on the workbench. "That little shit bit me."

"Is your hand okay?"

"It's fine."

"Let's look at it."

Mason stomped his foot, straightened up and let the arm hang at his side. "It's fine, Mom."

"Are you sure?"

"It's fine."

"What were you doing?"

"I'm fixing this damned disrupter. It's been shorting out."

Jake tried to spy a look at the hand, but Mason tucked it behind his back. Jake shrugged away any concern he had left and asked, "Why don't you let Savant do that?"

"Oh. That's a good idea, Jake. We'll let the technician do the technical work. I should have thought of that. You kids are so damn smart. Or maybe I'm just old and stupid."

Jake tried not to smile. Mason was only a few years older than himself, but he wore each year of difference like a decade. To him, Jake was just one of those damn kids these days. He often reminded Mason of their closeness in age but now he just nodded. "He's not here."

Mason grabbed a screwdriver from the floor and turned back to the workbench. "Of course he's not here."

"He should be. Where is he?"

Mason shrugged and shoved the screwdriver back into the backpack-sized device, aiming for a screw head Jake couldn't see. "He's running somewhere. He's climbing something. Or he's falling off something else. Don't worry. I'm sure he'll tell us all about it when he gets back. Then he'll tell us all about it again."

"Just leave it for him."

"No. It needs to get done. If I leave it for him, it'll never happen. Besides, it's my gear so it's my ass if it doesn't work right. Savant'll be just fine back in the truck. The lazy brat."

There was a *zzzt* from inside the disrupter and Mason jumped back a step onto one leg with his forearm over his face. He held the pose for a moment and looked cautiously over his arm.

"What's wrong with it?" Jake asked.

"It's a piece of junk."

Jake sighed, preparing to explain once more how no money meant no new things. "Look, I'd get a new one but..."

"No, thank you. The new ones are even worse. Everything now is just made to break. So you have to buy a new one. Not like it was before. Now if you don't mind, I have to be careful not to shock myself again." He placed the screwdriver back in the device once more.

"Shouldn't you unhook the power before you do that?"

"Why? I'd just have to hook it back up again anyway."

Jake rolled his eyes. "Duh. Stupid me."

"Your words."

Jake turned and stepped away as the lights dimmed, the sparks flew and Mason screamed, "*Sonofabitchinlittleprick!*"

He trudged back across the shop and back up the metal stairs toward his office with numbers running through his head. All of them had minus signs in front of them.

Glitch stopped him short of the door with an upraised hand.

"I don't want to talk about ankles or 16<sup>th</sup>-century exhibitionists, Glitch. I just want to go to my office."

"Your uncle's here."

Jake looked at the office door and sighed. "I don't want to go to my office." He opened the door anyway.

Uncle Aaron was sitting behind the desk, bouncing back and forth in the chair. His grin grew larger when Jake stepped in. "There he is."

"Hey, Aaron."

"'Hey, Aaron?'" The older man stood and moved around the desk with a spring in his step that said *I need a few bucks but I'll pay you back*. He stretched out his arms. "You don't have a hug for your favorite uncle?"

Jake didn't move.

"Okay," said Uncle Aaron. "I guess it is kind of weird to hug your business partner, isn't it?"

Jake shook his head, embraced the man and grimaced as three hard smacks landed on his back.

"That's a good boy. Now I won't have to tell your mother you weren't happy to see me."

Jake worked his way around the desk and sat in his chair. He felt the spring pop a little more than usual before the seat locked in a position that wasn't comfortable. He would have to add it to the list. "What can I do for you, Aaron?"

The old man sat on the desk and leaned forward. "How's our business?"

"It sucks."

"Then sell. I'll sign whatever I need to."

"There's nothing to sell. Everything's broken." Jake jerked a thumb toward the office door. "Even Glitch."

"The money's in the name."

"Ashley's Robot Reclamation of Green Hill? Do you think?"

"Well, then make it an acronym."

"No one is going to buy ARRGH," Jake said.

"You never know until you try."

Jake Ashley's eyes narrowed on his uncle. The grin on his face was a little too big to be truly genuine, but there was something new in it. "What's her name?"

Aaron stood up and waved the question off. "I don't know what you're talking about."

"Your new girlfriend. What's her name? Skylar? Tiffany? Cinnamon?"

Uncle Aaron sat in the guest chair and smiled. "Meagan."

"Hmm," Jake said. "She doesn't sound like a former stripper at all."

"She's not."

"Then she must be crazy."

"I'll have you know she is an executive director. Does that sound crazy?"

"Depends on what she's an executive director of."

Uncle Aaron turned his chair as he answered, possibly hoping the squeak would cover his response. "Society for the Preservation of Humans."

"Society for the..."

"Yes. Yes. Society for the Preservation of Humans. So what?"

"A humans first organization? The big one, even. She sounds well balanced."

"It's just a job. Look, do you have anything for me or not?"

"Not."

"Damn it, Jake." Uncle Aaron stood and gestured toward the office door. "This place is going down. We have to get out while we can."

"You're pretty much out already."

"Then save yourself and my five percent." He slammed his palms onto the desk.

Jake let out a cough. "Three percent."

He slammed his palms on the desk again. "My three percent. It's time to end it."

"Quit?"

"Yes, quit."

"Dad always said that Ashleys aren't quitters."

"He was full of shit. Of course we're quitters. We're born quitters. I quit things all the time. C'mon, Jake, be a quitter with me." Uncle Aaron smiled his uncle's smile and sat back down. The smile faded into one of his rare serious moments. "Look, Jake. The business is dying. Not just ours, but the whole industry. They're making bots better. And even the shitty ones come with a longer warranty. Pretty soon it will be just the corporate boys junking their mistakes. There's no room for the little guy anymore."

The independent shops were closing. Or selling. Or failing. But Jake wasn't ready to give up just yet.

"I heard from a buyer, Jake."

"Who would want to buy this place?"

"It doesn't matter who they are. All that matters is that they're interested and they've got more money than a whore after the Super Bowl."

Jake leaned forward in his seat. "I'm not quitting." He stood and crossed the office.

"Be honest, Jake." Uncle Aaron stood and pointed to the phone on the desk. "When was the last time that phone rang?"

The phone rang.

Uncle Aaron dropped his arm. "Well that is just the worst timing ever."

Jake grabbed the phone. "Ashley's Robot Reclamation."

"I mean a guy is just trying to make a point and the stupid thing just rings all over it. I hate machines."

Jake held up a finger to shush his uncle and turned back to the phone. He answered the caller's question. "Yes, we're junkers."

## 2

The Beast was named for its size and lumbering gait in traffic. But that didn't mean it didn't sound like a beast, too. The engine roared. The brakes shrieked. And there was a growl from a source that Kat had never been able to quite pin down.

The sixty-year-old vehicle charged through traffic like an elephant with hurt feelings, trumpeting over the quiet hum generated by the electric cars that filled the road.

By law, passenger cars had to be aware of their surroundings, and a hundred sensors in each vehicle were screaming at their guidance systems to get out of the way of the big red truck as it barreled through town. Traffic parted before the team as the Travelall bullied its way to the edge of the city and into the night.

They lined the bench seats and did their best not to bounce against each other as the Beast swayed back and forth on exhausted shocks. The interior smelled of fuel and exhaust and the odor mixed with the unending motion turned Jake's stomach. He fought the queasy sensation and focused on what lay ahead.

He made sure he knew where the window crank was and said, "Tell us what we're looking at, Mason."

"Okay." Mason produced a tablet and began to read the

information. "Two hours ago some fat farmer walked into his cornfield and..."

"Mason." Jake interrupted and instantly recalled a dozen conversations that had started this way.

"What?"

"Forget the commentary. Just give us the facts."

"It is a fact, Jake. The dude weighed like three hundy."

"It's irrelevant. And rude."

"Well, I'm sorry, Miss Manners, but I think it is relevant to know that the bot we're looking for took down something the size of a buffalo with no trouble. Now, if it was me going in there, and it is by the way, I think that's something I'd want to know."

Jake gave a reluctant nod and looked out the window.

"This is about safety, Jake. And, honestly, I'm a little hurt that you'd think this was about anything other than the wellbeing of my coworkers."

Jake waved him back toward the tablet. "Just get on with it."

"No." Mason set the tablet in his lap. "I'd like an apology first."

"Are you serious?"

"Are you sorry?"

Jake rolled his eyes. "Fine. I'm sorry I accused you of being insensitive."

"That's more like it." Mason lifted the tablet once more. "As I was saying, this fatty in the dell here waddles into his corn crop about two hours ago, possibly to check on a malfunctioning piece of equipment or, more likely, to make a sandwich."

Jake pounded the door. "Mason!"

"They found him dead with corn embedded in his chest," he read. "Oh big surprise, food killed him."

Jake pinched the bridge of his nose. It didn't help the growing headache as much as he'd hoped. "Just tell us what we're up against."

"It's a ZUMR, Model number R34-P3R Organic Compliant Deterrent System." He held up the screen to show everyone a blue-line schematic of the machine.

"It looks like a scarecrow," Glitch said.

"Points for you, Tin Man. That's exactly what it is." Mason turned the tablet back so he could read more. "Here's an ad for it. It suggests putting a hat and shirt on the thing for that old farm feel. Gives everyone a touch of the nostalgies I guess. But underneath the stupid hat it's a state-of-the-art murder murderer. You can tell from the oh so clever headline, 'Scares Crows Dead.'" He read further ahead to himself. "That's weird. The thing's brand new."

"It does what to crows?" Glitch asked. "How does it do that?"

"It fires corn kernels at about 2500 feet per second from this mini-gun on its right arm. And cuts them up with the scythe-looking thing on its left." He held the screen toward Glitch and waited for the cyborg to process the image.

"That's a terrible idea!"

"It's quite genius, actually. I can't imagine corn makes a very good bullet. So, what better way to make up for accuracy than with an insane amount of volume?"

"That's not what I meant and you know it. I mean, how can they get away with killing the birds?"

Mason shrugged. "It's a part of ZUMR's guilt-free farming line. The corn is all natural. So is crow blood. Crow feathers. Crow guts, too. So the crops remain completely organic, legal, and free of flying vermin." Mason paused and chuckled. "Scares crows dead. I get it now."

"You think this is funny?" Kat asked from behind the wheel.

"Pretty funny. Yeah."

"You're a horrible person, Mason," Kat said.

Mason shrugged again. "Okay."

Jake turned back from the window and glared at Mason. "Enough! Just tell us where to hit it."

Mason tapped the pad several times before shaking his head. "I'm not really seeing any weak points. If the mini-gun overheats it will start popping the kernels. That seems to be the biggest beef on the forums. Actually, that could be kind of fun."

"Nothing else?"

Mason searched the information. "No. It's weatherized. But that shouldn't be a problem for our disruptors."

"Good," Jake said. "Let's make this takedown quick. And take it easy on the equipment. Don't pull the trigger any more than you have to. Most of all, stay safe."

Kat spoke to Jake without taking her eyes off the road. "If this thing is so new, why did they call us?"

"The warranty team gave them a window of several days before they could come. I guess the farm decided that stopping a robot's murderous rampage was something that couldn't wait."

"We don't get many of those anymore."

"Corporate calls or owners with a conscience?"

"Yes." Kat pulled onto the exchange and followed the ramp onto another freeway. A small car swerved out of the way, waking its sleeping passenger.

It was another hour on interstates, highways and farm-to-market roads before the truck turned down the mile long driveway that led to the farm. Corn grew in fields on either side and Jake watched the stalks sway in the gentle, late-day breeze.

He rolled the window down to let the smell of the field into the car and the smell of the car out. Cold air blew in. He fought back a shiver as Kat pulled into a parking lot and stopped the Beast beside a black SUV that was only a fraction smaller and newer than the Travelall.

She killed the engine and waited for it to ping to a stop. She pointed to the black truck and spoke. "I thought you said they weren't coming."

Jake watched as the door to the truck opened and a woman stepped out into the chilly night air. She shivered and pulled on a windbreaker bearing the ZUMR Robotics logo. She smiled at Jake and shut her door.

"Hey, that's..." began Glitch.

"What's this bullshit?" Mason asked.

"Wait here." Jake turned to Kat. "All of you. I'll see what's up."

The Travelall door squeaked as it opened and clanged as he forced it shut behind him.

"Your team can turn around, Jake," the woman said. "ZUMR will handle this."

"The hell you will."

"It's our equipment, Jake."

"It's our call, Hailey. You left them hanging." He smiled for the first time. "Which doesn't surprise me at all."

Her smile faded. "Well, I'm here now."

"You certainly are." He looked over her shoulder. He knew she was hiding long and rich dark hair beneath her corporate cap. He knew it smelled like warm coconut. He shut out the memory. "But where's your team?"

A whirring sound came from inside her truck and a small robot emerged from the window. No bigger than a coffee can, the Whirbert flew on small rotors and bleeped and blooped as it perched on Hailey's shoulder.

"Your team's gotten smaller since the last time," Jake said.

"They'll be here. There was some kind of mix-up at dispatch."

"Sure there was."

Before she could respond, a door to one of the office buildings flew open and a man in a suit jogged across the parking lot to the couple. He steered toward Hailey and stuck out his hand. "Ashley? Thank God."

The woman put out her own hand.

Jake stepped in front of her. "I'm Ashley." He tried to intercept the handshake.

The man in the suit pulled his hand back. "You're Ashley?"

"Yes, sir."

The man offered his hand again, but with some obvious hesitation.

"Is there a problem?" Jake asked.

"I guess I just expected someone less mannish."

Hailey laughed at this.

"Jake Ashley," he said with emphasis on the Jake. "We're here to help you with your malfunctioning equipment."

"Oh, I see. I'm Dan Forester. I'm sorry. I'm sure that happens quite a bit."

"It does," Hailey said with a laugh.

"You're probably used to it then."

Jake shook his head. "You'd think so."

Forester turned to the woman with the robot on her shoulder. "So, are you with him?"

"Hardly." Hailey stepped in front of Jake and took the man's hand. "Hailey Graves. ZUMR Robotics, Warranty department."

"But, I thought you couldn't be here. I was told you couldn't be here."

"They aren't," Jake said. "Miss Graves is alone. My team is here and we're ready to go."

"My team will be here shortly," Hailey argued.

"But it's moving." There was panic in the corporate famer's voice. "I told your company this, Miss Graves. We don't want it to harm anyone else."

She nodded where she was supposed to nod, made a sad face at the sad parts and then responded with practiced confidence. "My team should be here in an hour, Mr. Forester."

"An hour!" Forester and Jake joined together in their disbelief.

"It could be gone in an hour, Miss Graves," Jake said. "We need to take care of this menace right now."

Whir-bert looked at Jake and blasted a series of angry bleeps.

Hailey protested as well. "Sir, if you'll just be patient, ZUMR will handle this situation."

"And what is the reward for his patience, Miss Graves?" Jake asked. "How many more have to die? And how many stories have to be written about all those dead bodies that piled up while we just stood here and waited?"

"Jake," she hissed.

Jake turned back to the man in the suit. "We can have this taken care of in no time, Mr. Forester."

"Any actions taken by an independent contractor will void the machine's warranty." How she loved to lecture.

Dan Forester cared about people. That was obvious. But the talk of capital investments shook his principles. Jake could see the hems and haws coming. He had to get in front of them.

"Warranty?!" Jake said. "How can you think about warranties at a time like this, Miss Graves? What is the cost of a single machine versus a human life?"

Forester wrung his hands together. "Quite a lot actually."

"Is it more than the price of integrity?" Jake asked.

Forester shrugged with a nervous smile.

Hailey showed Jake an invoice.

Jake nodded. "Fair enough. That is a lot. But is it more than the price of a PR team to keep Happy Dell Independent Family Farms Incorporated off the news streams?"

The man sighed. "Please take care of the matter, Mr. Ashley."

Jake turned to the Beast and yelled. "We're up!"

The doors opened and the crew filed out of the truck. They moved to the rear and began unloading their gear.

"You unctuous jerk," Hailey said under her breath.

"I've asked you before, please don't insult me with words I have to look up. We don't have time for that. We have to stop this killer." Jake started for the truck.

"You're a prick," she said louder.

He turned. "There. Wasn't that easier?"

Forester followed. "So, we're all good now, right? I can go? Home? You'll call when it's done?" The executive farmer turned to leave.

"Mr. Forester, before you go, there is one thing I have to ask you."

"Yes?" He bounced on the balls of his feet. Each bounce took him closer to the safety of his car.

"Has the machine ever exhibited any artistic qualities?" Jake asked.

"What... what do you mean?"

2

"Has it ever written you a poem? Sung a song? Written a book?"

"No."

Mason popped his head around the corner of the truck. "And it just shot the employee? It didn't dress him up like a scarecrow and put him on a stake?"

"What?" Forester squirmed. "No!"

"It didn't pin a sign to him that said, 'If I only had a brain'?"

"No! My God. Why are you asking this?"

"It's just something we have to do, Mr. Forester." Jake said. "Sentience complicates things. But it sounds like we're in the clear."

Forester looked more frightened by it all than annoyed by the technicalities. "Can I go?"

"Yeah," Mason said. "You can run away now."

Dan Forester nodded and jogged to his car. He slammed the vehicle's door and sped away.

Mason held up Jake's disruptor pack and motioned for him to turn around.

"'If I only had a brain'?" Jake asked.

"And then the robot takes the brains out of the farmer's head. That's poetic justice, Jake. Which is a form of poetry, and poetry is art."

"You know why no one likes you, right?"

"Yep." Mason held up the pack again.

Jake slipped his arms into the shoulder straps and switched on the pack. He pulled the discharger from the holster and checked the safety. It was broken.

They stood at the edge of the cornfield, staring down the rows of the golden green crop as the sun began to set. The breeze danced through the field and the stalks swayed at its command. The motion and the darkness made it difficult to detect any movement that wasn't corn.

Jake didn't like it. "Send up the drone, Mason."

"What drone?" Mason asked.

"What do you mean, 'what drone'?"

"You mean the Seeker 4000 with thermal imaging and focal plane arrays capable of detection and pursuit?"

"Of course I mean that one."

"Ah, well then you would also mean the one that is sitting in thirty-two separate parts back at the office waiting on a new focal plane array, firmware realignment and a valid operator's permit."

"Perfect."

A gust of wind startled the cornfield and the stalks dipped further into the rows. A dozen shrill whistles rose from the field.

"Do you all hear that?" Glitch put a hand to his ear and made an adjustment on a knob hidden behind his earlobe. "What's that sound?"

"That's the wind whipping through the plains," Mason said.

"What?"

Mason stared at the cyborg. "Didn't you ever blow on a blade of grass?"

Glitch shook his head.

Mason grumbled, "Stupid kids," before saying, "It whistles." He pointed to the field. "Like that."

"Oh, good. I thought my ear was buggy again. I think a wire is loose."

"Does any part of you work?" Mason asked.

"My fist works. Want me to show you?"

Kat stepped between them. "Knock it off, the both of you. We don't want this thing sneaking up on us just because you two can't keep your mouths shut."

"We'd never hear it anyway," Mason said. "This thing has sound baffling like you wouldn't believe."

"For a scarecrow?" Kat asked.

"The thing was designed to sneak up on birds, Kat. And a crow's hearing is better than a human's. And way better than Glitch's, apparently."

"Shut up, Mason. I can hear you, you know."

"Perfect." Jake ignored them both and peered into the rows of corn. He turned his head, listening for the silent killer. "So we can't see it. And we can't hear it. Any good news?"

"Yeah, since it doesn't really matter, I can keep on insulting ED-Four O Nine pounds here."

"Hey," was Glitch's only comeback.

"Seriously, Glitch?" Mason shook his head. "Is there anyway you can upgrade your wit? Because you're just making things too easy for me."

"Just shut up and let me think." Jake paced the edge of the cornfield, peering down each row as far as the darkness would allow.

Kat stepped beside him and asked quietly, "What are you thinking?"

"I'm thinking it couldn't be much worse. A silent renegade machine equipped for killing and hiding in a maze of noisy darkness."

"I don't want to be the one to say it, but you could hand it over to Hailey and her team."

Jake turned back to the team. "Here's the plan. We'll split up—"

"Because that always works," Mason said.

"Shut it, Mason," Jake said.

"No, really, I saw it in a horror movie once."

"Enough." Jake walked to the head of a corn row. "We'll split up. But keep no more than one row between us and stay abreast of each other at all times."

Mason held up a finger and opened his mouth.

"And no abreast jokes," Jake finished.

Mason closed his mouth and lowered his hand.

"Mason, hand out the comms."

"What comms, Jake?"

Jake closed his eyes and took a deep breath. "Fine. Keep an ear out for one another and have their back. This isn't your typical murderous laundry machine. It's quiet, has a machine gun for one arm and a sword for the other. It's dangerous. Let's find it and put it down quick."

The team nodded and spread out across the edge of the cornfield.

The discharger was shaped like a small carbine and he pulled if from a holster on his hip. He pulled the stock to his shoulder and made sure the cable that ran from the pommel was free of obstruction. His thumb found the safety and switched it off as if it actually worked in the first place. Within seconds, the pack on his back warmed as the circuits closed and the capacitor charged. A pull of the trigger would send the disruption charge through the baton and out a directional Tesla coil at the end of the instrument.

A single charge could incapacitate most consumer and low-end industrial models. The R34-P3R was weatherized, however, and

Jake questioned how effective it would actually be. He looked over to Glitch.

Each team member carried a similar backpack, but the giant cyborg had another tool slung across his back. The cannon looked like a rifle built to ridiculous proportions. The barrel could double for a sewer pipe, and the receiver was a block the size of a car battery. Its bulk made it too cumbersome for anyone that wasn't augmented like Glitch.

Glitch caught Jake's look and acknowledged the stare.

Jake nodded. "Keep the IMP handy."

Glitch nodded back and stepped into the cornfield. The rest followed his lead and each team member took a row.

Jake wasn't but a few feet in when the sounds of nature swallowed the footsteps of his teammates. Having never had the opportunity to wander through a cornfield, Jake had always pictured them as quiet, serene places, but the snap of the stalks and crackle of the plants made it anything but relaxing. Every creak could be their prey, every snap could be an ambush, and every sound put his nerves on edge.

The ground was moist beneath his feet and rich with an earthy smell that rose with every cautious step. He moved slowly, straining to hear in the darkness.

A gust of wind pushed the crop deep into the furrowed row. He jumped back and gripped the disrupter tighter in his hand. Two rows over he heard Glitch swear. Four rows over he heard the faint traces of Mason laughing at Glitch's discomfort.

The wind calmed and for a brief moment Jake could see further into the crop. Something was there and it was staring back at him.

Maybe.

It was as tall as the crop itself and thin like a stalk but, unlike the corn, it didn't sway.

A shout rose in his throat but before it could escape his mouth, another gust of wind obscured his view. He held still and waited for the wind to rest. When it did, he peered once more into the darkness at what he thought he had seen. But it wasn't there. He shuddered.

"It's ahead of us," he called to either side.

"Where?" Glitch's voice was faint in the field of plants.

"I don't know."

"Real helpful!" Mason screamed back. "Thanks."

Jake walked faster, calling for positioning every few meters to make sure the team was keeping together. The wind came in spurts and slowed their progress. It soon became almost rhythmic. With every pause, Jake scanned the field for the shadowy figure. But shadows were everywhere and he could never be certain the movement he spotted was anything other than corn.

Another gust blew a mass of leaves in his face. He grabbed at the plant. "I'm starting to really hate corn," he shouted and swatted the plant away.

It was in front of him. An evil face etched in metal beneath a rotting, floppy hat.

Jake screamed and stumbled backward as the machine swung its left arm.

He fell beneath the scythe as it cut a silver arc through air and corn. He hit the ground and the sliced plants crashed down on top of him.

The machine held up its left arm and glanced at an ear of corn impaled on the long and slender blade. The Reaper raised its arm to strike again.

Jake pulled the disruptor's trigger. A blue burst of voltage lit the field around him and crackled through the air as the arc connected with the tip of the scythe.

The arm stopped. The blade shuddered. The speared corncob popped.

The appendage fell dead at the scarecrow's side, but the robot did not fall. The machine looked at the dead limb and tried to move it again. Its torso bucked but the arm would not respond other than flopping a bit.

"It's here!" Jake shouted.

A whir filled the cornrow and the Reaper raised its other arm. The kernel cannon's barrels blurred as they spun up to speed.

Jake scrambled back on knees and elbows.

The scarecrow fired.

Plumes of earth chased him backward as the kernels spit from the mini-gun and dug into the ground. They stitched the earth closer and closer until they had reached just below his feet.

Jake fired again. The disrupter's charge leapt to the floating barrels but did nothing to stop their spin. The arm did not fall.

The Reaper continued to fire.

The musky smell of damp earth was quickly overtaken by the scent of ozone and freshly popped popcorn as the fluffy white snack poured from the barrels and began to pile up on the ground.

An explosion of cornstalks erupted next to the machine as Glitch charged through the rows shoulder-first at the Reaper. The giant man plowed into the machine, lifting it from the ground and sending it several rows deep back into the field.

The cyborg glanced at Jake quickly and dove into the field after the machine.

"Glitch, wait." Jake started to get to his feet as Mason and Kat found their way through the web of leaves.

Kat grabbed Jake's hand and helped him up as Mason grabbed a handful of popcorn off the ground.

"Where did they go?" Kat asked.

Jake pointed down the row. "Follow the wreckage."

"Did yoush mape dish, Jakgh? Dish ish delicishous," Mason said through a mouthful of popcorn. "Neesh buttersh show."

Jake and Kat forced Mason toward the new path that Glitch had cleared through the field. It twisted and turned in indiscriminate directions.

Fallen stalks tripped at their heels. The uneven nature of the furrowed field grabbed at their toes. More than once, Mason almost choked on his popcorn. For five minutes they rushed after their coworker, shouting his name as they fought to remain on their feet.

The path cut right, and they were met with a wall of corn. The team nearly fell over Glitch. The large man sat tenderly picking at his arm. His sleeve was dark with blood and he twitched with every touch.

"Glitch?" Kat put a hand on his shoulder.

"Damn thing shot me in my real arm."

"Are you okay?"

"Of all the arms I've got, he had to shoot this one."

"I'm sorry, Glitch," Kat said.

"Ah, it's okay. I was thinking about getting it replaced anyway."

"Why didn't you fry him?" Mason asked.

"I did. Right after he shot me." Glitch stood and brushed at the wounds on his arm. "Stupid thing used that spinny-gun to soak up the shot. Then he shot a bunch of popcorn at me and ran off."

"It's mini-gun, Glitch."

"Whatever it is. He's using it as a shield."

"It did the same back there," Jake said. "Mason. Kat. If you're going to shoot, try and hit it from the left side." He turned to Glitch. "Can you handle the IMP?"

Glitch pulled the large rifle from his back, seated it in his hand and smiled.

"Good. Try to keep the damage down." Jake turned to the others. "We distract. Glitch melts." He turned back and parted the corn. "Oh, thank God."

The team stepped through the crop into a large clearing. The heart of the farm consisted of several large steel barns surrounding a paved lot filled with equipment. Several service lights glowed above each door. It was the first light they'd seen since venturing into the fields. Unfortunately it didn't produce much more than atmosphere and shadows.

The group stepped onto the pavement and surveyed the area looking for movement or any clue as to where the machine had run.

"Any ideas?" Kat asked.

Mason raised his disruptor and started walking. "He went this way."

"How can you tell?"

He pointed to a trail of fluffy white popcorn. "Come on Hansel. Come on Gretel."

There wasn't much, but the wind had left enough of the popcorn undisturbed to establish a trail.

"Everyone stay behind Glitch." Jake spoke softly.

"That's because he likes you least," Mason said.

"It's because of the IMP, you jerk."

"Shut up, both of you," Kat said. "Before the wind takes the trail away."

The crew formed up behind the cyborg's bulk in a small "V" as Glitch followed the white specks.

They had taken only a few steps when a sound in the cornfield had them all spinning on their heels. Glitch pulled the trigger on the IMP and it kicked in his hands. The sound it made was subtle, a high-pitched *bloop* like a pebble falling into a hundred-foot well, but the shot itself tore a four-foot hole straight through the crop.

The stalks that weren't obliterated burned. The kernels popped all at once, creating a cloud of popcorn. Once it settled to the ground, it looked like Christmas and the team could see clear through to the other side of the cornfield.

There was nothing else behind them.

Mason clapped. "Nice shot, Redenbacher."

"Shut up, Mason."

He patted Glitch on the belly. "Whatever you say Jiffy-Puffy."

"I'm not fat. They're servos."

"Yeah, okay."

"Would you two please just follow the trail before the wind blows it away?" Kat asked.

"Right." Mason pointed ahead of Glitch. "Follow the popcorn. Like a professional."

The still air didn't last long, but it didn't have to. The popcorn led them around the corner to a metal barn that was larger than most neighborhoods. Once they turned the corner, they found the steel door ripped from its hinges and tossed ten feet away.

"I think he went in there," Glitch said.

"Very good, Glitch." Mason asked. "That new processor is really doing wonders for you."

Jake shook his head and stepped through the hole into the barn. He reached out to the wall looking for a light switch, not really expecting it to be there. It wasn't. The barn felt even bigger inside. He pulled out a flashlight and hit the switch.

The beam didn't penetrate far into the darkness, but the cavernous nature of the barn was exposed. It rose three stories up before there was anything resembling a ceiling and was filled with massive pieces of farm equipment. Several harvesters were lined up near a pair of monstrous doors. They were set to roll as soon as the computers said the crop was ready.

The rest of the team filed in behind Jake and spread out along the wall.

Jake splashed the flashlight around the group. "Someone find the lights."

Before anyone could respond with a "how?" or "yeah right" the metal cavern filled with a mechanical whir.

"Spinny-gun!" Glitch shouted and shoved Mason out of the way a half second before the corn came raining down from the rafters.

Mason hit the ground as the rest of the crew dove for cover.

Glitch stood. The big man's machine mind snapped on. As the corn struck the floor around him, one of his oddmentations began to calculate the trajectory of the corn and triangulated its origin in the darkness.

The data load was immense due to the number of kernels, but it finally returned an answer.

"I've got you now," Glitch said as he raised the IMP and fired. The gun sounded and a round section of the roof melted away, letting in just enough moonlight to expose the Reaper's silhouette as the machine leapt from its place in the rafters.

The IMP was knocked from Glitch's hands as the mechanical scarecrow kicked the giant back against one of the harvesters.

The Reaper's left arm still hung limp at its side, but it swung the mini-gun barrel to great effect, bashing Glitch back into the machine every time he took a step forward.

"Shoot it!" Mason yelled as he searched for his disruptor.

Kat kept tabs on the Reaper with her own disruptor but couldn't get a clear shot. "The current will run right through it into Glitch."

Jake stepped out from behind a crate and the mini-gun spooled up instantly to fire. He dove back behind cover as the kernels dug into the wood.

Glitch made the most of the momentary distraction and seized the machine by the waist. The metal muscles in his arm twitched as he lifted the Reaper above his head. He bashed it into the ground as he yelled, "You hurt my real arm!"

The Reaper's eyes turned brighter and it brought the gun to bear on the cyborg. Then its head and torso melted.

Mason flew back across the room and dropped the IMP as he slammed into the barn wall and collapsed.

The collision caused the entire structure to roll like thunder.

Glitch dropped the remains of the machine and rushed to his side. "Are you okay, Mason?"

Jake slid to his knees and examined Mason as best he could. "Would someone find the lights?"

"I'm on it." Glitch stood and ran off into the darkness.

"Firing the IMP?" Jake said. "That was..."

"Brave. Courageous. Selfless." Mason said as he stood on shaky legs.

"Stupid," Jake said.

"This sounds an awful lot like the start of one of your insurance premium rants."

"You're an idiot."

"Oh, now we're doing performance reviews?"

Bright lights filled the barn with a boom.

"Good job, Glitch," Jake shouted over his shoulder.

Glitch's voice came back from somewhere deep in the barn. "That wasn't me."

Jake turned. The lights weren't coming from overhead. They were coming from one of the massive combines. The work lights were focused on the two men in front of the barn doors.

"That's weird and terrifying," Mason said.

"Maybe it's just trying to help," Jake said not believing a word of it.

"Yeah, I don't like the way it's looking at us."

"I'm sure it's just the farmers back at the office trying to help." Why did he keep saying things he didn't believe?

The combine's engine turned over and the giant machine began to rumble. The blades began to spin.

"How sure are you?"

Jake started to edge toward the access door they had entered. "Not much. Actually I kind of regret saying it because now it sounds really stupid."

The combine lurched forward as the two men dove aside. It crashed into the door and produced a thunderclap that shook the barn and rattled the team.

Glitch ran out of the darkness and joined the two men. "What did you guys do?"

The combine backed up and redirected its lights at the trio.

"Run!" Mason shouted and turned for the door.

Jake and Glitch followed.

The three men ran out of the barn and were halfway across the tarmac when the combine exploded through the barn doors in a shower of sparks and screeching metal. The combine's reel snapped in two and spun away across the parking lot. The machine turned on the fleeing trio and choked out the moon with its work lights.

Jake fired a blast from the disruptor, knowing that it would do little to slow the massive machine. The streak of electricity ran the length of the farm equipment to no effect.

They zigged and zagged across the open space and the machine course-corrected each time.

Cybernetics notwithstanding, Glitch's bulk slowed him down and he was falling behind. "It's following us."

"You think, dumbass?" Mason shouted as he tried his own disruptor against the machine. It worked as well as Jake's.

"Lose it in the corn," Jake yelled and turned into the field.

Glitch followed him as Mason took the next row over.

"I'm not going to make it, guys." Glitch yelled.

"You can do it, Glitch." Jake turned to encourage him. "Redirect power or something."

"Nope." Glitch crashed to the ground and slid through the dirt as the combine tore into the corn behind him. "I was right."

The machine sucked the giant man into its maw and Glitch's screams disappeared inside the machine.

Jake screamed himself and fired his disruptor at the combine until the system shut down to prevent it from overheating.

The machine chewed through the corn toward him.

Mason burst through the row of stalks and fired his own weapon to failsafe.

The machine kept coming.

The two men turned to run but bounced off one another in the process and fell to the ground.

The combine's blades snapped at a blurring rate as they neared, and the two men kicked into the dirt trying to push themselves away.

The machine loomed over them.

The lights were blinding them.

The two men rolled out of way as the blades sheared the corn stalks from the earth and the combine passed between them.

Jake got to his feet and beat against the machine looking for a hollow spot, a belly in the beast. He screamed the cyborg's name. "Glitch!"

"I'm okay." The voice came from behind the combine.

Jake rushed to the rear of the machine and found Glitch lying in the cleared field naked to the skin.

"Glitch! Glitch, are you okay?" Jake asked.

"Yeah. I think so."

"How the hell are you okay?!"

Mason ran around the far side and saw the two men. "Why are you naked?"

"That thing ate my clothes." Glitch stood, revealing that every shred of material had been thrashed away on his journey through the machine. Also, that his crotch glowed in the dark.

"Geez, Glitch. Even your junk? Can't you leave anything alone?"

"Shut up, Mason."

"Let's talk about Glitch's little light show later," Jake said. "It's turning around."

The combine roared as it turned and bore down upon them once more.

"Man that thing is surprisingly nimble." Mason checked the status on his disruptor.

Jake held up his own and saw that it was ready to fire once more. "Maybe if we both hit it at once?"

"Sure," Mason nodded enthusiastically, "that will never work."

"Just shoot."

Both men fired and the front of the combine turned blue as the disruptors let flow a steady stream of electric bursts. The engine sputtered, wheezed and died, leaving them in silence but for their panting and something on Glitch that beeped.

The work lights flickered, popped and went out leaving them in the dark with only their flashlights and Glitch's junk providing any kind of light.

Mason looked at the weapon in his hand. "That really shouldn't have worked."

The combine boomed and all three men jumped. A hatch squeaked open and Kat jumped to the ground. "It looks like I saved you all once— Glitch, why is your dick glowing?"

# 4

Bruises and fatigue made it a long walk back for everyone, but even more so for Glitch, as the tarp they'd found in the barn covered his nakedness but did little to hide the glow in his crotch.

"Tell me it's just to make peeing at night easier."

"Shut up, Mason."

"I'm not judging," Mason said. "Just asking."

"No, you're judging."

"Okay, you're right. I'm judging."

They reached the office parking lot to a round of applause.

The rest of the ZUMR team had arrived and were busy unloading their reclamation equipment. Four robots standing seven feet tall and four wide at the chest stomped into the parking lot from an old model moving truck. Designed to take a beating from anything the company had ever manufactured, they were built thick and shook the ground when they walked.

The technicians turned at the team's approach and clapped fervently, whistled and made other congratulatory comments that they obviously didn't mean in the least.

Mason told them all to go to hell and walked back over to the Beast.

Hailey didn't clap, but she was smiling when she walked up to Jake. "How did it go, Jake?"

"It went fine."

"You have a funny definition of fine, Ashley." The man's name was Colton Porter. And he was a dick.

He walked up to the couple and held up his phone. A splintered ray of light shot from the end, projecting a large screen into the air that was playing drone footage of the exact moment Glitch was dropped naked from the combine into the cornfield. "So that's how morons are born. So much for the cabbage patch."

The ZUMR technicians laughed at this.

Glitch turned red and rushed to the Beast, where he sat inside wrapped in his tarp and sulked.

"You're a class act, Colton," Jake said.

"Sorry, Ashley. I wasn't thinking." He put his arm around a reclamation bot and smiled. "You see, our machines don't have feelings. They just do what they're told and keep their pants on."

"You put a little too much faith in your machines. I wouldn't trust them to fold my laundry, much less stand by me in the field when it mattered. One little hiccup and I've got two renegades to worry about."

"That's not how it works, junker. A machine can't turn other machines."

"Don't be so sure."

"I wouldn't expect you to understand." He patted the machine on the back. "I coded the Guardian series myself. They are completely incorruptible and incapable of anything but compliance."

"Yay for you. I'll remember that the first time I'm called to bring one down."

"You wouldn't stand a chance."

Jake smiled at Colton and took Hailey by the arm. He led her a few feet away under protest.

"What are you doing?" She snapped her arm out of his hand.

"I need to talk to you about something. How long did you have your drone overhead? How much did you see?"

"I saw it all. You managed to destroy a barn, a crop, a combine and Glitch's pants all in a few minutes. I'd call it your highlight reel."

"You saw it then?"

"Saw what?"

"The second anom."

"What? No, there was no second anomaly."

"Then what do you call that giant corn cob chomping monster that tried to run us down?"

"If I had to guess, I'd say salvage error."

"You think we turned it on ourselves?"

"Oh, I'm sure it was an accident." She put air quotes around "accident." He hated it when she used air quotes. "I'm sure a stray shot probably triggered its programming. And I say that because I'd never accuse you of intentionally sabotaging a machine just to justify a second bounty."

"You'd never do that? That's sweet of you."

Hailey nodded. "Just like I'd never even think for a half a second that you would fry a machine and make it go renegade just to extort more money out of the poor farmers here at Happy Dell Independent Family Farms Incorporated."

"Isn't that nice of you to say."

She smiled at him and nodded.

He leaned in close. "Look, you and I can play I Hate My Ex all night long, but I'm being serious here."

She folded her arms and cocked her hip. "Yeah, because you're Mr. Serious."

"Hailey, we never touched it. Not once. It went renegade on its own. I swear."

"First of all," she said. "We are not exes. We would have to have been a thing before we could even be a couple. And we'd have to be a couple before we could be exes. That's how it works. And you and

I were never a thing. You get me? Second of all, you don't get to swear. I get to swear. If anyone has a right to swear it's me, dammit."

Jake took a deep breath, focused on removing all sarcasm from his voice and looked her in the eyes. "Hailey, both of them were ZUMR tech. Don't you think that's at least worth looking into? At the very least to cover your company's ass?"

Hailey looked away and sighed.

"Look," Jake continued, "I want to be wrong. And I want you to be the one that proves me wrong. Because I know how much you'd enjoy that. So please, prove me wrong and call me up and tell me you told me so."

She looked at the ground and ran her fingertip over her lip as she thought. Then she nodded. "I'll look into it."

"That's all I ask." Jake turned and stepped toward the truck. His mind was working on how to explain everything to Forester.

"Jake," Hailey called with no trace of hate.

This surprised him and he turned. "Yes?"

"Thank you," she said.

And she meant it. He could tell. His heart tripped and tried to tell him all of the things that her tone could possibly mean because it wasn't what she said, it was how she said it.

So, how did she say it? She had said it softly. That could mean she didn't want others to hear, which wasn't necessarily a good or bad thing.

How was she standing? That mattered. Body language was ninety percent of communication. It was open. She had unfolded her arms. That meant she wasn't opposed to further communication. That was a good thing.

How was she dressed? That mattered, too. She was in a one-piece blue ZUMR jumpsuit, which meant that she was working and he had lost all perspective on the conversation and was possibly going crazy and why did she have this effect on him?

And how long had he been staring now? Oh, no, he was well beyond thoughtful pause and considered silence and was moving deep into awkward moment territory. He had to say something. "Hey, Hailey?"

"Yes, Jake?"

Something playful, but nothing serious. "Were we at least an item?"

"Good night, Jake." She turned and went back to her truck.

He watched her walk away and sighed. He decided to bill the farm first thing in the morning. He hoped they paid quickly. Hopefully before they came back out here and saw the damage that had been done. But it could wait until morning. He just wanted to go home.

**Read the rest now!**

**in**

**JUNKERS**

# Also by Benjamin Wallace

## About the Author

Benjamin Wallace lives in Texas where he complains about the heat.

You can email him at: contact@benjaminwallacebooks.com
To learn about the latest releases and giveaways, join his Readers' Group.

Visit **http://benjaminwallacebooks.com/join-my-readers-group/** to join and get your free book now.

If you enjoyed REVENGE OF THE APOCALYPSE please consider leaving a review. It would be very much appreciated and help more than you could know.

Thanks for reading, visiting, following and sharing.
-ben

**Find me online here:**
BenjaminWallaceBooks.com

facebook.com/benjaminwallaceauthor
twitter.com/BenMWallace
instagram.com/benmwallace

Made in the USA
Middletown, DE
28 August 2023

37449845R00156